IN PURSUIT OF
PERFECTION

Copyright August 2019

ISBN: Paperback   978-1940758947
ISBN: EPUB   978-1940758954
ISBN: MOBI   978-1940758961

Cover Design: Rae Monet

Published by:
Intrigue Publishing, LLC
10200 Twisted Stalk Ct
Upper Marlboro, MD 20772

IN PURSUIT OF PERFECTION

Chapter One

Every minute mattered and traffic on Market Street in Philadelphia crawled. Walking to the Crowne Plaza might be faster. It couldn't be any slower. *Did the cabbie even have his foot on the accelerator?* Macy Rollins considered climbing over the seat of the taxi, strangling the driver, and taking the steering wheel. She pushed forward to peek at the speedometer. He turned to face her, his brow raised, then returned his gaze to the snarl of cars in front of him.

"Can you drive faster, go around?" Macy pointed to the empty right-hand lane.

The driver stared straight ahead. "No ma'am."

"What if I told you I had an emergency?"

"No ma'am," he repeated.

"There's an extra twenty in it for you if you manage to catch all the green lights."

The driver locked eyes with her in the rearview mirror. Her stomach tightened around the knot that began forming earlier that morning. From the moment she got up, nothing had gone a planned.

"If I don't get my manager's signature on this contract…" Macy reached into her wallet, pulled out a bill and held it high. "C'mon, mister I could lose my job."

"If I speed, I could get a ticket. Lose my license. That ain't worth twenty bucks." His clipped tone matched hers.

"If you don't get a ticket, you could be twenty dollars richer. Besides, driving through a yellow light is not against the law." She waved the crisp bill at him.

"Not worth the risk." The light turned yellow and he slowed to a stop.

Her horoscope suggested she border on the extreme today. There wasn't anything more extreme than rushing with a deadline clock ticking in her ear. She fell against the seat with a huff. The world conspired against her.

The meter in the cab ticked higher at every traffic light right along with her blood pressure. She could almost feel time pulsing through her veins.

A block away from the hotel the driver slowed again. Macy handed him the fare and jumped out with a curse. The heels she'd worn to match her dress made walking any kind of distances uncomfortable.

She ran toward the entrance of the hotel. With a little luck, and she was due for some, she just might get the contract signed and to Pipeline Delivery in time to reach the customer tomorrow. The promotion to VP that she wanted and needed was in sight, but that didn't mean she could coast into it. How many sleepless nights had she spent worrying about money, worrying about paying her bills, or worrying about helping pay for her brother's college tuition if the scholarship didn't come through?

She stopped just outside the ballroom and took a deep, hopefully calming breath. She needed to appear in control, even if a riot was happening on her insides. She hadn't thought about the high-priced lawyer named Dennison Malveaux, the man who'd represented her father, in a long, time. But Roxy, her boss mentioned his name this afternoon and all those memories resurfaced like debris churned up from the ocean floor. Now she was getting ready to walk into the same room with him.

Music blared. Dennison Malveaux's campaign reception was well under way. With any luck, she wouldn't even have to see him. If she did, she didn't need to speak to him. He wouldn't remember her anyway. She was only twelve with pigtails when he used every loophole available to make sure her father's divorce from her mother left them destitute. Dennison had uncovered every loophole available to help her father hide his modest investments.

She took another deep breath before stepping inside. One look at the expensive, glittering gowns and the carbon-copy tuxedos let her know this wasn't her crowd. The room was packed with the aristocracy of Philadelphia. It even smelled rich. Seafood and beef delicacies, she probably had never heard of filled the air with mouthwatering goodness.

Her goal was to get in and out of the hotel before someone exposed her as an interloper. She pushed her way through the throng to find her manager, Roxy English. The goal was to get her signature and get out.

Everything that could have gone wrong in the office today, did. In spite of following her horoscope and wearing the lucky red dress, the day was a disaster. *Why did the flu have to take her assistant down today?* The replacement sent from the pool lost the contract file when her computer crashed. Roxy's disappointment was palpable the minute Macy showed up at her office door empty-handed. The promotion Roxy had promised wasn't a done deal yet. Nothing with Roxy was ever easy.

Macy slowed her gait. Her new shoes were cute but too tight. In less than an hour, she could be home and out of the corporate armor. The plan to sink into her favorite sweats, and comfy slippers, while preparing for the company audit had to be better than hobnobbing with this crowd.

She scanned the room in search of Roxy. She would be easy to spot with her signature blond hair resting at the center of her back. Macy pushed up on her toes to get a good look around the room. Roxy had two flaws: She loved to talk, which meant the courier would close if Macy let her slip into one of her monologues, and she possessed a nasty temper, and was known to explode without warning.

Why Roxy wanted Macy to meet her here was a mystery. Roxy liked rubbing shoulders with the powerful branch of society, but this was not a place to conduct business. The atmosphere in the room was too high-brow for the casual business conversation. Tonight was about letting the affluent sniff your arrogant presence.

Everything Roxy did was calculated. Since she'd insisted Macy meet her here, she had a reason.

Macy spotted Roxy engaged in conversation with a small group of people in the corner of the room. From the animated way Roxy moved her hands, she was dominating the conversation as usual. Macy sighed. She could almost hear her watch ticking off the seconds before the courier closed. The man listening to Roxy didn't seem to mind her prolonged story. His face was familiar. But Macy didn't know a soul in this room other than the people who worked at English International, and this thirty-something hunk didn't work there. If he did, every single woman, including herself, would have been standing outside his door with a file in hand, in dire need of his opinion.

The guy engaged with Roxy had dark, expressive eyes and lashes as thick as any woman's. He flashed a smile that lit up his face, and Macy froze. It was Avery Malveaux, the oldest son of Dennison. It wasn't the thick head of hair, or his tantalizing build that she recognized, but his warm eyes and wide smile.

Avery's picture stayed on the front page of the society page. He was one of Philly's most eligible bachelors. But not for long. Wasn't he engaged? Why was Roxy chatting him up?

Macy tightened her hold on her bag and pressed forward. She had one hour to get Roxy's signature and drop off the contract in time for it to arrive at the customer's location on

Friday as promised. She greeted everyone in the group, and then directed her attention to Roxy. "I have the contract for you to sign." She had to force the words out because Avery stared at her, and it felt as though his gaze penetrated her soul.

"Ah, Macy, you're late," Roxy said. "I wondered how long it would take you to get here. You're cutting it close." She scowled before accepting the envelope. "Let me introduce you to Avery Malveaux. We've just completed negotiations with his law firm. Starting today, Avery's firm will be our outside legal counsel. He's going to help English International with our expansion efforts. His expertise in Europe and the Far East will come in handy. This fundraiser tonight is for Avery's father, who is running for re-election to City Council." Roxy grinned. "This is Macy Rollins, the Sales Manager at English International. Nobody knows our products, inventory, our account structure, or our business objectives better than she does."

Avery extended his hand to shake. Macy tried to swallow past the huge lump in her throat and accepted his firm grip.

Roxy continued. "The two of you will be working closely while Avery gets up to speed. I think it might be good as we get ready for our annual round of contract renewals, to let Avery see that side of the business. It will help him understand the business and get to know our current customer base."

Macy's lucky dress tightened on her like a tourniquet. How could today's horoscope have been so wrong? How could she work with anyone related to Dennison Malveaux? Why was Roxy's smile so enormous when the world was being shaken loose from its core?

Chapter Two

Macy locked her knees in place. Falling in front of everyone wouldn't further her career or convince anyone she wasn't a flake. When she got home, there would be plenty of time to figure out how she was supposed to work alongside of a Malveaux, but for now, she needed to stand up straight, look him in the eye and act like a professional.

"Welcome aboard, Mr. Malveaux, I look forward to working with you. We'll certainly keep you busy." Heat ran along her palm and wrist where his hand had touched hers.

"Thank you." His acknowledgment wasn't warm or welcoming. He probably had the same cold, calculating streak that his father possessed. And why not? They were both lawyers and had the same genes.

Avery clasped his hands in front of him. "Based on the information I read about this particular customer, shouldn't this contract be on the customer's desk tomorrow? It's late."

Macy's tongue refused to cooperate, lying flat in her mouth, like a balloon with no air. Useless. What had she done or who had she crossed to cause the stars to fall out of alignment? She was a good daughter who helped her mother as much as she could, a hard worker, putting in long hours even though most of the time Roxy didn't acknowledge her efforts and the best of friends to her roommate, who seldom remembered to buy her share of groceries.

She pushed aside her anger. Snapping at Avery Malveaux wouldn't do much to advance her career. "The administrative assistant just completed the changes. I contacted the company president today, and they are willing to accept the contract a day late." She kept her voice level.

Avery Malveaux was outside counsel. She wouldn't have to see him every day. Managing cordial would be easier if he spent more time at his offices than at the corporate headquarters. She could work alongside a rattlesnake as long as it didn't slitter into her path. The Malveaux family had robbed her family once, but she wouldn't let Avery jeopardize her pending promotion.

"I'm sure Macy will find a way to straighten this out." Roxy patted Macy's shoulder "Somehow, she manages to get the job done, every time. Don't you?"

"Yes, of course." Macy addressed Roxy alone. Avery's comments reinforced her determination to stay focused.

Roxy scribbled her signature on the contract and handed it back. "Besides if I hadn't demanded she come down here for your announcement, this would have been in the mail earlier."

Macy glanced at her watch. Every second the angst in her stomach inched higher. The contract felt like a grenade in her hand. The trickle of perspiration that dripped between her breasts was no surprise. She patted the envelope containing the contract, holding it tight to her chest. She eased back a step, to make a graceful exit and bumped into Celeste English, Roxy's sister.

"So sorry, Celeste."

As usual, Celeste wore a stunning emerald green couture dress, cut tastefully for the conservative crowd. She wore five-inch heels in the exact same color. Celeste had the fashion sense of a great designer but as much charm as a slug.

"Macy, what are you doing here? I didn't know you were invited." Celeste tilted her head and looked down her nose at Macy even though they were the same height.

"I'm just here to get Roxy's signature," Macy said. "Now that I have it, I'll be on my way."

"Too bad you didn't have time to change into something more appropriate."

"I don't have time to discuss my attire. I'd better be going." Macy took another step.

Roxy grabbed Macy by the arm. "Before you leave, I need you to represent English on Saturday night."

Macy saw her weekend slipping away even before Roxy finished the sentence. Her plans of curling up on the sofa and reading a book vanished as the smile on Roxy's face widened. Whenever Roxy wanted more than the standard fifty-hour week, she slipped into her ultra-nice persona and her inflection became syrupy sweet.

"Avery has another venture he just launched. A new nightclub opening Saturday night, which is also the corporate sponsorship night. I need you to attend because I can't make it. We want to support his venture, especially since he's working with us now. Who knows, with all the other businesses there, you may be able to snag a new client or two."

Avery directed his attention to Roxy. "I'm a silent partner. It's a financial venture for me." The features on his face softened for the first time since she'd arrived. "I'm sure Macy has more interesting things she'd rather be doing on a Saturday evening."

"Nonsense, it's the least we can do. I'm sure Macy won't mind. Will you, dear?" Roxy spoke up before Macy could reply.

Like hell. But she needed this job and the promotion that Roxy dangled in front of her like a golden ring that she jerked away whenever Macy got too close. "I'd be happy to." She produced a smile as fake as the tone of Roxy's voice.

Avery pulled his wallet from his pocket and handed Macy a card with the club's name, *Ambience*, embossed in large gold letters. He flipped the card over, showing her the address on the opposite side before placing it in her outstretched hand. His touch lingered a little longer than required, but she didn't bristle.

"I'll be there." She met his eyes. He seemed poised to say something more, but she excused herself from the group before giving him the opportunity.

Halfway across the room, she looked back at the gathering. Celeste had slipped her hand into Avery's, but his gaze remained on her.

Chapter Three

Avery watched Macy weave her way across the room, taking everyone's attention with her. In the warm lights of the ballroom her brown skin glowed like a bronzed statue waxed to perfection. Her ruffled mini-dress hugged her behind, and her strappy sandals accentuated her shapely legs. He wasn't the only man ogling her as she made her exit.

He'd rattled her. But his comments were all about business, she shouldn't have taken them personal.

"Well, isn't Macy flying out of here like the place was on fire?" Celeste's sultry voice sounded like a cat purring. "Why do I get the impression that she's always trying so hard, always sucking up to you, Roxy? There is something about that girl that I don't like."

"Macy seems a little distracted lately," Roxy said. "That's not like her. She's usually so focused."

Celeste turned to him. "Roxy always says the nicest things about Macy. Even when they aren't warranted."

"That's not true. I treat everyone who reports to me the same. And, I have the same expectation of each of them," said Roxy.

"Sometimes, I think you like her better than you like your own sister." Celeste pouted just enough to look seductive. "If you want, I can talk to her tomorrow and see if I can figure out what's going on."

"Good idea, Celeste. Let me know if there is something I need to be concerned about with Macy." Roxy turned her attention to Avery. "As you may have read in the literature I gave you about the company, we've started our Dragon negotiations. During these negotiations, we will renegotiate over half of our customer contracts. It's onerous on the staff, but we find it's a proficient way to evaluate our offering all at once. Macy knows our customer base better than anyone. I want you to spend some time with her, to get a better understanding of what kinds of customers are attracted to our products. That knowledge will be beneficial as you work on expanding our market share."

Avery nodded. "Don't worry. I'm on it." Working with Macy could pose a challenge. There was something in her eyes that spoke to him. Something in the way her curls framed her face and came to rest on her shoulders, like silk that made him want to touch her hair.

"I can be helpful too." Celeste reached for his hand and held on to it. "Even though I don't handle anything as glamorous as the customer portfolio, I have all the systems knowledge. We rely heavily on our customer portals, so you'll need to understand them."

He pulled his hand from Celeste's. She was like a vine, locking him down, threatening to overtake and choke him. Roxy and his parents wanted him to find something appealing about Celeste, but it wasn't happening.

He sipped his wine. "I'll set up some time on your calendar, Celeste." He offered an excuse and made his way through the crowd, hoping it wasn't too late to spot Macy one more time.

Celeste caught up to him and slipped her hand back into his. He groaned loud enough for her to hear. "What can I do for you, Celeste?"

"Roxy is always talking about customers. She has very little interest in the Information Technology side of the business. My domain. But without my staff, the business would be crippled."

"I'll make sure to spend some time understanding the systems."

11

"Good." She slipped her arm through his. "Now that you officially work for English, I want you to spend more time with me."

"Why is that?"

"Roxy is watching, and she expects us to make a love connection." She rose on her toes and planted a wet kiss on his cheek.

"Do you always try to please your sister?" He pulled a handkerchief from his pocket and, with one broad swipe, he wiped his cheek.

"I do if it keeps the checks flowing. Want to kiss me so we look authentic?"

"Let's not and say we did." He turned around his attention to the door.

"Maybe we can go on an official date soon. That would make Roxy happy."

"Making your sister happy is not a reason for us to go out."

"When Roxy is happy, she's much more generous. My life is good when my sister is generous. And lately, she hasn't been pleased with me. But since she's got it in her head to match the two of us, she's practically giddy, and I want her to stay that way. You do want to keep the English account, don't you?" She stopped and stared at him.

"Whether you and I are dating has nothing to do with our law firm and English International."

She pressed her index finger into his chest. "You see, that's where you're wrong. Of course, the two are connected. If I'm happy and out of Roxy's hair, then she's happy. You're kinda like my goose with the golden egg. So for now, let's pretend we have something in common."

Avery pulled away from her just as his father approached.

"Good evening, Celeste, I'm glad you could stop by tonight." Dad planted one of those fake air kisses near her cheek and produced his infamous campaign smile.

"Councilman! Of course, I'd be here. I'll do whatever I can to help you get reelected."

"You hear that, son?"

"Yes, another supporter," he said weakly.

"I can't have too many of them." His father nodded.

Avery frowned. Celeste didn't need encouragement.

"I'm happy your firm will be working with English now," Celeste said.

"It's not my firm anymore." He slapped Avery on the back. "Malveaux and Malveaux belongs to Avery and his brothers, now. My job is serving the constituents of Philadelphia. Sealing the deal with English was all Avery's doing. It's about time we were able to bring our businesses together. This partnership should be beneficial for both parties."

"I'm sure it will." Celeste's tone was a little too sweet.

Avery watched his father place his hand on Celeste's shoulder. "Avery will have to bring you to the house for dinner. His mother and I would love to have you."

"I think that's a lovely idea. We'll come up with a date, and I'll call to set it up," Celeste said as she wiggled her hips next to Avery and flashed the Councilman her dazzling veneers.

Avery watched his father walk away before turning to Celeste. "You can be quite manipulative, I see."

"I've got all kinds of skills." Celeste pulled him toward the bar. "How about you buy me a drink?"

"It's an open bar."

"Not for the brand I want." She looped her arm through his. "Besides, we could have fun for a little while. Who knows where this could lead? You're certainly cute enough. So, here's the deal." She pushed her hair behind her ear. "Play along for a while. Let's let Roxy think we're interested. It will keep her from meddling in my life for a while. I'm working on some ideas and I don't want her asking me a lot of questions yet."

"I don't play games." He shook his head. Not anymore. He'd been burned by women who liked to pretend one thing while doing another. He'd come across enough of them to know when they were using him. Celeste wanted something more than what she was saying, and it wasn't to spend more time with his easy-going personality.

He paid for her premium drink and left her at the bar cozying up to a wealthy investment banker. At least with Celeste, he knew exactly what she wanted. There was no guessing with her. His steps quickened as he maneuvered his way across the room, shaking hands and greeting his father's guests along the way.

He took long strides towards the hotel lobby. Everything came with strings attached. Why couldn't the English account just be about business? Now he'd have to deal with Macy, who was pretty and probably competent, and Celeste who was incompetent and probably devious.

He spotted Macy standing outside the hotel in a cab line at least ten people deep.

When was the last time a woman had grabbed his attention so quickly? He slowed his pace, enjoying the view of her backside for a moment. Yes, his last relationship had turned out disastrous. But maybe Macy was worth another try.

Chapter Four

Macy focused her attention on the slow-moving cab line. She closed her eyes for a moment and prayed that the rest of day would be uneventful. Her horoscope had been all wrong today.

It would have been so much easier to blame this delay on Avery Malveaux, Mr. Good-looking. If she could have gotten Roxy's signature and departed immediately as planned, the nervous ruckus in her stomach would have settled. But she had to small talk with all of them. Her toes screamed for release from her shoes.

What was it about Avery Malveaux that made her feel warm and hateful at the same time? Maybe it was all those news articles about how he treated women. According to them, he wasn't loyal, and his last name told her he wasn't honest.

She folded her arms over her chest. His success at English depended on her willingness to help him understand the customer relationships. No one understood the temperament of English customers better than she did. For once she had something that would benefit a Malveaux. The thought made her giddy.

She craned her neck to see down the street. If another taxi didn't come soon, she was going to have even more problems in the morning.

Her phone rang, and she pulled it out of her purse. The number following the 202 area code wasn't familiar. There was no reason to waste time on a wrong number. She shoved the phone back in her purse.

The courier closed in fifteen minutes. If she got into another slow cab, she wouldn't make it. She tapped her fingers against her thigh.

The phone rang again. Macy snatched open her purse. Annoyed with the phone, and the delay in this stupid cab line, she didn't check the caller I.D. before accepting the call.

"Yeah," she yelled.

"I must have caught you at a bad time." Gayle sounded hurt.

"I'm sorry." Macy adjusted her tone when she recognized her roommate. "This day just keeps getting worse. I didn't mean to yell."

"Where are you? Aren't you coming?"

Loud rap music came through the phone, muddling Gayle's words in the persistent beat. Macy held the phone away from her ear.

"Macy!" Gayle shouted again. "Can you hear me? I asked if you were coming."

"I don't think so. It's almost seven, and I haven't dropped off the contracts yet."

"There you go again. I'll bet you're grinning at your boss like you don't mind giving the company all your time."

"Cut me a break. It's late, I'm tired, and my shoes might look cute, but I swear they're issuing an all-out assault on my toes. I found out I've got to work with Avery Malveaux and I've got the upcoming audit, that I've only began preparing for."

"So you're not coming."

"No. Please understand. I'm exhausted."

"You're twenty-seven, for god's sake. You're supposed to have fun now and then. Instead, you work as if you have a family of ten to support. We haven't been out together in months."

"I know, I know. I shouldn't have to keep up this pace much longer. Roxy will make a decision about the VP assignment in a few weeks. Then I might get my life back."

"Fine. Then I'll have fun for you."

"Good idea. Bye, Gayle."

Macy ended the call. She wanted to kick off her shoes and stand barefoot on the cool pavement but decided to wait until she was in the cab.

She couldn't remember the last time she had fun. But Gayle didn't have a brother who needed help funding college, or a mother who needed extra financial help every month. If only her life could be that carefree.

Chapter Five

Macy leaned forward to give the driver the courier's address. She glanced at her watch. Only a miracle would get her there in time. Based on the congestion still clogging the streets, nothing magical was going to happen to change that.

The contract was her responsibility. She should have been on top of this weeks ago. Maybe she was leaving too much in the hand of her assistant.

"He has some nerve, second-guessing my ability to evaluate my work," she said aloud to no one.

"What was that, ma'am?" the driver asked.

She shook her head. "Nothing. Look, I know there are speed limits and everything, but can you drive any faster? I'm in a hurry."

"I can try, but there's a lot of traffic, and speeding is against the law."

"So is human torture," she whispered, thinking it was just her luck to catch every law-abiding taxi driver tonight. She kicked off her shoes and wiggled her toes. Her grip tightened on the envelope containing the contract. She needed to focus on one thing at a time. After she dropped off the contract, then she'd think about the next problem. Like the audit or finding the time to get a manicure and pedicure before Avery's opening.

The cab approached the courier's location. She slipped her shoes back on and gathered her things.

The courier's office was dark, with no sign of activity inside. A sense of dread swelled in her. Her heart pumped faster. She paid the driver then stepped out of the cab. With just a little luck, maybe someone was still inside, in the back, closing up for the night. She pulled the door handle.

Locked.

With her hands shielding her eyes she stared through the glass door.

Nothing.

With her open palm, she slapped the glass door and cursed. "What else can go wrong?" She slumped against the brick wall. If only she could have gotten the signature and out of the ballroom sooner. After a few moments, she divided the blame in three equal parts; her administrative assistant, the computer goblins that ate critical files, and the world that didn't want to see her get ahead.

She gnawed her bottom lip and envisioned Roxy's wrath. Macy steadied herself against the wall as her flash of anger subsided. After a moment, she was calm enough to push off the wall and headed towards the intersection. She needed to sort out her options.

Her instant reaction to Avery was irrational. Could she dislike him for something his father did, when he was just a little boy? He wasn't to blame for what happened tonight, and neither was Celeste or Roxy or even the damn computer. She always had to run faster, and jump higher to stay ahead, this was no different.

Chapter Six

Friday morning Macy stood at her dingy kitchen counter and took several deep breaths, fighting the mounting tension in her neck. She hadn't slept much. How could she? Her life was a bundle of loose ends waiting to be straightened out. If she could get the promotion, then maybe she could convince her mother that sending her brother to college wasn't going to be a colossal financial burden. Especially if they could talk Brian into applying for some scholarships and stopped putting all his faith into getting a full ride from Maryland to play football. And maybe, she and Gayle could move into a decent place. One where the paint wasn't peeling, the floor tiles weren't loose, and the HVAC system worked when you needed it.

Her blue and white floral dress was a simple shift with a handkerchief hem. Understated compared to her dress yesterday, and it wouldn't draw any unnecessary attention. Proper for casual Friday, and her feet were thankful for the lower heels.

She scrolled through her phone and found her favorite horoscope site. Sure horoscopes were silly, but there was a connection between the stars, the planets, and her mood. Hadn't her horoscope told her that her last boyfriend wasn't a jerk, who she couldn't trust? Then there was the time it predicted Hurricane Sandy would hit the Jersey shore before she made the deposit on her vacation. And then, last week her horoscope said she'd have a surprise and then she'd found a twenty-dollar bill in the bottom of her purse. Sure most days the post meant nothing to her, but why take a chance? So, what did today offer?

Today your interactions with others will be warm, friendly, and congenial. Any sort of get-together you attend will benefit you. Something romantic looms for the weekend.

How could she be discouraged with such great news? All she needed to do was adjust her attitude to match the stars, and everything would work out fine. She read the words again and nodded head. For the next few weeks everything needed to work like a precision watch. The contract negotiations, the audit, her brother's scholarship search. She exhaled through her mouth. She'd be extra chipper at work today.

Gayle paddled into the kitchen. Her hair was tossed and knotted, her mascara had smudged around her eyes into black circles.

"Is that the dress you wore to the party last night?"

Gayle glanced down at the wrinkled silk and nodded.

"Hard night, huh?" Macy said.

"I had a blast. Too bad you missed it." Gayle opened the refrigerator and pulled out the metal tin containing her special blend of coffee, her breakfast of champions. "Aren't you late for work?"

"This contract was supposed to be on the customer's desk today. But the courier was closed last night." She patted the envelope lying on the counter. "So, I'm going to stop by there this morning and talk to someone in person. Roxy will rage when she finds it hasn't arrived in Virginia as expected. And the new lawyer will probably help her." She paused for a second.

"Why not use one of the national couriers? Roxy doesn't have to know, and if you pay for it using your own money, she doesn't have to know anything, except you kept your promise and you can stop worrying."

"I wish it were as easy as that, but there are two things wrong with your proposal. First, it's against company policy. The purchasing department selects all outside vendors, so I can't just go to another company. Roxy has insisted on Pipeline Delivery. I think there's a family connection or somebody blackmailed her into using them. With the luck I've been having, I could be fired for using an unapproved carrier." And I don't have any extra money to pay for special deliveries."

"Sounds like you could be fired for breathing over there." Gayle found the coffee press in the cabinet. "Either way, I think by the end of today, you might end up looking like me this morning."

"That's just what I needed. A reminder of how tenuous my job can be." The knot in her stomach doubled. "I'd better get going." She shoved the contract in her backpack, grabbed her purse and headed out.

By the time Macy eased into the English office building her confidence was not at the top of her game, but it was closer. With her backpack gripped in her hand, she made her way to her office on the third floor. A few minutes to catch her breath and pull together a story before anyone drilled her with questions and she'd be fine. The contract was with the courier as of nine this morning, with only a one day delay. Any good Sales manager could smooth over a one-day delay.

Right?

In her office, she closed the door and flopped into the chair behind her desk. Everything was going to be just fine. She took several short breaths until the churning in her stomach eased.

She looped a curl around her finger and gazed at the top of her desk. The sooner she told Roxy the contract was late the sooner she could get her ass chewed out and move on. But her feet refused to cooperate. Her body remained still except for the rapid breaths she continued to take.

The knock on her door cracked her quiet bubble. "Yes."

Her assistant stepped in. "I didn't hear you come in." Michelle's eyes narrowed, and she tilted her head. "Are you okay?"

"I'll be fine." Macy sat up straighter, smoothing down the front of her dress. "Michelle, the audit begins soon. I've gone through some accounts, but I need you to pull the paperwork on my selling expense account. With all the activity to get ready for the Dragon negotiations it's going to have the most activity. I don't want any surprises."

"I usually just check everything. Leave that to me. Okay?" Michelle said.

"No, the yearly audit is much more detailed. I'll need to review the accounts and sign off on them. Pull the documents, label them and have them on my desk early next week."

Michelle rubbed the side of her nose and glanced down, before looking back to Macy. "Are you sure you're okay? You look like you've eaten something rotten."

Macy nodded. "Give me a few minutes."

"Well, you might be able to have a minute, but the new legal guy wants to meet with you this morning. I told him you get in at nine, and he's already been by here twice," Michelle said. I think he's a type A personality. Like we needed another one of those around here, right?"

"Thanks, Michelle. I'll handle him. I had an errand to run this morning, so I was in a rush." She reached for her purse. "I'll just go to the restroom and finish applying my make-up and fluff my hair. Then you can tell Avery I'll see him."

"Sure thing." Michelle turned around and walked out the door. She stuck her head back inside. "No luck. He's coming down the hall now," she said before disappearing.

Macy closed her eyes for a moment and squared her shoulders.

He rapped on the door and walked in.

She stood. "Come on in. Have a seat."

"I've been waiting for you. Do you usually get into the office so late?" He pushed up his cuff and examined his expensive watch.

"It's only ten and no. I had to make a stop before coming into the office this morning. But, I don't think your new responsibilities include monitoring my activities."

He smirked. "I can assure you I have plenty to keep me busy. I was only checking to make sure the Bunting contract made it there this morning."

She cleared her throat. "The courier was closed last night when I arrived. I dropped the contract off this morning, as soon as they opened." Her words jammed together.

He bent his head and pinched the bridge of his nose. She could almost see the anger spilling from his pores.

"Look." She cleared her throat. "I'll handle this. It's not your problem."

He shook his head.

"I will call Mr. Bunting personally. I'll explain the situation and let him know the delay couldn't be helped. I've worked on this account for over two years. I don't think it's going be that big of a problem."

Avery stood. He towered over her desk making her feel even smaller. She stood, too. With her shoulders pushed back she mustered as much attitude as she could.

"I'm only saying this is not the way to start the contract negotiating season. That's all." His tone softened.

"This was an unfortunate incident."

"Can I make some calls?"

"No. I'll handle it."

A stiff silence blanketed the room. Avery's first day in the office and already he wanted to help her do her job. Did he think she was incapable? They weren't off to a good start.

"I must inform Roxy of what is going on," he said.

"No, no," she said. "I'll tell her."

He gave her a long stare. She held his gaze before he turned and walked out.

She stood and grabbed the sides of the desk for balance. This had to be the moment when someone at work was going to be frustrated. Roxy expected results. The last thing she wanted for her staff to come to her with every little issue that came up. But if Avery ran to her office to tell her about the Bunting contract before she did, then everyone was going to be unhappy.

Roxy's door was open. Macy stuck her head inside. "You got a minute?"

"Yes." Roy waved her in.

Macy sat across the desk from Roxy. "I wanted to let you know the courier was closed last night when I arrived. For some reason they closed ten minutes earlier than what's posted on their website."

Roxy's jaw dropped. She stared at Macy as if her words required translation. "It was supposed to be there today, right?"

"Yes." Macy moved to the edge of her chair. Her heart pounded. "I dropped the contract off this morning at the courier and impressed how important it was to get there tomorrow. I'll call Will Bunting this morning, explain what happened and ask him to work with us."

"His committee was quite clear they wanted all proposals to arrive no later than close of business tomorrow. You're not leaving yourself any extra room. I don't understand what you can say to him to smooth this over." Roxy pushed her fingers through her hair and off her face.

"I'm trying to fix this. I'm not sure why the courier would close early."

"This is not about the courier, Macy. Don't try to shift the blame, it won't fix the problem. You're the Sales manager. No matter what happens these negotiations are your responsibility. If you lose this contract I'm not going to lower your sales objectives this year. You're going to have to find a way to make up that revenue." She placed her palms on the desk, her nostrils flared. "I'm not sure what to say. We are all under a lot of stress, I'm expecting everyone to do their share.

"Of course. We're in agreement. I'm taking full responsibility." Macy stood.

Roxy snorted. "You have to."

Chapter Seven

Saturday's were always spent doing the same thing. Avery was ready to break this routine. His father no longer ran the company, so they didn't need these update sessions anymore. Avery used to enjoy them, back when he wanted to impress his father. But he'd long since outgrew that need.

Avery shifted his position in the overstuffed, winged-back chair in his father's study.

His parents still lived in the spacious Gladwyne home, north of Philly, where he'd grown up. And he still hated his father's office just like he did when he was twelve and had to listen to his father lecture him for traipsing through his mother's garden.

Avery nodded as his father continued to talk. When he was in his twenties, he cherished every word of wisdom his father imparted. Now at thirty-three, he'd learned to tune him out and follow his own counsel. The Councilman loved to make speeches, even if he was only talking to one person. The lecture was always the same, the family name, dignity, and discretion. Avery could repeat the speech verbatim but endured his father's litany anyway.

A whiff of his mother's famous meatloaf drifted into the room. Listening to another monologue was worth the effort for a taste of a good home-cooked meal, as long as he could get the meal to go.

His father inhaled in preparation for a new barrage of the same old speech. Telling his father to stop match-making and meddling was poised on the tip of his tongue. Even though his father wasn't fond of "I told you so's," Avery wanted to remind him about Monica and their ugly breakup.

"I know you have your hopes set on Celeste and me, but that's not going to happen. I'm not interested in Celeste English. Just like I wasn't interested in Monica or Teresa or whatever that woman's name was at the last dinner party you and Mom put together."

His father dragged his glasses down his long-pointed nose and glared at him. "What do you mean? Celeste is a lovely girl. Did you see her work that room Thursday night? She's as good at schmoozing as your mother."

"I want more from a woman than just her ability to work a room. Or one who is only interested in her career or sleeping around, like Monica was." Avery hurried the conversation along. The club opening was in a few hours.

"Avery, I know you think you know what you want, but life doesn't always present us the answers in black and white." His stocky father rose from his chair and strolled from behind his desk. Avery pressed his fingers into his tight abs. One day would his chiseled pecs turn into man-breasts like his father's? Tomorrow morning he'd do an extra set of stomach crunches and eat one less muffin.

His father continued. "You think the most important thing right now is the next woman you're going to spend the night with." His father spoke slowly, in a measured tone while jingling his pocket change. The fastest way to end this conversation was to remain quiet. If he corrected his father's impressions now, he would be here another hour. "Stop chasing women. You're the oldest. You need to set an example for Austen and Cameron. Your brothers watch every move you make. They've looked up to you from the moment they were born." His father threw his hands in the air. "Invincible. You've got the big firm. You've won some significant cases. You're with a different woman every week. But none of that is going to be important when you get to my age. And the last thing I want this campaign season is another Malveaux tabloid headline."

"I've worked hard for ten years." Avery measured his words as he spoke. "My private life has never interfered with my work or yours." A vision of Macy behind her desk after their confrontation clouded his vision. After the way he'd spoken to her, she might not be willing to share everything she knew about the business. Finding a way to mend fences with Macy moved to the top of his to-do list.

"You need to settle down and get married," he paused, and Avery could predict the next words. "Celeste will make the perfect wife for you."

"I'm not interested in a wife right now. I'm focused on expanding the firm."

"English International and Celeste are both good opportunities."

Avery stood up and stretched his legs. The small measure of domination he got by towering over his father made him smile. "Dad, I'm a grown man. I don't need any help picking a woman. And I know Celeste is not the one for me. That's not going to happen. I'm not interested in marriage. I want more from a woman than someone who can fuel your political aspirations."

"You can say that now because you've never run for office. I know men who had to shelve their dreams because they married the wrong woman." His father strode to the bar, unscrewed the cap on the Jack Daniels, and topped off his glass. "Don't be so hasty, Son. All I'm saying is give yourself a little time. Let the relationship marinate a little longer. If Celeste is not the one, give it some…"

"Dad." Avery's voice was cold. "I know Roxy thinks she was doing me a favor by introducing me to her sister, but not every good deed is a favor."

"I don't want your pictures plastered on the society page for another ridiculous scandal. That story about you and Monica and your broken engagement, went on for weeks. It was ugly." His father's jowls wobbled with each word.

Instead of worrying about Avery's love life he needed to spend some time in the gym.

"If you had let me handle Monica my way, that nonsense would have never happened." Avery raised his voice.

"You're thirty-three-years-old."

Avery made a grand gesture of looking at his watch. He walked to the door of his father's study and placed his hand on the knob. "I'll settle down when I find the right woman."

Outside the office, he exhaled. His father needed to get off this "get married" bullshit or their Saturday morning visit would become a lot less frequent.

Avery made his way through his childhood home in search of his mother. He found her in the solarium reading a book at arm's length. In some ways she showed her age, but there was no doubt she was still a striking woman. The fine lines around her eyes were more pronounced than they used to be, and her laugh lines stayed in place long after the laughter. But, she was still the yardstick by which he measured all women. And not only when it came to looks; what he wanted was a woman with her grace and sincerity. Any man would be lucky to have his mother. He hoped his father shared his sentiment, but he doubted it. His father was too self-centered.

He greeted his mother before he bent to kiss her on the cheek she offered.

"How was your discussion with your father?" She closed her book and gave him her attention.

He sat beside her. "Pretty much as I expected."

"You know why your father is a politician. He has a way with people."

"Yeah, but is what he does a negotiation or a manipulation?"

"With your father, it's a little bit of both."

Chapter Eight

Macy pushed away the worry that tried to disrupt her monthly visit home. The kitchen in her mother's house hadn't changed much since Macy was a preteen. The cabinets were chipped. The door to the spice cabinet hung lopsided on its hinges. It wasn't state-of-the-art, but last year the purchase of a new stainless-steel refrigerator with ice and water in the door was an upgrade.

Her mother pulled oatmeal-raisin cookies from the oven and left them cooling on top of the stove before she sat at the table across from Macy. "Aren't you going to eat a cookie? I made your favorites." She pushed a teetering plate of cookies toward Macy.

"You always make too many." Macy reached for one. "I shouldn't. I'm going to a work thing tonight and I don't want to look bloated in my dress." She took a small bite. "Has Brian applied for any scholarships like we talked about?"

"He did. You know your brother. I'm sure of at least three and he promised to look for more. He's so sure he's going to get to play ball at Maryland, it's hard to keep him focused."

Macy shook her head. "Was I that hard-headed when I was his age?"

Her mother's face broke into a smile that made her eyes sparkle. "You were too serious. About everything. My children are extremely opposite. I think you missed most of your childhood because you worried about your grades and your friends and world peace."

"Well, I didn't have much choice, did I?"

Her mother placed a hand over Macy's. "We were fine."

"Yeah." Macy nodded. "I know. We had each other, didn't we?" She mocked her mother's voice.

"Well, it was true."

Macy took another bite from her cookie. Somewhere between the time her father had left and now, Macy had become the default head-of-the family. Her mother was so consumed with sadness back then, that Macy assumed the role of cleaning the house, making sure her brother showered and cleaned behind his ears. She was ready to hand the part back to her mother. "Do you ever think about Dad?"

"Not in the way that you mean. I look at you or Brian, and I see some parts of him reflected in you both, and I feel sorry for the stuff he missed. He was trying to hurt me, but he was too stupid to see how he hurt his children too." She shook her head. "I don't have the bitterness anymore. I had to let that go and raise my babies."

Macy placed the remaining part of the cookie on the napkin. She tapped the blue vinyl cover of her checkbook. "We need to talk about expenses. I can't stay too long."

Macy's mother picked up a cookie. "We're good this month."

"What about the hot water heater? I thought it was on the fritz. And how did you cover Brian's college applications?"

"I think the hot water heater will last through the end of the year. But, the applications…"

"I'm going to write you a check for five hundred dollars."

"You don't have to, baby." Her mother stood. At the stove, she moved the cookies from the cookie sheet onto the wire rack.

"Mom, you know I don't mind helping. Take the check. Just in case."

"Just in case, what?"

"For emergencies. I will be traveling soon, and something might come up. This way you'll have a little extra. How about that?"

Her mother turned to face Macy. "Okay. Now finish that cookie. I'll pack up some for you to take to Gayle."

Macy wrote out the check, then entered the amount in the ledger. There wasn't anything left for frivolous purchases this month.

After a quick shower, Macy pulled the dress from the closet. She'd found the dress whiling wading through the racks at a discount store. It had been marked down twice, and with her coupon, she felt like a lottery winner. She slipped on a pair of black pumps before examining herself in the full length, bathroom mirror. The fifty dollars she'd spent for the black knock-off Versace was worth the money. It was a sleeveless V-back and silky fabric, that hugged her slender frame and accentuated her full breasts. It was finished off with a leather belt cinched around her small waist. The dress made her feel like a supermodel.

Tonight, she was going to have fun, if she remembered how.

The words from today's horoscope stared up from her phone.

Your day will be anything but ordinary. Today's celestial energy indicates you might not find love, but you'll find excitement and you'll go back for more. Be careful when dealing with those you don't fully trust.

There was enough excitement in her life, and none of it made her beam. Instead, it knotted her stomach and left her uncertain. Tonight she was going to have some fun. She was entitled to stop worrying about work and her brother's college funds and enjoy herself for a few hours.

She twirled around in front of the mirror several times before applying lip-gloss and coiling her hair into a loose

33

knot. After a final glance in the mirror, she found Gayle waiting in the kitchen.

"Aren't you glad you decided to keep that dress?"

"I am for now, but when the credit card statement comes, I might not be happy. I could have used the money spent on this to help pay one of Brian's college applications." She ran her hand along the soft fabric.

"No. You need to put yourself in front of your brother sometimes."

"Yeah, that's easy for you since your family is very supportive. Every time you ask them for something, they deliver. I'm the one who does that for my family."

Gayle's jaw tensed, and she looked away, hurt.

"I didn't mean it in a bad way, Gayle. It's just that as an only child you're used to getting everything you want and your parents have plenty to give you. My family is nothing like yours."

Gayle jumped up from the stool. "No worries. Ready to go?" She never stayed angry for long. She grabbed Macy by the arm and pulled her to the door, then handed Macy her cell phone. "Take my picture before we leave. I'm posting lots of pictures tonight on all my social media accounts, so my ex can see what he's missing."

Thirty minutes later, the taxi pulled behind several cars dropping off women at the double wide entrance doors. Music from inside the club pulsated through the air. A line of fashionably dressed people waited to get inside.

Macy's heart quickened as she and Gayle made their way to the VIP line. With any luck, she could put in her appearance, avoid Avery, and claim an evening of fun before crawling back into her comfortable bed and starting her regular grind again. She squared her shoulders and sucked down a big breath.

"My name is on the list, so we don't have to wait in line." Macy waved for Gayle to follow her.

"Wow, this night just keeps getting better. A special invitation, no waiting in line. How could you even think about missing this?"

"I hope this makes up for me bailing on you the other night," said Macy.

"Oh, it does. It does." Gayle walked ahead of her into the club.

Lights flashed and the sound of camera shutters opening and closing saturated the air. Macy shielded her eyes from the blinding lights.

"I feel like a celebrity." Gayle struck a super-model pose for the photographers. "Come on, Macy give them what they want. We might be in the paper tomorrow."

"Oh, wouldn't that be great. The tabloids can write a fascinating article about how an unknown woman showed up in a fake designer dress." She nudged Gayle forward.

The bouncer scanned his list and struck Macy's name off before he opened the chain gate and allowed them to enter. The colored lighting in the club was dim and moved around them slowly. The music blared, making it difficult to have a conversation. Along the edges of the dance floor, a few dancers waited for an opening in the crowd before inching onto the parquet floor. Gayle bobbed her head to the beat of the music.

The huge place was packed with hundreds of people milling about. "Wow, this is a huge turnout, considering it's corporate sponsorship night." She shouted at Gayle, who was already wiggling her hips to the music.

Each level had a balcony overlooking the first floor. Chrome and glass adorned the bar that stretched the full length of the back wall. Ornate liquor and wine bottles illuminated by track lights glistened in the back of the first-floor room. The crowd surrounding the bar waiting for drink orders was thick, but they seemed patient. The women wore stylish dresses that didn't look like they were bought at a discount store, and they wore heels too high to be comfortable. The men in their dark suits and creased slacks stood around in clusters, as if they were surveying the terrain for action later in the evening.

Macy scanned the room. "I don't think there are any empty tables. Maybe one will open later." She spoke loud into Gayle's ear.

"Who wants to sit down? We didn't come here to be wallflowers."

They waited their turn at the crowded bar. When they finally stepped away with their martinis, new, thirsty patrons filled their space.

Macy surveyed the cramped club in search of Avery. With his height, he should be easy to spot. She needed to find him, so he could report that she had shown up. "That jerk." She mumbled.

Chapter Nine

Avery's adrenaline pumped faster than the music. With his business partner and brother, Austen, by his side, Avery stood on the third level of the club looking down onto the crowd. People continued to stream in. Soon they would have to limit access until some of the patrons left. Without a doubt, they could repeat this performance when they opened to the general public. If this were an indication of the club's future patronage, his investment would pay off sooner than he hoped.

He watched the entrance for Macy's arrival. He'd been rough on her about the contract. He hadn't meant to question her ability, but his charm seemed to fail him when he talked to her. If she didn't show, it wouldn't surprise him.

He spotted Macy on the edge of the dance floor. The dress she wore was killer. With a rack like that and her tiny waist, it's no wonder so many men stared at her as she walked across the club. Her signature bun sat a little lower on her neck, but the only loose curls were the ones framing her face.

"What? What do you see?" Austen turned his attention to the first floor too. "Ouch man! She's hot. Do you know her?"

"I think Cinderella has just arrived." He fist bumped his brother.

"Wipe your mouth, Avery. I think you're drooling." Austen laughed. "I don't believe this can be happening to the biggest player in the game. It's a good thing Mom and Dad left before the party moved into full swing."

"Don't worry. This is only about work. I'm still in the game. Excuse me, Austen." Avery left his brother and made his way to the stairs without taking his eyes off Macy. There was no need to tell anyone about his feelings for her, just in case she flipped him off again. He exhaled the rush of air filling his chest. Why had he given this woman a hard time the day before?

Several patrons stopped to shake his hand, and he lost sight of her in the crowd. He craned his neck and used his full height to peer over the room. The dance floor was packed tighter than a beehive. There she was, standing on the opposite side of the dance floor.

She couldn't be the same woman he'd met at his father's fundraiser. Tonight, she had an aura that bordered on regal, as if she had stepped away from her throne long enough to mingle with the subjects of her kingdom. Without disguising his stare, he eyed her from head to foot. She hadn't noticed him yet, so he took his time. While staring at Macy the dream from last night came back to him. He was chasing her along the beach, but no matter how close he got, he couldn't catch her. He had awakened sweating and panting and horny.

What made Macy different from the other women in his past was something he needed to figure out. And why had he been so bull-headed with her? He charged his way across the crowded floor.

He reached Macy and took a deep breath before she saw him. "Macy".

When she didn't respond, he tapped her arm to get her attention above the blare of the music. "Macy, I hardly recognized you. You look amazing."

"Hello, Avery." She half-smiled while continuing to rock her head to the music. He didn't expect a warm welcome, but the distant expression in her eyes said there was a lot of work to do before they would become fast friends or anything more than distantly pleasant.

"I'm glad you made it."

She nodded. "Duty calls, so here I am." She took a step away from him. "The last thing I wanted to do was give you the impression that I don't care about my job, or make commitments that I don't keep."

"I deserved that," he said.

She pushed a wisp of hair behind her ear; the graceful gesture drew his attention to her delicate wrist and ear.

Like a high school boy, he fumbled for something to say. Talking to women was a trait he'd developed in grade school, so talking to Macy should be easy. Why was he struggling?

"I might as well get this off my chest before you say another word. You were very presumptuous to question my ability without understanding the circumstances." She held his gaze. The intensity in her eyes let him know his remarks in her office on Friday wouldn't be forgotten. This hot-tempered woman spoke her mind. He liked the challenge.

"I'm new to English. I ask a lot of questions because I'm trying to understand the culture. It's my nature to question everything."

"Everything or everyone? There's a difference."

"I didn't mean to imply you weren't doing the best you could under the circumstances. That's just my way. I tend to ask a lot of questions."

She crossed her arms and struck the same stance she had the first night they met. He wanted her to say something that would ease the tension between them. But she held her ground.

He gestured around the club. "What do you think?"

"This is a nice turnout. I hadn't expected the place would be this full. Roxy thinks this place will have printing needs one day. From the number of people staring at their cell phones, I don't think this crowd even knows what words printed on paper looks like."

"Very funny. I do enjoy your sense of humor. You're not going to stay angry with me all evening, are you?"

Macy snorted and her long lashes fluttered. "I don't like someone questioning my ability. I've worked hard to climb the ladder at English. You've been there less than a week, and you think you have the right to second-guess me or that I need you to jump in and fix my problems for me. I don't work for you, I work with you. There is a difference."

He stepped closer to her. "I'll try not to misjudge you again."

"Why do you make that sound like it's going to be hard to accomplish?"

"You can't pin a guy in a corner. We like to leave ourselves a little wiggle room, just in case."

She glanced over her shoulder.

"Looking for someone?"

"Yes, my friend." She started to walk away.

Was she in a relationship? "You brought a friend?"

"My roommate, Gayle. I thought you'd want a good turn out and that every person would count."

"That's great." He paused. "I'm not sure we knew the crowd would be this big, but we hoped for it and we sent out lots of invitation. The response has been overwhelming."

"It's very impressive. The Malveaux personal image just went up again."

He leaned closer, pretending he needed to get closer to her to hear what she'd said. The intoxicating scent of her perfume made him want to nuzzle her neck.

"I hope so." He reached for her hand. "Come, dance with me."

She hesitated. Her eyes darted around the room. Avery led her to the dance floor. The opening note of a Mary J Blige song played, and she abandoned her glass on a nearby table. He sensed her reluctance but refused to release her hand.

He held her waist as they danced and pulled her closer. She fit into his arms, as if they were made for each other.

"So, do you forgive me for my callous comment?" He tilted his head to look into her light brown eyes.

"I'll think about it. I work very hard for English and wouldn't do anything to put the contract negotiations at peril on purpose."

"I get that. I was out of line."

She nodded. Her eyes softened enough to let him know that hurdle was now behind him. He relaxed a little. Her long, regal neck, the soft feel of her skin, and the sparkle in her eyes made concentrating on his dance step impossible. Seeing her in a different environment made her seem like a different person. So why wasn't she already taken?

The song ended, but he didn't want to stop talking to her or let her disappear into the crowd. Not yet. There was no guarantee he'd get another opportunity to hold her this close again.

The next song was slower than the last one. Macy released Avery. The intimacy of another slow dance wasn't in her job description. She'd made the necessary appearance, had the necessary conversation. Now her time was her own. She held onto Avery's arm with a light touch as he led her off the dance floor.

Avery had excellent qualities, all the things she thought she wanted in her perfect man. Tonight he was polite, handsome, charming, he even had a sense of humor. But, to expect the man standing before her tonight to be the same man she'd see in the office on Monday morning was about as ridiculous as expecting Gayle would give up her party lifestyle.

She wasn't ready to surrender her original impression of him simply because he was polite. Forgiving and forgetting too soon was a fatal mistake. A tiger doesn't give up its stripe, he just changes his disguise. Besides, if Avery was anything like his father, it was bound to show up if she gave him enough time.

"I should show you around. There isn't much to see down here. Upstairs is where the Ultra VIP lounges are located, and they are nice."

"Well, I'm here with a friend." She glanced around for Gayle. The crowd had grown thicker. She doubted she could locate her without a massive search. "I should try to find her."

"This will only take a few minutes." He led her off the dance floor. A new surge of dancers rushed to take their place and dance to the hip-hop song that filled the room.

"I guess I could look. At least I will be prepared to answer if Roxy peppers me with questions. And I know she will."

"Oh, good."

She hoped Avery wouldn't look close enough to realize her dress was a knockoff. Would he even care? She was pretending tonight. She was a jeans and sweatshirt kind of girl, not one who liked to have her picture spilled across the front of a newspaper, not even a supermarket tabloid. Sure, whenever she stepped across the threshold of English International, she had to dress to the nines. All the women did. It was one of those unwritten corporate rules. But at home, she always went for comfort over style.

Or were shallow women the only ones who cared about things like that? And was he flirting with her? How could he be so arrogant one day and so charming the next?

Avery steered her toward the back of the club. The music grew less intense as they moved away from the dance floor.

At the elevator he pulled a gold pass from his pocket and flashed it at the panel.

"On the second floor the music is not as loud. It's more R&B versus the hip-hop downstairs. The third floor is all jazz music. We wanted to have something for everyone. We call the upper levels the Ultra lounges. They're elegant and cozy with upholstered sofas and chairs. Not everyone can get beyond the first floor."

"How do people get to come up here? Do you need a special pass?"

"A special pass or deep pockets. Depending on the night, you just might need both. The lounge fees start at three hundred. They're intended for special occasion parties, or important guests." He placed his hand on her back and guided her into a private lounge on the third floor. The intimacy of his touch while dancing was expected, but they were off the dance floor now. She hurried her pace just beyond his reach.

He ended the tour at what she guessed was the Malveaux private lounge, that overlooked the first floor. On one side of the room was a small bar, stocked with premium brands of alcohol, tended by a mature bartender.

The inside was much more lavish than anything else he'd shown her. A tall, muscular man was seated on one of the cushioned couches.

"This is my brother, Austen," Avery said.

"So, you're the woman that had him flying out of here," Austen laughed.

Macy looked at Avery in confusion. Was he anxious to see her so that he could apologize about his comment yesterday, or did he doubt she'd show at all?

"Never mind him. Austen, this is Macy Rollins. She works at English."

After a quick handshake, Avery escorted her to the other side of the room to a grouping of upholstered chairs that overlooked the dance floor below. Macy slid onto the seat and crossed her legs.

"What was that about?"

"Nothing. Let me get you a drink."

He looked down at her thighs as her dress rode up. Macy tugged the edge of her dress. She kept her eyes on him as he made his way to the small bar on the far side of the room. What exactly was going on here? Was Avery testing her, or was his obvious interest in her genuine? Tonight he was the perfect gentleman. Escorting her around the club, getting her a drink from the bar. She had his full attention and not once did his attention stray to another woman, whose dress was shorter or tighter or to a woman that was prettier. She didn't have to compete for his attention. Whatever he was doing, was working, and dang-it, she knew better.

He returned with two glasses of champagne. She detested the taste but held the glass to her mouth and pretended to sip before setting it down. "If I hadn't promised Roxy I'd come tonight, I'd probably be home getting some much-needed sleep. Gayle dragged me out."

"I was only kidding about telling Roxy if you didn't show. But why would Gayle have to force you? Why didn't you want to come?"

"I'm not a partier. I'd rather sit in the corner of the sofa and watch a movie or read a book. By the time Monday drags around, I always wish I'd gotten more sleep. Gayle can go out every night, and it doesn't bother her."

"I would have never guessed that about you. I guess I had a different perception of you."

"Different how?"

"I'm not sure yet. I'll answer that question later." He rubbed his hands together.

"You're quite the charmer, I see."

"What do you like to do when you're not running around trying to please Roxy? What do you do for fun?"

"Fun is highly overrated."

"That means you're doing something wrong." He chuckled. The ease of his laughter relaxed the tension in her shoulders.

"So, there is no special man in your life?"

She reached for the champagne and contemplated an answer. "Ah, the personal question." She tilted her head, trying to ease the uncomfortable heat peppering her back.

He held up his hands. "You don't have to answer, if you don't want to. I don't want to make you uncomfortable."

"I don't share my personal history with my colleagues. But the answer is no. I'm not currently dating anyone. Who are you dating this week?"

He clutched his heart in exaggerated pain. "Why would you say that? I'm single at the moment. Truth is, I've been playing the field, as you say. But that's only because I can't seem to find the right woman." His eyes softened.

"Macy, we meet again." Celeste sauntered into the lounge wearing a dress that fit her like a glove and so short it was amazing her butt wasn't exposed. She bore her infamous fake smile. The smell of alcohol reached them before Celeste did.

Avery stood slowly and glared at Celeste. His comfortable manner disappeared. "Celeste, I didn't know you were coming tonight." He shoved his hands in his pocket and straightened his back.

"I can see that." Celeste glanced down at Macy. "Nice dress you're wearing, Macy. I see you know your way around the discount stores."

Macy gripped the stem of the glass tighter. If there was a way to slink out of the room unnoticed she would have taken it. She should have known Celeste would be here.

"For a worker-bee, you sure do show up in all the right places. Shouldn't you be out running errands for my sister, or something?"

"First of all, I'm not a worker bee. I'm the Sales Manager, responsible for both profit and loss. The last time I check IT was just a drain on overhead. Besides, it's Saturday, and I'm here because your sister asked me to represent English." Macy emptied the contents of her glass.

Jacki Kelly

Avery stood. "How did you get up here? You don't have a pass."

"At the elevator, I told the attendant, I was your guest. You don't mind do you, sweetie?"

Macy's entire body tensed. Once she was willing to give Celeste a pass on her outrageous behavior. She was Roxy's sister after all, but not after tonight, she wouldn't be as forgiving.

"What in the world are you doing up here, Macy? I'm sure Roxy doesn't pay you enough to hang out on the VIP level." She draped her arm around Avery's waist.

He stepped out of her embrace. "Macy is representing English, so I decided to show her around." Avery stood between the two women. "Why don't you get a drink?" Avery pointed to the bar in the corner of the room.

"Good idea." Celeste zigzagged her way to the bar. Avery returned to his seat. The strained tension around his lips matched the tension filling the room.

"I've met my obligation for the night," she said. "I'd better go find my friend, she must be wondering where I am." She put her glass down and stood.

"I'm sorry. I didn't mean to make it sound like…"

She held up her hand. "I'm here because Roxy can't be and that's the truth."

Celeste came toward them with a drink in her hand. "Are you sure you don't want another drink before you leave? Up here the drinks are free, and I know on your salary you can't afford to buy too many of them downstairs."

"Celeste, don't worry so much about what's in my wallet," Macy said with an edge in her voice.

"Oh, look at you, getting sassy. I didn't think you had it in you."

Macy nodded. "Thanks for showing me around, Avery." She almost extended her hand to shake with Avery but pulled it back.

Before leaving the room, Macy glanced over her shoulder. Celeste had taken the seat she'd vacated. There was something about her Macy was never going to like.

Chapter Ten

Monday morning Macy sat behind the desk in her cramped third-floor office nervously tapping the wooden surface. Saturday night had faded to a distant blur that was hard to decipher. Something was going on between Celeste and Avery, but that didn't dull her attraction to him the way it should. Maybe it was the way Avery always looked miserable in Celeste's company.

She checked her horoscope.

You are a good judge of character and that talent will be your major asset today. You know the truth when you see it. You'll need to be extra vigilant today to discern whom you can trust.

Oh, how true. Even though today's message sounded like a warning. If her horoscope continued to forecast gloom, she might have to switch to tarot cards. At least she hadn't made a fool of herself on Saturday night, by gushing or extending a compliment to Avery. He was the one she needed to be careful with. He was no more her friend than his father had been her mother's friend. The Malveauxs were wealthy aristocrats who used people to get what they wanted. She'd be fine as long as she remembered that.

Enough of that, she shook her head and placed her palms flat on her desk. The company audit was a week away. Today she needed to continue her examination of all her accounts. There was no such thing as too much prep. She scrolled through her computer, located her two largest financial accounts, then she removed the back-up paper documentation from her desk drawer.

Preparing for the audit should be the easiest thing she'd do all week. Her accounts were always in order, down to the last penny. She monitored them every month. Growing up poor was an excellent precursor on how to manage money.

She ran the computer cursor down the screen, giving each line item in the travel expense account a quick glance. The sum matched the numbers on the printed document. With satisfaction, she pulled up the selling expense account. The account included her team's salaries, travel expenses, product displays and delivering product to customers. She ran the cursor down the column of numbers in front of her and checked them against the paper documentation. The two didn't add up.

She closed her eyes until the sting of stress disappeared, and then repeated the act. Maybe she was missing something. She took her time, examining each transaction. Still no match. The pressure on her temples increased, tightening like a vice.

She punched the long string of numbers into the calculator. Taking her time, she pushed each key with a deliberate tap. After hitting the total, she stared at the final sum. Fear suffocated her, making her gasp. She blinked several times before staring at the documents again.

"How can it be $100,000 over the forecast?" she mumbled with her hand pressed against her throat.

She repeated the exercise three times.

Nothing changed.

"Michelle, can you come in here?" she called to her assistant.

A moment later Michelle appeared in the doorway. "What's up?"

Macy pushed the spreadsheet across the desk. "Take a look at these numbers. They're not adding up, and I need to know why. You said my sales account was balanced last month. Now it's coming up one hundred thousand short."

"That's crazy." Michelle picked up the papers and wrinkled her nose.

"I've looked at it three times."

"Well, there must be a reasonable explanation," Michelle scanned the sheet.

"Are you sure it balanced last month? You did check the account, right?" Macy tempered her anxiety. Yelling at Michelle wouldn't resolve the issue.

"Of course, it was."

"I was so busy I took you at your word, without checking. But if it balanced then, what's wrong now?"

Michelle straightened. Her weave fell across her left eye. "Let me take a closer look. I'll figure this out."

"I want every invoice and voucher for the last three months and put them in chronological order. Don't leave anything out. I want you to set up a conference call with the sales team. I want them to be prepared to discuss any unusual or unexpected activity that wasn't in the budget. I want them to make themselves available later today."

"I'll get right on it."

Macy's temperature rose. She flopped against the back of the chair. Just what she needed, another crisis. With this much money missing, she could lose her job. Problems were piling up like bodies. She drummed her fingers on the desktop. Still, no word or call from Bunting on the contract and it was already ten o'clock. Not a good sign. Even though Roxy hadn't yelled about the delayed contract, the drawn look on her face spoke the words she didn't.

Macy picked up the phone and redialed Carl Bunting's office.

When the assistant answered, she cleared her throat. "This is Macy Rollins, calling again from English International. I'm following up on the contract. Has Mr.

Bunting received it yet? I was guaranteed delivery by eight this morning."

"I'm sorry, but I can't verify that the contract has arrived. You should call your courier, and make sure the package was delivered."

Macy closed her eyes for a moment. "Yes, I will. In the meantime, if it shows up can you please call me right away? Let me give you my cell number so you can reach me if I'm not at my desk."

"Sure, Ms. Rollins."

She picked up the receiver and dialed the courier. "I dropped off a package on Friday morning that was supposed to be delivered by eight today. It has not arrived yet." She provided the tracking number to the lackadaisical man who answered the phone.

After several minutes he returned to the phone. "Yeah, I looked in our system, and I'm not finding that tracking number. Are you sure you're reading it right?" He had the enthusiasm of a snail.

"Of course. I'm reading the right number. Maybe you wrote something down incorrectly. Let's try again." She spoke slower this time enunciating each letter and number. "This is very important. I need to find that package."

"Hold on."

She pulled the phone away from her ear and stared at the receiver. She recognized the voice. It was the same guy that helped her on Friday. He lacked gumption then, and today he still didn't seem interested in serving the customer. As soon as things settled down in the office, she'd discuss changing courier services with Roxy.

When he failed to return to the phone after ten minutes, she hung up.

Telling Roxy that contract still hadn't arrived was not an option. Roxy had made that very clear. She picked up the phone and dialed Gayle.

"I need a favor. A big one."

"Do you know what time it is? I'm not up yet." Gayle sounded groggy.

"I wouldn't call if this wasn't important.

"What is it?"

"The contract hasn't arrived yet. And I can't take the chance that it won't be delivered today. I need you to ride to Virginia. This morning. It's a three-hour drive, if you leave in ten minutes you'll be there before noon."

"You're serious?"

"Please, Gayle."

"What's in it for me?"

"I'll buy groceries for the next six months. I promise."

"Deal."

"I'll text you the address and have Michelle bring the contract over right now. She'll be there by the time you're dressed," she paused. "Gayle, thank you so much. I wouldn't have asked if I had another option. I've got a meeting this morning that I can't miss."

"I know you have my back. You always do."

Macy ended the call. After giving Michelle the detailed instruction, she took several short breaths. She regained her composure before call Bunting assistant and assuring her the contract was on the way.

She pulled the pyramid of contracts closer. A debacle of another contract arriving late wouldn't happen again. She'd prepared for whatever surprises waited to ambush her.

After pouring over the details of each contract for hours, there was still fear the day was about to blow up in her face. There was always another bombshell lying in wait around the next corner to keep her off balance.

She pushed away from the desk just as the phone rang. She snatched the receiver from the cradle. The sight of her mother's number on the display made her smile. At friendly caller.

"I meant to call you this weekend. I just keep rushing from one thing to the next," she explained.

"I know you're busy. I won't keep you long." Her mother's soothing voice calmed her.

"Is everything okay? I dropped a check in the mail this morning."

"Macy, I didn't tell you about the water heater because I wanted money. Brian and I are doing fine. Really, we are. I might even take a trip after I get Brian settled at school." She paused. "I just want you to come for a visit soon. It's been a while since you were home."

The three-hour drive one way to southern Maryland required a whole day, which meant she only saw her family a few times a year. She needed to do better. "I'll check my calendar. I promise. And we'll do something fun, go shopping and out to dinner. Maybe I'll talk you into cooking chicken marsala." She glanced at the clock in her office. "Now I've got to go. I'm late for a meeting. Tell Brian I'll be there for his last game."

She gathered her papers and hurried to the conference room.

Roxy and Avery were already seated at the table.

"Good morning Macy." Roxy greeted her the moment she walked in.

"Sorry, I'm late. I had a call…"

Roxy waved her toward a seat. "Did you have an enjoyable weekend? I'm really sorry I didn't get a chance to go to the opening. It seems everyone is talking about how wonderful it was. I'll have to drop in another night and see for myself." Roxy talked while shuffling through the papers in front of her.

Macy took the seat opposite Avery. She gave him a quick glance. "My weekend was busy as usual," she said.

Roxy intertwined her fingers and placed her hands on the table. "By the way, Carl Bunting called this morning. He doesn't have the contract that you couriered on Friday. He's less than pleased and threatening to move his business elsewhere."

Macy lowered her head and exhaled a long slow breath. "He'll have it by noon today."

Roxy's eyed her. "You're sure?"

Macy nodded. "I am."

Avery sat up straighter. "We'll print another copy, get your signature, and have it hand delivered today if we have to."

Roxy looked across the table. Her eyes narrowed. "Fine. But if we lose this piece of business …"

"I'm handling everything, Roxy." Macy managed to get the words without croaking. "And I also think this is a good reason to look into switching couriers. We need someone more reliable."

Roxy glared across the table. "We've got enough demanding our attention for now. Before the Dragon negotiations get underway in earnest, we need to close negotiations with some of the smaller clients. That way we will know where we stand and what we need for those final rounds. That means we need to move on the Watney, Albabo, and Williams' contracts. As always, we'll meet face-to-face with these customers since they always seem to need a lot of hand-holding." Roxy released a loud sigh.

"I've already made my travel plans and I've reviewed the contracts. I'm not expecting anything significant to come up," said Macy.

"I reviewed those contracts this weekend and planned to accompany you when you meet with them," Avery said.

"Great, Avery. I knew I would be happy we hired your firm. I was hoping you were available. This way you can run any traps with their legal teams while you're in the room with them. But I can't make it to Asturias or Geneva. Something has come up, and I need to stay close to the office." She glanced at Macy. "You'll have to go to handle the Europe accounts without me. I should be able to deal with the Williams account."

"No problem." Macy's heart thumped faster. Nothing about this meeting was turning out the way it had in her imagination. But, if she nailed the contracts on this trip, there was no way she wouldn't get promoted. Under the table her leg swung back and forth.

Avery straightened his tie but didn't look across the table. "Are you sure you can't make it, Roxy? These contracts are the cornerstone of the business. They've been with you from the beginning. I think they may be offended if you don't show up this year for these negotiations."

Just like a Malveaux to climb over someone's head to advance their agenda. But she wasn't her mother, and she didn't mind a fight.

She leveled a glaring stare at Avery. The same one she used on people who stepped on her foot when riding Septa or who tried to push ahead of her in line at the grocery store. The idea of throwing daggers at Avery, cutting into his custom-tailored suit and shredding his cold heart pushed away her frown. He couldn't be trusted. "Avery, I'm sure I can give the customer that warm, fuzzy feeling they'll need. I'll assure them Roxy's absence couldn't be helped. As a matter…

Roxy put up her hand. "Yes, Macy is right. She can handle this alone. Besides, she's got more hands-on experience than I have. Nobody knows these contracts better than her."

"Thank you, Roxy." Macy looked at her manager but directed her sarcasm at Avery.

"I can't think of a better team than you and Avery. So, I hope you two get this business done. I would go, but I need to prepare for the remaining Dragon contracts. We've got some shipping issues and supply chain problems that required immediate attention, or we'll see a disruption in meeting demand."

"I'm ready," Macy said and forced a smile. She'd show Mr. Malveaux just how different she was from the women that usually surrounded him.

She'd prove to him that he didn't know her or what she was capable of doing. The idea settled in and she conjured up ways to make him look foolish. He wasn't the first man to underestimate her capabilities.

Roxy pulled her chair closer to the table. "I really appreciate your willingness to go on such short notice, Avery. Of course, if you have any questions just let us know." She looked at Avery and Macy. "If you don't have any other comments, let's review the remaining contracts this morning."

An hour later Roxy stood gathering her briefcase and purse. "I've got to run. I'll have my assistant make the travel arrangements for you, Avery. Any questions?"

Macy looked at Avery. "No. You don't need to worry about Watney or Albabo. I'll handle them."

"Good, I have lunch today with Celeste, I need to run. Avery, would you like to join us?"

"No, thank you. I'm going to pass." He didn't look at Roxy when he spoke. Instead, he glanced across the table at Macy as if he expected her to respond.

"Okay then." Roxy adjusted her purse on her shoulder. "You guys are sure you're okay with the plan, right?" Her eyes darted from Avery to Macy for confirmation.

"Stop worrying, Roxy, I know what I need to do." Macy stood with confidence.

"Avery, I might fly Celeste over later during your visit to Geneva. She needs a little vacation. Would you be willing to show her around?"

"I'm sure Celeste will jump at the chance, but this is a business trip. After we finish, I'll need to get back to Philadelphia."

"Well, let me know if you change your mind." Roxy rushed from the room. Hurrying was the way Roxy did everything.

Macy tried to read the expression on Avery's face, but couldn't. She shoved a contract into the folder and gathered the folders in her arm. Avery was her nightmare. He questioned her work and came pretty close to flirting with her all while dating Celeste.

Avery collected his papers and walked to her side of the table. "Are you surprised that Roxy won't make the trip?"

She glanced up at him without saying anything. He looked perfectly normal. Where did he hide his long, pointed tail and sharp teeth?

"What surprised me was your comment," she said without parting her teeth. "How dare you question my ability to handle the accounts. I'm the Sales Manager and I didn't get there without knowing what I'm doing. I don't appreciate your snide comments about my ability."

"I didn't mean to imply you weren't capable…"

"That's exactly what you implied." She brushed past him to leave the room.

He reached out and touched her arm. "Macy, Roxy pays me to help her make sound decisions."

She pulled away from his grasp. "She pays me to do the same thing. So, I would appreciate it if you stop second-guessing my work."

"Fair enough. We need to work together, and I think we can. I'm sure we can."

She gave him her coldest stare before marching out of the room.

Avery rubbed his chin. Her look stung like a blow. Macy was right. There was an extra punch in her stride that had to be caused by her anger at him. Kicking himself for the comment about her ability wouldn't help him. When had he turned into his father? He shuddered.

If he kept stumbling with Macy, it would be impossible for them to work together. The English contract had taken too long to acquire to allow his tongue to mess things up. He just needed to pull it together and let his charisma do its work.

He didn't need another miscalculation. Too many of those and he'd be standing on the outside of his prize account wondering what had gone wrong. He needed to gain Macy's trust. And fast.

Judging from the look she gave him, it wouldn't be easy. He could interpret the contract language, but Macy knew what the customers wanted. She knew the marketplace.

He inhaled the floral fragrance of her perfume lingering in the air. If he didn't find a way to control his tongue, he wouldn't last too long as outside counsel at English. Roxy was aware of the tension between him and Macy. That was no way to get started.

They were corporate peers, she didn't report to him, and he didn't report to her. Her work wasn't a reflection on him. So why was he saying things to offend her? Fumbling for the right words had never been a problem.

He followed Macy down the hall, not sure what he planned to say, only knowing he needed to say something and it had better be good.

Before she could shut her office door, he stepped inside. "Hello Macy. I'm Avery Malveaux. We're going to be working together. I think we'll make a good team." He shifted his briefcase to shake her hand. She gave him a blank stare without extending hers. "We've gotten off on the wrong foot, all my fault. I'm trying to make it right. I know I might sound corny but play along with me, please."

Her facial features relaxed. Good, he was making progress. "I'll stop by your office this afternoon, so we can discuss the trip. I have some questions. I'm sure you have some inside tips to share on how you plan to approach these customers. Your flexographic plates are expensive, so I'd like to understand what value English brings to them."

The line around her mouth tightened. "If you think I'm letting you off the hook that easy, you're mistaken."

"I'll pick you up for lunch, and we can talk at the restaurant."

"Lunch? What makes you think I want to eat lunch with you?"

"We both need to eat, and my afternoon is booked so it's the only time I can talk. I'll pick you up at noon." He walked away before she detected the lie.

Chapter Eleven

The morning evaporated in a blur of paperwork and phone calls. Macy glanced down at the surface of her desk. From the stack of papers remaining, very little had been accomplished. She wanted to have lunch with Avery about as much as she wanted to have her nails pulled from their beds. But, she'd done much worse things for the sake of her job.

Just because the Bunting contract was out there somewhere dancing in limbo, didn't mean she could give up. She scrolled through her contacts, looking for the number of the woman she met last month at the Graphic Arts Conference.

When Constance picked up, Macy introduced herself.

"Yes, I remember you. That was quite a display English had," Constance was pleasant.

"I was hoping I could set up some time to meet with you, so we can discuss your company needs and how I can help you achieve them."

"That would be great. We're located just outside D.C., so let me know when you'll be in the neighborhood."

Macy pulled up her schedule. "How about two weeks from today, on the twelfth. I can be there at nine."

"Sounds good."

"I'll have my assistant send you some materials to help you get familiar with our offering."

Macy ended the call, then checked the time. She dialed Gayle next. "How did you make out?"

"No problems. They have it. You could hire me as your courier service. That was easy."

Macy released the air in her lungs. "Gayle, if you were here right now, I'd kiss you."

Gayle laughed. "Just remember, you can't nag me about groceries for six months."

"It the least I can do. You saved my ass. At least now if Bunting doesn't like the terms of the contract, it won't be wholly on my shoulders for not arriving in time."

She dropped her chin. One hurdle done. She sent Roxy an email, with the good news.

At noon, Avery stepped through her office door. His bright, shiny face said this lunch was something he'd been looking forward to having. She wished she could have shared his enthusiasm, but she had every intention of heeding the words from her horoscope.

"You know, Avery, I'm swamped this morning. Instead of eating lunch I need to drop by the courier. Something is going on over there and I need to know what. When I called them this morning I didn't get a satisfactory answer." She pushed away from the desk to stand. "We can get together later this week." If she didn't come up with another excuse before then.

"I think that's a good idea. I'll drive. We can pick something up on the way back."

"That's okay. I can manage alone."

"Now you don't have to." He stepped aside to allow her to exit the office.

"Are you always this assertive? I'm waiting for you to give me advice on how to breathe."

"I don't know if I'd call myself assertive. *Efficient* does a better job of describing me." He pushed the elevator button. "If something can be done right the first time, that's always the option I'm going to take."

"You didn't invent that theory. Unless you are bat-shit crazy, that's the option that ninety percent of the world

61

would naturally take." She directed her attention to the elevator panel.

The doors parted. She walked into the elevator car ahead of him.

"Have you tried calling the courier? You might be able to save yourself a trip."

She pushed the lobby button before he could, then pointed her index finger at her head. "You know, I never thought about picking up the phone. I can see why Roxy hired you. Even though this doesn't concern you, the contract was hand delivered this morning."

"Good to know."

"But the one I dropped off at the courier on Friday hasn't arrived yet. Something is going on over there and I need to find out what it is.

"So why are you mailing another contract?" He pointed to the envelope in her lap.

"It's a test. If they can't delivery this contract a second time, then maybe I'll be able to convince our purchasing department it's time to switch."

He nodded twice with a smile that almost took over his face. Who knew he was capable of something so extraordinary? She kept looking, waiting for the smile to fully bloom. In it was the charm that buckled knees.

"I like your sense of humor. At least you're not as uptight as you appeared that first night in the ballroom."

How did he go from being gruff one moment and almost easy going the next? She turned her attention on her shoes. Safe territory, seldom did shoes cause her shortness of breath, unless there was a really good sale at Nordstrom's.

Pipeline Delivery was only a few blocks away. They rode in silence. Leaving her too much time to think about Avery.

He pulled into the lot. Before he could turn off the engine, she opened the car door.

"Wait up. I'm going in with you."

"I've got this."

He turned off the engine. "I know you're tough. But, I'm curious." He climbed out, closed the door, and caught up to her.

"This place is as messy this time as it was on Friday. No wonder they can't find anything in here." She managed the disgust in her voice.

"Are you sure we're in the right location?" Avery straightened his tie while looking around as if he'd stepped in gum. "This explains a lot about what's been going on."

A woman, several years younger than Macy, approached the counter. She wore jeans torn at the knees and a t-shirt that stated she was still hung over from last year. "Yeah. Can I help you?" the woman asked without missing a beat on the chewing gum she smacked. Her name tag read Ruth, but she didn't look like any Ruth Macy had ever met.

"I'd like to get some information on this tracking number. I dropped this package off on Friday morning." She pushed the piece of paper across the counter.

"Okay." Ruth slunk away, in no hurry. She wouldn't move any faster if her butt were on fire.

Macy folded her arms. If this was like the call she made, they'd have a long wait. Why English continued to use such a deficient operation begged investigation.

"Tell me, do you give everyone a hard time or just me?" Avery's eyes wandered over her. She looked down at her silk slacks and ran her hand over the zipper.

"Everyone. But I saved a little extra for you."

"Why is that?"

She mocked his pose. "Because you're so smug. I don't think I've ever met a man who emitted so much privilege."

"Is it privilege or confidence?"

"Actually, I was going to say *entitlement*, but I thought that might be too much." She pushed off the counter and stepped away from him. "Whatever it is, you have way too much of it."

The expression on his face didn't change. He continued to stare at her with the same expression.

"Here you go." Ruth handed her a sheet of paper. "It will be delivered tomorrow or Wednesday."

"Why isn't this package arriving today as requested? I paid for early morning express service. This is unacceptable." Avery said, no longer looking amused.

Ruth shrugged her shoulders and released a loud smack of her gum.

Macy pulled the duplicate paperwork from her bag. "Can I mail this now with the assurance that it will arrive tomorrow?"

Ruth looked at the clock on the wall before strolling to a nearby desk to glance at a bulletin board. All the while she continued to smack her gum. Her nonchalance was maddening. She returned to the counter. "No. This won't get there any faster than the other one. If you'd brought it in this morning, before ten, then maybe we could."

"Can you get your manager out here?" Macy couldn't control the anger in her voice.

"He's not in yet."

Macy closed her eyes and inhaled. She managed to count to five before turning to Avery and saying, "You see what I'm working with here?"

He grabbed her by the elbow. "Let's get out of here before the top of your head blows off." He steered her out the door and back to the car. "I think we've earned that lunch, along with something stronger than a soda to drink."

In the car she buckled her seatbelt. "You know that contract isn't going to arrive either." Macy said with a sigh.

"It doesn't matter. Bunting has the contract and you've got enough information on this courier operation to suggest a changing." Avery started the engine and backed out of the space. "The Bunting contract's late arrival is a company failure, not a personal one. It's a wonder they're still in business."

"They've had some turnover in personnel. They weren't always this bad."

At lunch she sat across the table from Avery. "It's a good thing you pulled me out of Pipeline before I lost my temper," she said.

"You mean, that's not what I already saw?" he chuckled.

"I could have been worse." She took a bite from her sandwich.

"I'll have to make a note of that and remember not to get on your bad side. At least not again. But we are a team now." He lifted his soda as if he was toasting her, before taking a sip.

She nodded. "You're joking, right? I mean after some of the things you said, don't you think my reaction to you was justified?"

"I'm not usually so aggressive." He looked down at his half-eaten sandwich. "My father has coveted the English account for years and I'm the one to get it. So, I guess I feel a need to outdo him. Show him I'm a better lawyer than he was."

His confession shocked her. Maybe he wasn't as cocky as she thought. If she wasn't careful, really careful, she could fall for his charm, his good looks, his warmth, and the prettiest eyes she'd ever seen on a man. "Are you and your father close?"

"I'm not sure I'd use the word close. He's my father. I used to look up to him. Growing up in his shadow wasn't easy." He picked up a French fry but put it back down. "That's enough about me…"

"We had better get back to the office. It's getting late."

"Before we go, tell me why English calls contract renewal Dragon."

She twisted a curl around her finger. "Roxy likes to give projects special names. That way in a word the whole team knows what she's referring to. The Dragon negotiations is that time of year when several contracts need to be renewed. Instead of spacing them out, Roxy likes to do them all and get them over with. It's easy for her, all she has to do is basically sign contracts, it's the rest of the team that gets stressed."

"Have you thought of changing it?"

"I'm working on it. But most of our contracts run on calendar years, so whether they're two or three years, they'll still come due during this period."

"Can I ask you a personal question?"

"I need to get back." She stood and pulled her purse on her shoulder. She wasn't ready to pour her heart out to him. The less people knew about you, the less they could use against you. She didn't tell every Tom, Dick and Avery, her father was a total ass-hole and had screwed up her ability to have a decent relationship with the opposite sex.

Back in the safety of her office, she collapsed in her chair. Working with Avery was going to be more of a challenge than she'd calculated.

She shook his image away. A quick scan of her email said nothing had changed since she'd left. Her assistant had left a pile of messages on her desk. One message was from Carl Buntings assistant, confirming the contract arrival. For just a few minutes she needed the world to stop, to give her time to map out the pieces and gain some clarity. From the moment Roxy hired the Malveaux firm, there seemed to be an onslaught of problems, and she wasn't fast enough to bat them down. Regardless of all the flowery talk over lunch about them being a team, working together and starting over, she wasn't falling for any of it.

This pace was unsustainable, but this wasn't a race with rest stops at designated intervals where she could slow down to catch her breath before continuing. Either she was in it all the way, or she could give up and go back home.

She glanced at the time on the right corner of her computer screen. It was only two in the afternoon, and she was already wrung out like wet laundry. She closed her eyes and massaged her lids.

Dread crept up her back. Pouring over the sales numbers this morning produced nothing. Every invoice, every voucher, and every expenditure was accounted for, but the numbers refused to add up.

She pushed away from the desk and stood, stretching her arms overhead. Maybe she was trying to apply logic where none existed. Balancing the accounts wasn't like her checking account where she was the only one making the deposits and withdrawals. The whole sales team charged expenses to her codes. But she had to approve everything, which meant she should have been able to track each item.

The phone startled her. She yanked the receiver off the cradle. "Macy speaking."

"This is Debra in accounting. I'm calling to set up a meeting with you and the auditors. Are you available on this coming Monday?" Debra's clipped tone was all business. Any other time talking to her would have been enjoyable, but not today. Not when she needed more time.

"I'm leaving for a business trip and won't be back on Monday." She reached for her calendar. "How about the following Monday, the twenty-second?"

Debra paused for a moment. "We want to get this completed as soon as possible, but if you're away, I guess we have no choice. We'll review your accounts in advance. If we have any questions, I'll reach you by email. If all goes well on the twenty-second, you can just sign-off."

Macy opened her mouth. The review wouldn't go well. But those words wouldn't move beyond her tongue. They sat in her throat like a boulder. "Yeah, sure. See you then." She hung up the phone and flopped back into her seat.

"Are you okay? You look like you saw a zombie." Avery stood in her doorway.

She needed to have a little talk with her heart tonight as soon as she got home. A couple nice conversations were no reason to take him out of co-worker category and place him in friend category. She knew better. Just because they'd found common ground on which to work didn't mean he was any more trustworthy than the corned beef sandwich they'd shared at lunch. He might corral his rough critiques, but that didn't mean he was her ally.

"Are you going to stop in my office to talk to me every time you walk by?" she asked.

"That's my goal.ll mm   m"

"You're not going to get much done. And we have new legal counsel who frowns on that. You had better watch out."

"Ouch, girl. Your words pack a punch. I thought you would have forgiven me by now."

"I'm thinking about it."

He came in and took the seat in front of her desk. "Between the audit and the Dragon negotiations, I don't know how you guys can juggle so much. Does English always schedule things this close? The staff is stretched too thin."

"Listen, about the audit…" Macy started.

"What about the audit?" He perched on the edge of the chair.

"It's nothing." She waved her hand, dismissing her comment. "We have a good team here at English. They're used to this manic pace. You'll get used to it, too."

"I hear that audit group on the fifth floor is brutal this year."

Macy's stomach constricted. "They're brutal every year. But we…the staff…manage."

Long after Avery was gone, she continued to stare at the chair he left empty. When she was growing up, she couldn't wait to be in control. No more taking orders from anyone else and no more worrying about what others thought. But life couldn't have turned out more unlike what she'd hoped. Control still eluded her. The only thing that seemed to matter is what others thought of her. She released the breath she was holding.

"Hey, Michelle, can you come in here?"

"Yeah, I'll be right there." There was urgency in Michelle's voice.

Macy clicked several icons on her computer, dividing the screen in half. With the mouse, she examined the numbers on the spreadsheet against the accounting entries. She scribbled down the record numbers on the legal pad before studying the transactions.

"Michelle, are you coming?"

Several moments later, Michelle stuck her head in the door. "What's up?"

"Have you had any luck in tracking the money?"

"I haven't had any time to look. But I'll get on it."

Macy bit back her disappointment. "Diving into the numbers is your priority." With her elbow planted on the desk, she pointed at Michelle. "I need answers today."

"Can't today, Macy." She sunk her teeth into a chocolate bar. "I'm leaving early today. I've got something to take care of this afternoon."

"We've talked about this before, Michelle. You need to clear time out of the office with me. I need your attention on this right now."

"Yeah, I know, but this just came up. I'll get to it in the morning. Promise."

"Are you sure I've seen all the vouchers that needed approval?"

Michelle looked over her shoulder, back at her desk before returning her attention. "Yeah. I'm sure." She looked over her shoulder, again.

"Is everyone available for the call this afternoon?"

"Yes. The conference call is all set up."

Okay, Michelle. Go ahead, but you need to come in early tomorrow and get working on this."

"Yeah, sure thing," Michelle said, already halfway out the door.

Macy rubbed her forehead. Right now wasn't the time to fire Michelle and start interviewing for a new assistant. The world needed to stop spinning for just a few moments. Her job depended on finding that money. She picked up the phone and dialed accounting.

"Connie, I need your help," she said. "Can you run monthly balance on my account, starting with January?"

"You want everything? That's a lot."

"Yeah. How soon can you get it to me?"

"Give me a day or two."

"Connie, one more thing. I'm seeing a lot of new accounts. Several that I don't recognize. I know we're going after market share, but I didn't expect this many. If I send you a list of the names, what information can you provide on them?"

"Well, I can tell you when the account was set up, by who, and purchasing activity. What else would you need?"

"That's a good start. Thanks."

Macy ended the call, but the nagging didn't subside.

Chapter Twelve

Avery hustled his way through the open area toward his office. No matter how friendly he tried to be with Macy, she remained standoffish. Who could blame her? For a man with a reputation as a playboy he hadn't used his skills to woo her. His ambition to be a better lawyer than his father got in the way.

Sure, Macy smiled and was cordial, but her shoulders tensed any time he approached her. Maybe she needed more time to loosen up and get used to the new person he was trying to be.

The glamour of chasing empty relationships and fast women had dulled. There was a finite number of relationship games a man could enjoy. He needed something more substantial in his life. For now work was satisfying, but it wasn't long-term fulfillment.

"Avery, do you have a minute?" Roxy approached him from behind.

Without waiting for him to reply she passed him and continued toward her office, waving him to follow. She closed the door.

She stood behind her Mahogany desk. "Will you be ready for the trip?"

"Yes." He remained standing as well.

"Good." She opened a folder on her desk and removed a sheet of paper. "When Macy returns, I'm planning to promote her to VP of Sales. I'm getting some pushback from the other VP's. They think she's too young and doesn't have enough experience. We've butted heads on this several times and I'd like more ammunition to get them to agree with me.

Celeste is always telling me I don't see the real Macy and maybe she's right. I'm hoping you can help."

"She knows her accounts. I doubt anyone's better. She's been bringing me up to speed, and for every question I ask, she has an answer. She's sharp."

"I know, but you know how some of the older guys can be. Do me a favor." Roxy spoke fast. "When you guys get back from your trip I want to meet with Harvey and Ray. They're giving me the most push back. With your help, I'm hoping to give them an unbiased opinion of her."

"Sure thing." He reached for the doorknob. *How hard could that be?*

"One more thing. I'm not one to pry, but how are things going between you and Celeste? She told me the two of you had dinner last night."

"Roxy…"

Her phone cut him off.

"I need to get that. Let's talk when you get back and thank you." She picked up the receiver and motioned for him to close the door on his way out.

Chapter Thirteen

The last two weeks were a blur of gathering, and doing, and checking and packing and preparing. Macy leaned back in her office chair and inhaled. The days had passed so fast she wasn't sure she was ready to go to Europe. There still wasn't an answer on the missing money. The conference call with her team hadn't yielded anything to account for one hundred thousand dollars. Connie had pulled everything she requested. But the mystery still hung over her head like a cloud. Michelle was searching, without any luck.

The flight to Geneva would leave at seven, and she had poured over the contracts like there was a secret treasure buried in the legalese.

Her cellphone buzzed on her desk. The same 202 area code showed on her screen. She dismissed the call. Later she'd investigate blocking the number. It had to be some tele-marketer trying to sell her car insurance she didn't need.

She faced the computer and pounded on the keyboard. Clearing e-mails was a beneficial way to channel anxiety. While she waited for the computer to catch up with her fingers, a sense of contentment settled over her. Her interaction with Avery had found a comfortable pattern. The earlier tension had vanished. Either he was a good faker, or he'd begun to trust her judgment.

Avery popped into her thoughts at odd times, while she showered or waited for a taxi, anytime she was alone. He even had a starring role in all her late-night fantasies.

From the other end of the hall, Roxy's voice drifted into her office. Macy held her breath, hoping Roxy wouldn't stop in. With Roxy, one question could turn into an hour-long conversation about some irrelevant thing. Her footsteps drew near. Macy tried to look busy. Maybe Roxy wouldn't stop and interrupt her, but the clicking of Roxy's heels slowed at her door anyway. Her heavy cologne drifted across the room ahead of her. She wore a kimono sleeve cardigan, white silk pants, and leopard peep-toe pumps. Her infamous blond ponytail swung from side to side as she came into the room.

"I didn't expect to see you in the office today. I thought you would be home packing. Aren't you ready to go?" Roxy sat in the chair in front of the desk. Macy braced herself for the long conversation that was sure to come.

"Yes. I just wanted to review a few things before leaving."

"You're so diligent." Roxy crossed her legs. "I have all the confidence in the world that you can handle this customer. By the time you finish with Watney and Albabo, the Dragon negotiations will be well underway. If these two agree with our terms, then we'll be in a better bargaining position with the others. They're key in the industry. I enjoy this time of year. It's when I get to use all my skills of persuasion. I feel like a puppeteer, controlling the whole process."

How Roxy could breathe while talking so fast fascinated Macy. At any minute she expected Roxy to hyperventilate.

"I know we haven't talked much about what happened with the Bunting contract, but I'm sorry we lost that business." Macy leveled her gaze at Roxy.

"That was most unfortunate. I was disappointed."

"The next time, I won't cut it so close. I'll make sure all the paperwork is prepared days in advance."

"You do good work, Macy. Even with all that stuff that went wrong with the Bunting contract, you fixed it. I have faith in you," she paused. "I like the way you and Avery are working together. You've helped him understand the company, which is going to be critical for him to help us with the expansion."

"These clients are tough, but I'm ready." Macy stood up and collected the items she planned to take with her on the trip. Now that Roxy was comfortable, it would be impossible to get any more work done.

"I wish Celeste was more like you, more serious about a career and her life. I'm always telling her she should spend more time with you. That you have so much to teach her." Roxy stared out the window behind Macy. "She's only twenty-four, still young, but she should be more concerned with the direction of her life." Roxy spoke low. For someone who was always animated, she was very still.

"Celeste is a free spirit and I'm trying to get her to settle down. That's why Avery is good for her. He's patient, stable, and mature. But…" Her eyes were unfocused as if she was watching a tableau of what she wanted for her sister playing out in front of her. "My husband is getting a little tired of Celeste's antics. He thinks I need to step back and stop being her safety net." Roxy stood up and ran her hands over her pants. "Well, after I pay for a lavish wedding, I won't have to worry about her anymore, will I?" The bewildered expression on Roxy's face evaporated in an instant. "I've probably said too much. I don't know what got into me. Have a successful trip and keep up the good work."

Macy slumped in her chair and forced her nerves to relax. Roxy might not have as much confidence in her if she knew Macy was starting to have feelings for Avery and she was even more certain he had feelings for her.

"I see you and Avery have lunch almost every day. Don't you worry about office gossip?"

Macy jerked in her seat and lifted her head. Celeste stood in her office doorway with her hand saddled on her hip. Today she wore a simple dress, no exposed breast or hip-hugging dress with just enough material to cover her butt.

"I thought you had better things to do than survey the lobby."

"Just so you know, he's out of your league."

"Is there something I can do for you, Celeste, or did you stop by to give me an update on office activity."

She smiled, but it was as fake as she was, before taking the seat vacated only moments before by her sister. She crossed her legs. "Are you ready for the audit?" Her voice dripped with insincerity.

"As a matter of fact, I was gathering paperwork now." There was no way she was going to share any details with Celeste. The woman was about as trustworthy as a hungry cat. "Are you ready? Did you have some issues last year?"

She smacked her palms down on her knees. "I'm always ready. The issues raised last year were minor. I'm sure IT will be stellar this year. Besides my team isn't as large as yours, so it only took me a day to prepare. You must be sweating through the audit and the contracts." Celeste shook her head.

Macy grabbed a stack of papers and made a display of organizing them. "Don't worry about me. My accounts are in order."

"Okay, I'm going. But I meant what I said. Unless you want to get your feelings hurt, Avery's probably not the guy for you." Celeste uncoiled her long legs and slinked out of the office.

Macy faced her computer. She moved her mouse to the accounting system icon and clicked twice. She entered her username and password and waited. The circle kept spinning but didn't connect. A quick glance at the clock in the corner of the computer said she had just enough time to print out last month's selling expense transaction before heading to the airport.

She entered her username and password again. ACCESS DENIED flashed on the screen in bold red letters.

"What the hell…" Macy mumbled. There was no time for this. She reached for the power button and shut down the computer. After waiting ten seconds, she turned the computer back on. She took her time, typing in her username and password one slow keystroke at a time. ACCESS DENIED flashed on the screen. This time the words were more disturbing than before.

She picked up the phone. "Stan, my access into the accounting system has been denied."

"Calm down, Macy. Did you enter the wrong password five times? If you did that will automatically lock you out."

"No, I didn't. I know that, and I only did it twice and I used the right password."

He sighed. "Let me check and get you back on line."

She heard him tapping on keys. She closed her eyes and took a deep breath. The the phone line went quiet for several moments.

"Are you still there, Stan? What's taking so long?"

"I'm here. I'm not sure what the problem is. Let me do some checking and call you back."

"I'm heading to the airport. I need to get into the accounting system. I've got things to check. I've got an audit coming up."

"Don't know what to tell you yet. I'll get you back on line as soon as I can. I'll shoot you an email when I figure it out."

"Stan, there has got to be something you can do."

"We're shorthanded. I'll get on it." He hung up.

Chapter Fourteen

After a layover in Barcelona, the flight to Oviedo, Asturias, landed just before the sunset. The dwarf-sized airport was almost empty. Philadelphia International airport had several terminals. Macy only saw one terminal at the airport in Asturias. Within minutes they had their bags and walked the short distance to the waiting car. The warm air outside felt good after shivering through most of the flight.

The tension in her neck throbbed. Something hung in the air that wouldn't let her relax. The negotiations she could handle, she'd done it before. There was only one thing dragging her down. The audit.

Avery snapped his fingers in front of her face. "Are you there? You've been in a zone from the moment the plane taxied to the gate."

"I've got a lot of things on my mind. I checked my email and I don't have anything from Stan saying my access to the system has been restored. And, negotiating the contract with Albabo won't be easy. The pressure for this meeting is higher than what we will deal with at Watney."

"Why is that?"

"Every year Albabo tries to squeeze us on price. What they can't get on price, they try to get us on freight cost. Roxy has complained about them for years."

Avery rubbed her arm. "You don't sound worried."

"I'm not. It's like a ritualistic dance we do with them. I'd be flabbergasted if they sign the contract without giving me a hard time first. Two signed contracts puts me closer to a promotion." Macy didn't look at Avery.

"Roxy says good things about you. You're probably closer to that promotion than you think."

In her hotel room, she released a long breath. The only thing holding her together was cheap glue that threatened to burst at every seam. How could she focus on the contract until she found out where the money was? No matter how well she did on this trip, the audit could derail her whole career. What if this wasn't a simple accounting error, where the wrong account got charged or someone added an extra zero to an entry by mistake? What if this was sabotage? With her palm on her chest, Macy forced herself to breathe.

The room was small, but it was decorated in soothing shades of maroon and gold. The queen-sized bed took up most of the room, but a small desk and chair was shoved into the corner. At the window she pushed the drapes aside to see a view of the deserted main street.

She pulled her computer from the bag and set it up on the narrow desk. If her accounts were balanced last month, then she needed to examine every day's transaction since the beginning of the month. The process might be long and tedious, but it had to lead to answers. She'd start with the first fifteen days and would ask Michelle to examine the last fifteen days. If she worked every night, together maybe they'd have an answer by the time she returned to Philadelphia. She tried to get into the accounting system again. But the same warning flashed on her screen.

The phone startled her from her thoughts.

"Yeah," she said.

"How about dinner with me tonight?" Avery sounded upbeat.

"I can't. Not tonight. I want to get a little work done and crawl into bed." She continued pounding on the keyboard.

"You need to eat something. There is a small restaurant downstairs, we can eat there. It'll be quick..."

"I can't, Avery. I'm working."

"Okay," he hesitated. "How about breakfast?"

"We aren't meeting with Albabo until three," she said.

"Then that gives us all morning to have a nice breakfast and go over the meeting details."

His optimism had no bounds. It must be nice to stroll through life without a worry. One day she hoped to have the same experience.

"Yeah, okay. Thanks for checking on me."

She hung up the phone. Falling for Avery could be easy. Nobody had pursued her with that much enthusiasm in years. At least not anyone worth a second glance.

In the morning before going down to breakfast with Avery, she pulled out her phone and checked her horoscope.

Take nothing for granted today, double-check, then check again all your sources today. Most of the feedback that crosses your desk will be severely tainted by several sources. Today is not the day to be trusting. Others stand to gain from your misfortune. Proceed with caution so that you're not a pawn.

The words flashed at her like a warning sign. Today she needed good news. There was already enough doubt pushing on her shoulders. She jumped up. At least now she knew what she needed to do. If she were any more cautious, she wouldn't trust a soul.

She tried the accounting system again. Still no access. It was too early to call Stan, so she sent him an email. If he didn't response today, she'd have to call his boss, Celeste. This was getting ridiculous.

In the hotel dining room, seated across the table from Avery, she stared at the pork-n-beans on her plate, next to the scrambled eggs.

"I don't get the beans with breakfast." She pushed them aside.

"It's a European thing," Avery said.

"Do they eat them with dinner too?"

"Not as much as we do in the States." He shoved a fork full of beans into his mouth and chewed like it was the best thing he'd eaten. Did you get the work done last night?"

"I've started."

"Was it contract related? Does it have to do with Albabo?"

She shook her head. "I'm preparing my documentation for the audit. No matter what happens here, Roxy takes the audit result just as serious as she does these contract negotiations."

"Was your access renewed yet?"

"No. I'll call Celeste as soon as she gets in the office."

He swallowed the rest of his orange juice. "Finish your breakfast. Then I'll go pick up my computer and meet you in your room to review the Albabo contract, if that's okay."

She sat back. Today wasn't the time to get sentimental because Avery was being nice. But her heart did that skipping thing anyway. His plan was a good one. His company was better than good but sitting on her bed next to him was more than she wanted to think about. "How about we meet at those chairs over there." She pointed to a grouping near the exit.

"Fine." He pointed his fork at her plate. "Eat up."

In her room, she pressed her back against the door. As long as she stayed focused on the reason she was in Europe, she'd be fine. She just hadn't planned on liking Avery so much. Life was so much simpler, when all she had to worry about was work and the promotion. Now she'd added Avery and the audit into the mix. She gathered her computer and her bag and hurried toward the elevator.

Avery was already seated when she reached the lobby. She took the chair across from him and turned on her computer. "Albabo is a private company. The president is involved in all parts of the business. They will try to squeeze us for every penny. But if we stand our ground they'll give in." She scrolled through the contract on her computer screen without looking at Avery.

"I haven't seen the changes they're proposing yet. Do you have a copy?"

"Albabo never sends an advance copy. Some low-level personnel will give us their mark-up when we arrive. I'll review the changes, take special note of the sales terms, price and termination clauses. Our thermal plate processing eliminates the needs for solvents, cuts down on process time. Our product is clearly the best, so I won't let them intimidate me. Which they'll try."

Neither of them spoke for several moments. The only sound in the lobby was the clicking of the computer keys and a few other guests' whispered conversations.

"I have to call Michelle." She reached for her phone from her purse. "She's working on some audit analysis for me." She glanced up at the corner of her computer. "She should be at her desk now."

She dialed Michelle's number. "English International." The voice was unfamiliar.

"This is Macy Rollins. Is Michelle in the office today? I need to speak with her."

"Macy this is Pepper. Michelle is not in the office. She quit."

Macy tilted her head. "Did you say she quit?"

"Yes. Yesterday."

"Did she say why?"

"No one has heard from her. She called HR, said she was quitting and would send an email saying as much. That was it. Your calls are forwarded to me, and I'll be helping you out until you get back and can hire someone else."

Before hanging up, Macy scribbled the temporary assistant's name on the legal pad. Her stomach contracted around the remains of her breakfast. Had something happened with Michelle? She wasn't the kind of person to just quit her job. How many conversations had they had about living paycheck-to-paycheck? She tried to replay the last conversation she had with Michelle, had she said something to offend her?

"You don't look too good."

"Michelle quit yesterday."

He pushed to the edge of his chair. "People quit all the time. You'll hire someone else."

"I know that." She shook her head. "But this came out of the blue. I had no idea she was unhappy."

"Maybe she wasn't unhappy. Maybe she got a better offer, or maybe she won the lottery and is now independently wealthy."

"Don't you think that's odd? She quit the day I left for a four-day trip and she failed to give so much as a head's-up?"

"Your leaving for this trip and her quitting may not be related. That's circumstantial. One doesn't lead to the other."

"Now you sound like a lawyer." Macy couldn't ignore the worried voices whispering in her head. He didn't know about her audit issues, so he couldn't know how much they could be connected.

Chapter Fifteen

Macy strolled into the Albabo conference room with enough confidence to slay the negotiations. The room was the same as it was last year. The oval walnut table and red cushioned chairs were reassuring. All she needed to do was convince Albabo that English was their best choice of printing plates, just like last year.

The Albabo team hadn't gathered yet, which gave her time to set up her presentation. She pulled her chair closer to the table and turned on her computer.

"Are you nervous?" Avery took the seat next to her.

"No." There was no way to explain to him how the preparation for the meeting had been intense and now she wanted to purge all the details and experience some relief. She'd spent the night preparing. This morning was the performance.

The executives from Albabo walked into the conference room at three. She pushed away from the table and welcomed the large contingent of employees whose job was to find advantages for their company.

"Avery, this is Pablo Mateo, the Executive Director. Pablo, Avery has just joined the English team as outside counsel. He's observing today, getting an understanding of our corporate culture." Avery smiled. He shook hands, and she led him around the room introducing him to everyone.

After the introduction, Macy returned to her seat and unofficially called the meeting to order. Her fingers danced across her keyboard as she went through her presentation. With each slide the tension in her shoulders disappeared.

"You are familiar with our product. We continue to make improvements that benefit our customers. Our highly productive plate processing technology will allow you to speed up processing, reduce cost, and help you to meet your goal of sustainability."

Pablo cleared his throat. "Macy, I'm going to save you some time. We are familiar with the product. We love the product. It's perfect for our corrugated packaging. But costs are too high. Every year another increase." He patted the papers in front of him. "We need to lower our variable cost."

The Albabo team nodded their heads in agreement. Macy jumped forward two slides. "We believe we can sell our product at a premium because we don't be just selling you the product and disappear. Our customer service is available twenty-four hours a day, seven days a week. We offer a whole line of peripherals that enhance your workflow and production efficiency. Our competition doesn't do that."

He held up his had stopping her. "Our shipping cost is three times higher. If we don't stop the bleeding, we won't be in business in a few years."

"Pablo, we pride ourselves in being a full-service company. We have an experienced logistics team. Let me have our experts talk with your team. I'm sure together we can provide some suggestions that may help reduce your freight cost. I'd hate to see you switch to a cheaper product, when what you really need is help with your supply chain."

A slow smile spread across Pablo's face and Macy settled back in her chair.

The moment Macy stepped outside of the Albabo office she let the exhilaration wash over her. She couldn't remember the last time she felt this much contentment.

Avery held out his hand to her. "You did it. They were tough, but you were tougher."

"Admit it. You didn't think I had it in me, did you?"

"Let's say, I no longer doubt you. Negotiating is in your blood, you could be my second chair anytime you want."

They walked toward the waiting cab.

"This calls for a celebration." He opened the car door and she climbed into the back seat. He slid in beside her. "The good restaurants won't open for dinner until eight or nine tonight. We can toast your success in the hotel bar."

"Sounds like a good idea." The hotel bar was a neutral zone. It wasn't a date. They were just having a cocktail. That was innocent enough.

The hotel bar was full of men in suits, with a few women peppered in. The place had a festive vibe, which fit with her mood.

"Grab the table. I'll get the drinks. What do you want?" Avery said.

"Slightly dirty martini." She weaved through a group of men blocking the walkway and sat with her back to the wall. She had a clear view of Avery as he waited at the bar. He was nothing like the stuff she read about him in the papers. If he was a playboy, he hadn't shown any of those characteristics around her. His head didn't snap around every time a pretty lady walked by. He seemed content to give her his undivided attention. And he never hesitated to pick up the check. Sure, he had plenty of money, but still he was a class act. If only...

She shook her head. Now wasn't a time to start having silly thoughts about him. She exhaled through her mouth and extracted her phone from her purse. She dialed Celeste's number. After several rings it clicked over to voice mail.

"Celeste, I've been working with Stan to fix my access into the accounting system. It's been a full day and I still can't get in. Can you follow-up with him to get this corrected. I have some things I need to check. Thanks for your help."

"Is everything okay?" Avery asked before placing the drinks on the table.

"I'm just leaving a message for Celeste about the system." She picked up the toothpick that held the three olives and pulled one off.

He held his martini glass in midair. "Let's toast to your bad ass skills."

She picked up her glass and tapped it to his. No one had ever called her a bad ass. Was this the way it felt when you had someone to share your life with, someone to recognize your hard work and help you celebrate it? She tried not to blush.

"Thank you, Avery."

"Offering to help them reduce their freight cost was ingenious."

"We often offer to help our customers, with financing, sourcing issues, even marketing." She sipped her drink. The raw taste of Vodka was rough against her throat. "You seemed surprised. Did you think I was going to fluff the meeting?"

"No. In the beginning I was a knuckle-head. I judged you before I even knew you. I was wrong. But I will tell you, some of it was your fault." His eyes sparkled with mischief.

"My fault?" She drew back.

"Yeah. You caught me off guard. I was fumbling with words and forgot all my game. You made me look like an amateur."

She chuckled, unable to remember the last time she was this relaxed around a man. Even in his club, she was cautious. Gayle was right, she needed to get out more, have fun. Flirting like this was only good in your twenties and thirties. Once she hit forty, she would come off as desperate. "You think you've got game, huh?"

"Didn't you notice? Then I must have been worse than I thought. Promise you won't tell anyone."

She made a haphazard effort of crossing her heart. "We'll see."

Chapter Sixteen

The flight from Asturias to Geneva was less than two hours, but exhaustion clung to Avery like his wrinkled shirt. He blinked his dry eyes several times as he walked alongside Macy to the waiting car. There was a price to pay for drinking and laughing until after midnight.

Spending an enjoyable evening with the right woman has a way of making a man's steps more purposeful. And as he walked out of the airport with Macy, he was that man. Last night hadn't been just any night.

They had connected on a different level, moving beyond co-workers and beyond acquaintances.

Something about the way she laughed at his comments and the way she held his glance gave him hope that a spark of attraction for him brewed just below her surface. They were moving toward interest or at least curiosity.

For a man with enough relationships to fill a small theatre, he should have been used to the heady unbalance of attraction, but this was new to him. This time there were stakes. If he misread her, he'd fall hard. This was more than binge dating without commitment. With Macy he wanted to go all the way in, not wade along the shore.

"I did all the talking last night," he said when they got into the car. "Tell me something about yourself that nobody knows."

She glanced at him from the corners of her eyes. "Okay, let me see." She tapped her finger on her jaw line. "I collect Hard Rock Café pins and I hate brussel sprouts."

"That's a good start, but I was hoping for something a little more in-depth."

"I guess my life story is not that deep. I grew up in Queen Anne's County. I went to a small historically black university. I live in Philly now with a roommate in a place we can barely afford. But we're close, so we make it work."

He nodded. It didn't take a law degree to know she was holding back something.

"Would you like to get together for dinner this evening?"

"I think I'll eat in my room. I don't want to arrive at the customer's tomorrow morning suffering from jet lag. The time difference from Philly is catching up to me."

"Then how about lunch. We have the whole day ahead of us. Would you like to walk around a little?"

She didn't respond right away. He could almost see her brain searching for an answer.

"Would you like to go over anything before we meet with the customer?" He didn't want to hear no. He had too much energy to retire to his room this early.

"I feel confident that I can handle the negotiations, but I'm not cocky. The deal isn't sealed until the customer signs the contract." She stared straight ahead. "I have some things I need to check in preparation for the audit. When we get back, I might not have enough time."

"Can I help you?"

She faced him. Her smile was weak, but at least it was a smile. "I can't ask you to do that. Besides, it's a one-man-task."

Macy closed the hotel door, dropped her bags and rubbed the bridge of her nose. Hanging out with Avery would have been a whole lot more enjoyable than being shut up in the small hotel room, looking at numbers that refused to cooperate. But until she solved the mystery, she needed to stay focused. Missing money, Michelle quitting, the audit, no accounting access and the Dragon negotiations all at the same time…the world had turned on her.

This morning she hadn't even taken the time to look at her horoscope. Unless the stars proved a lead on where to find one hundred-thousand dollars, it was useless.

Today the stars are drawing you toward someone surrounded with an air of mystery. You are a person who likes to unravel intricate puzzles, since the predictable bores you; the urge to run full on is natural. But first, find out what you're up against. This pursuit will challenge you in ways you can't imagine.

Macy reread the words. There had to be a fly on the walls of her life. All she had to do was substitute Avery's name or English International into the horoscope, and it was like having her fortune told. She didn't need another challenge right now. What she needed was to find the missing money, get a promotion and help her brother get into college. Was she asking for too much?

Dinner with Avery in the bar last night was memorable. What was supposed to be a drink, turned into a night of laughter. It wasn't a date, but if it was, it was the best one she'd ever had.

From the soft mattress in her room, she flipped through the channels on the television trying to find a station to block out the noise in her head. The hullaballoo encouraged her to spend time with Avery, not just working, but accepting the olive branch he was offering. She settled on a BBC broadcast before arranging the pillows on the bed and getting comfortable. She dialed the cell phone number she had for Michelle. Maybe Michelle would tell her why she quit. Even though they weren't friends, they had a causal enough relationship to share information. The phone rang four times before going to voicemail. She left a message. She dialed Celeste again. Still no answer.

She reached for her computer and turned it on. Curling up in the full-size bed for a nap would have felt better, but until she solved the puzzle of the missing money, sleep was something she could do at night.

She tried the accounting system again. No luck. The small printed line on the pages she'd printed were hard to make out, but nothing caught her attention.

The selling expense account had the largest balances. With the Dragon negotiations heating up, she expected to see the huge expenditures in the account. Sending contracts back and forth via courier, sometimes for several reiterations, wasn't cheap. Couple that with customer visits all around the world to ensure they had extra face-time; it all added up. She flopped back against the pillows and stared at the ornate ceiling.

The hotel phone rang, pulling her out of the cocoon of papers surrounding her.

"Yes," she answered

"Macy, this is Roxy. We've got a change in plans. Can you take some notes?"

Macy scrambled to find a pen. "What's going on? Is everything okay?

"We're hearing rumors that Watney is thinking about switching companies. They're looking for extended payment terms. I don't want to lose that account."

"We could adjust the bulk price. If they increase their minimum order quantity, we could offer them forty-five day terms. I think there is room for healthy margins." Macy pulled the file from her bag and examined the numbers. "Yes, there is. Let me take a look at the contract, and I'll call you back later today."

"I knew I could count on you. Get Avery involved. This is the kind of thing he needs to understand, so he'll understand our challenges. He's there to help."

Macy hesitated. "I can handle this without him. I can go over this with him later."

"I want him involved. That's what I'm paying him to do. I don't want any legal snafus."

"Sure thing." The words rushed off her tongue. "Give us a couple of hours. I'll let you know what we come up with." She hung up the receiver. After a pause, she climbed off the bed.

She took several short breaths while shaking her hands. "I can do this," she said. "Working with him this late in the evening is not going to be an issue as long as I don't make it one. No drinking tonight and no staring into his eyes until after midnight."

She called the hotel operator and waited while she was connected to Avery's room. He picked up on the first ring.

"Avery, I just heard from Roxy. We need to make some changes to the Watney contract before our meeting in the morning. Can we get together and talk?"

"I was on my way out the door to an early dinner. Let's make it a working dinner. I'll grab my stuff and meet you in the lobby in five minutes. Does that work for you?"

"Well…well, I was going to suggest we grab something quick and get to work."

"Don't be silly. I'm hungry, and I want to eat."

She scratched her head. Was he just being stubborn to get his way? She sighed. "I'll come right down."

Chapter Seventeen

Avery walked around the edge of the ornate rug in the lobby. He had a win, she was having dinner with him. Serial dating had taught him that sometimes women said no, but he didn't want to hear that from Macy.

Macy stepped off the elevator before he completed his third trip around the lobby. He tried not to stare, but he couldn't drag his eyes away from her slim frame. Loose curls framed her face. She seldom wore her hair down, but tonight it was free as if she wanted to shout her femininity at the world. At work she kept it tucked into a knot at the nape of her neck. He wasn't prepared to see her like this. Gone was the professional façade. The woman striding toward him looked more carefree than he'd ever seen her. There were two people rolled up into her tight jeans and neatly tucked blouse, and he liked them both.

Each step she took towards him was like seeing something she'd been trying to hide. She wasn't just another woman, the kind he'd dated in the past. She was different. Without trying she tugged at his heart.

"Do me a favor," she said.

"Sure. What?"

"Call Celeste. I've been dialing her number and it keeps going to voice mail. I want to know if she'll pick up for you. I need to talk to her."

"Okay." He fished his phone from his pocket, found her number and called.

"Hey, Avery. I thought you were out of town."

"I am. I'm in Geneva. Look I have Macy here with me, she'd been trying to reach you. I'm going to put you on speaker." He changed the setting.

Macy grabbed the phone from him and held it between them. "Hey, Celeste, have you gotten my messages?"

"No. I've been swamped. What's up?"

"My access to the accounting system was revoked. Stan is having a problem getting it restored. Can you see what's taking him so long or help him out?"

"Are you and Avery having a good time?"

Macy looked up at him. "We're conducting business. Can you help me?"

"Did you tell him it was a priority one complaint?"

"No. I didn't use those words, but I told him I need it right away. Wasn't that enough?"

"Sure thing, Macy. Now which system are you having a problem with?"

"The accounting system." There was hysteria simmering in her voice, he'd never heard before.

"I'll look into it."

He leaned closer to the phone. "This is important, Celeste. Can you get it taken care of today?"

"Oh, look, Macy has Avery helping her out. Isn't that cute."

"Celeste, if you straightened this out, I'd really appreciate it," Macy said.

"Consider it done." There was a hint of sarcasm in Celeste's voice. "You two have a good time. Enjoy yourself." She disconnected the call.

Macy handed the phone back to him. "How much do you wanna bet, she doesn't do a thing."

"Of course, she will. Stan reports to her. She'll make him do it."

She shook her head. "Men are so dumb," she mumbled.

"I heard that," he said. "Whose decision was it to call me tonight anyway, yours or Roxy's?"

"What difference does it make?" She snapped her head back.

"I'm curious." He waited while she pouted. "Did you decide to reach out to me just so I'd call Celeste?"

"Umm."

Her hesitation provided the answer, but he waited, forcing her to admit she was still hung up on something that blocked them from working comfortably together.

"Okay. Roxy insisted I call you, even though I could handle it without your help."

"Aren't we supposed to be working together. If you don't let me see the kinds of issues the company can run into, how can I help with the expansion?

She hesitated for a moment, looking down at her shoes like a scolded child. "You're right. Now can we talk about the changes?"

"I've spoken to the concierge. He recommends a small restaurant that's within walking distance." He wanted to reach for her hand, but there was nothing welcoming in her eyes.

"I thought we'd eat here. This is more about resolving the contract issues than it is about eating."

"We're going out." Without giving her an opportunity to reject his suggestion, he started toward the door. Outside he pointed in the direction they needed to go.

The cool evening air made him glad he'd brought his jacket.

"It's colder than I thought." She rubbed her free hand along her arm.

"Do you want to take my jacket?"

"I can run back and get mine," she said.

"No. Take this." He placed the jacket around her shoulders."

She pulled it tighter. "Thank you. I left the room so fast…" She quickened her steps. He had walk faster to stay even with her.

As soon as the waiter took their dinner order, Macy pulled the contract from her bag. "I'm thinking there is room to lower the price a little without starting an all-out price drop." She flipped through the pages.

"Aren't you at least going to eat first?"

The look she gave him should have been enough to signal her intentions. "This is a business trip. A long one. I think we should take care of business. With any luck, we can have this sorted out before our meals arrive."

"Are you always this driven?"

"You know, before you came along I was pretty certain Roxy was finally going to promote me this year. Roxy just as much promised me. But since your arrival, nothing seems certain. In just a few short weeks, the courier lost the Bunting contract not once, but twice. The audit is coming up, and I've got some major issues to address before meeting with the auditors. So yes, I'm usually driven, but right now I'm driven on steroids. I want us to settle into a working relationship where we don't step on each other's toes."

If she had any idea Roxy wanted him to report back on her abilities during this trip, she would without a doubt heave her glass of sparkling water across the table at him.

He caught the eye of their server. "Yes, we'd like a bottle of wine." He retrieved the wine list still lying in the middle of the table and examined the choices. "Bring us a bottle of the house Cabernet Sauvignon. I don't want to be too extravagant. This is a business dinner, after all."

He couldn't read the expression on Macy's face. "You do like Cabernet, don't you?"

"Can we take a look at the contract now?" She shoved the paper across the table with her index finger pointing at the pricing section.

By the time dinner arrived they had finished a glass of wine and managed to agree on the restructure for the payment clause.

"That wasn't so hard, now was it?" Avery cut into the Porterhouse steak and popped the medium rare meat into his mouth, without looking at her.

"You remind me of my brother," she said. "You don't think anything bad can happen to you. He's so sure he's getting a scholarship to play football at the University of Maryland he didn't want to apply to any other schools or any other scholarships. My mother and I had to berate him, and even then, he only applied to two more schools. He believes everything will just work out in his favor. And you. The only time I've seen you serious was when you were complaining about my work. So, tell me something." She put her fork down. With her chin nestled into the palm of her hand, her eyes beamed with a seriousness he hadn't seen before. "Are you only out to get me?"

"I'm not gunning for you. Never was. That day you rushed into my father's campaign party, you looked like you were frightened to open your mouth." He poured more wine into her glass before topping his off, too. "I see a very different woman now."

"Everybody is entitled to a bad day."

He pretended to think. There was no way he'd share the last year of his life and how his ex-girlfriend had made him look more than a little foolish. She had played him with the skillfulness of a surgeon, and he'd been too self-absorbed to know she was cutting up his heart. "Have you found out why your assistant quit?"

She shrugged. "No. I've sent a few emails asking my staff, but no one knows anything. I've tried to call her but didn't get any answer."

He glanced at his watch. "Try reaching her now. It's early enough in the evening you might catch her."

"Now? At dinner?"

"Sure, why not. If you really want to know."

She pulled her phone from her purse and punched a few keys. "It's ringing." Her face brightened. "Hey, Michelle, it's me, Macy," she said.

Her face darkened, she pulled the phone from her ear and stared at the screen.

"What happened?"

"She hung up on me. She didn't say anything, she just hung up."

"What was that about? Is she mad at you?"

"Why would she be mad at me? This makes no sense. I was her manager, but we had a good relationship. We've hung out together. Gone shopping together. I've had her over for dinner and I've been to her place for game night with her friends." She shook her head.

"Well it sounds like something between the two of you is broken. Maybe you'll find out when you get back to Philly."

Chapter Eighteen

The next day, Macy exited the Watney Building ahead of Avery, her heart thumping so hard, she could hear it. She gripped her briefcase and stepped into the waiting cab. With her eyes closed, she eased the air out of her lungs, making sure not to come off as an amateur. What she wanted to do was dance on the sidewalk with her arms in the air. She'd done it. Faced down two customers and walked away with two contracts that were even better than the deals Roxy negotiated last year.

Avery climbed in the cab behind her and closed the door.

"Whew." She couldn't contain her jubilation another minute. "Yes! Yes! Yes!" She pumped her fist.

"You were good in there." Avery's face brightened with a smile. "Because of your determination, I think the customer was speechless. I am quite impressed."

"You sound surprised. Don't you know by now, I have the magic touch?"

"Your abilities are no longer in question. I must have been nuts to doubt you and I see you're not going to let me forget that."

"I'm slow to forget. I remember things well past their usefulness."

"That's good information to know." He placed his hand on her knee but removed it quickly. The warmth from his touch spread through her. "My compliment was sincere."

"Okay, got it." Macy tried not to gush. She needed to remain professional at least until she was back in her hotel room. "It's what Roxy pays me to do and expects me to do."

"The customer is happy, that's all that matters, and working with you has been my pleasure," Avery said.

"Okay, two signed contracts call for some kind of celebration. I don't mean drinks in a dark bar. I've never been to Switzerland. I want to see something special."

"We're in the city center. I have the perfect thing."

"You've been here before?"

"My family used to come often to ski. Not so much anymore. Everyone is busy."

"Okay where are we going?"

"Sir, can you take us to the Jet d'Eau," he instructed the driver before turning to her. "Since we don't have much time before sunset, I think this will be perfect."

"It's nothing stuffy like a museum, is it?"

He shook head. "No. The Jet d'Eau is a water monument, that shoots lots of water into the air and it's located on the Rhône. This way you get to see a well-known river and a monument at the same time." He sounded as enthusiastic as she felt. Usually when she made a special request that didn't include a television or a bottle of beer her dates would scrunch their noses and protest with a deep sigh.

The driver dropped them off in Bains des Pâquis. Assuring them, they could also get something to eat at one of the best restaurants in the city.

Avery stepped out of the car and offered his hand to assist her. "Wow, this is perfect. I can tell Gayle I did more than just work." She pulled her cell phone from her purse.

"Come this way, we can get a little closer." Avery held her elbow and directed her down the path.

She caught the landscape in the center of the frame and held the picture button. At least one of the pictures in the collage had to turn out perfect.

"Be careful, if the wind shifts you can get drenched."

"Aren't you going to take some pictures?" She glanced over her shoulder at him.

Jacki Kelly

"Watching you is enough for me."

She stopped for a moment and gazed at him. When was the last time anyone of the opposite sex had been so nice to her?

When the sun settled low in the sky, the wind picked up. Macy looked at her watch. Right on cue, her stomach grumbled. "I didn't realize it was so late and how hungry I am."

"If my memory serves me, there is a great Swiss-French restaurant that's pretty close to here." They walked along the path together, back the way they'd come. "We should be there in about a few minutes."

"I hope they have fondue. Everything I've read advised me to eat some while I'm here."

He shifted towards her. "Then it's your lucky day all the way around. The place I have in mind has fondue, served with both bread and vegetables. Just in case you need something a little more substantial."

"I hope it's not too far. I've already done a lot of walking in these heels."

"Should I carry you?"

She pretended not to hear him. They weren't on a date, but she couldn't help wishing they were. Everything about the day had been perfect and Avery had been perfect too. If she could change anything about him, it would be his father. And after all these years, that should be such a minor thing. No one remembered those days, so long ago. Her mother probably didn't even remember the name of the lawyer that had screwed them so royally.

"You're staring at me." She felt the blush creeping into her cheeks.

"Yes. Yes, I am. I consider myself a good judge of character. But your determination with these negotiations has been awesome. You shot down every argument they had."

102

"Watney is always difficult. I learned that last year when Roxy and I handled the negotiation. A lot of what they ask is just a test, so I was expecting them to run us through their gauntlet."

He gave an appreciative nod. "I'm not sure you even needed me."

"Don't tell me I wounded your male ego because you played a smaller role."

He straightened. "No, not at all. Let's just say the meeting was a little different than I expected. But I must admit, I don't like standing on the sidelines. I'm always all in."

They stopped in front of a small windowless storefront. The only indication of the restaurant was the elaborate gold lettering on the glass door.

"This place doesn't look too appealing from the outside." Macy glanced down the deserted street.

"Trust me. You'll love it." He held the restaurant door open.

Macy paused for a moment before climbing the set of narrow, steep stairs leading to the second floor.

At the top of the stairs was a huge dining room with a wall of windows across the back of the room that overlooked the city.

"What a gorgeous view." She placed her hand on her chest and took in the white linen table clothes, the sparkling wine glasses, and the fine bone china. The panel of windows catching the setting sun off the lake more than made up for the drab exterior. Several tables were occupied, with couples chatting in low voices. The servers moved about unhurried.

"And the food is just as good." Avery stepped to the desk and gave the hostess his name. He spoke low, but she heard him request a table by the window.

Once they were seated, he ordered a bottle of Cabernet Sauvignon.

"I'll have a glass of the house Riesling. No matter what happens, I'm not drinking as much as I did the other night. We have an early flight in the morning. I don't want to miss it." She spoke while looking out the window

"We have to toast our success. We've managed to work together quite well."

The server returned with the bottle. When they were alone, Avery raised his glass towards her. "Congratulations, Macy. You were amazing today." He tipped his glass to her.

The pressure of performing had vanished, releasing her from the terrorizing grip that had clutched her since leaving home. She swallowed almost half of the glass before placing it back on the table. Tonight, she could enjoy his company and pretend anything she wanted.

"There was one point today when I thought Rogier was going to have a heart attack," he said.

She nodded. "That was the moment when I wondered if I was pushing too hard. But he got over it fast enough."

"All of the contract renewals won't be this intense, will they? This kind of activity can age a person." He picked up his wine glass and took a big swallow.

"The contracts in the States should be easier. I'm not saying the customers won't demand a lot, but they seem to peter-out after a reasonable amount of time."

"What do I need to know about English International that I don't already?"

"Secrets. You want to know secrets," she paused. "The vending machine on the third floor will give you two candy bars for the price of one, but only after you buy a bag of chips. And never drink the coffee if Alberta makes it, she doesn't always wash her hands before leaving the ladies room."

"That's disgusting." He mocked shock.

They laughed together like old friends.

His tie was loosened, but still around his neck, and his posture was casual. The guard she'd put up to keep him at arm's length slipped away just like the tension in her shoulders. He wasn't the enemy. Seeing her father in the eyes of every man wasn't healthy, but it was a pattern that wouldn't vanish anytime soon. It had become her security blanket. The one thing she could count on to keep her heart safe.

"Last night I talked about myself," Macy said. "Tonight, why don't you tell me something about you? Tell me something I haven't read in the paper."

"You can't believe everything you read in the paper. Most of that stuff has been taken out of context to make it more salacious."

"Then give me your version of the party where two women got into a fight outside of your place over you."

He dropped his head and grinned. For the first time, a more sensitive side of him showed up. He looked embarrassed. She didn't think he was capable of such a human emotion.

"Yeah, I want to hear all about that." She pulled her chair closer to the table.

"The real story is not as juicy as the one they printed. First of all, only one of those women was my girlfriend." He put air quotes around girlfriend. "We had only been on a couple of dates. The other woman was her co-worker that had a beef with her. Something to do with stealing her promotion or talking to the manager to get it quashed. Either way, after that night our fledgling relationship was over. They weren't fighting over me at all."

"Okay, how about Engagement-gate? Isn't that what the tabloid called it?"

He ran his hand down his face and moaned. "I knew you were going to ask me about that. I wish that one was as easy to explain." He put his index finger on his fork tines and rocked it back and forth. He didn't seem willing to talk about that incident.

"You don't have to talk about it if you don't want to. I guess that one had more truth than the big fight, huh?"

"We were in a committed relationship. At least that's what I thought. Then I found out she was cheating on me. I told her, I wanted out. She'd humiliated me and I was just a bank account to her. When I shut it down, she went straight to the tabloids."

"Wow, that's awful. But I'm not surprised. Isn't that what all famous do when they're upset?"

"You think what she did was okay?" His facial expression darkened.

"No. I'm not saying that, but you're known for being a playboy, so she probably thought you were still dipping your toe in other pools."

He shook his head as if she had started speaking a foreign language. "We were serious. I wasn't fooling around. What kind of person do you think I am?"

She sipped from her wine glass. "I'm just saying, you're a player, so she probably was just trying to keep up with you."

He placed his palms on the table. "You have me all wrong. I don't know what kind of circle you travel in but what you're describing is something that only happens in bad TV movies."

"Oh, wow. I'm sorry," she said. "I didn't mean to upset you." Empathy filled her chest. Avery had everything. He could do anything he wanted. He never worried about paying bills or putting up with crap to help someone else. But he had problems, too. She needed to lighten the heavy mood that had settled over them. "I guess, even rich, good-looking people have problems."

"So, you think I'm good-looking, do you?" The sadness in his eyes was gone and he was back to his confident self.

"You're all right. I guess." She picked up her glass of wine.

Two servers arrived with their dinner and side dishes.

"Since you're in a sharing mood, why don't you tell me about you and Celeste? What kind of thing do the two of you have going on? I wouldn't peg her as your type."

"Ah, you have a good sense of judgment. She's not my type, and we don't have anything going on. She's Roxy's little sister. I'm only trying to be nice to her. She doesn't make it easy though."

She sat forward in her chair and searched his face. "You aren't lying to me, are you?"

"Why would I lie?"

She shrugged a shoulder. "I don't know. The way she's always hanging around you, I just thought…"

"Don't. She's Roxy's sister, and I'm not interested."

"Roxy is almost planning a wedding."

He closed his eyes for a moment. "I think it's time Roxy and I had a serious conversation. I have no plan to marry anyone, least of all Celeste."

"Please keep my name out of it. Tonight, we're just making conversation. I don't want to be involved in any of this."

He placed his hand on top of hers. "I was planning this conversation long before you said anything. Everything that is said here tonight stays here. Just before we left she mentioned something about Celeste and me having dinner, and that didn't happen."

"Then why do you think Roxy thinks the two of you had dinner?" She left her hand under his. He didn't seem to be in a hurry to pull away.

"I think her little sister has opposition to telling the truth. She likes to twist things until they benefit her." He extracted his hand.

Macy couldn't suppress her smile. "It's good to know she's evil with everyone and not just me. I was beginning to think there was something about me that turned her into a witch." She slipped her hand away. The weight of his hand on hers was too intimate. "I'd like to share something with you." But the urge to tell him about the shortage in her account wouldn't go away. If she didn't talk to someone soon the stress would eat her up.

He made the dramatic gesture of placing his elbow on the table and tucking his chin in his palm, giving her his full attention. "What's up?"

"You know we've got the audit as soon as we get back to work?"

He nodded. "Any luck?"

"No, I still don't have access." She picked up her near empty glass and swallowed the remaining contents. The wine made it easier to talk. "One of my accounts is missing a hundred thousand dollars. I can't figure out where the money went. I mean I have checked everything."

He straightened and backed away from her as if she were highly contagious. For several moments he said nothing. "I'm sure there is a logical reason." He rubbed his chin. "Have you reviewed every line item?"

"Yes. I've checked all the paperwork I brought with me. Without access I can't comb through the accounts like I want."

"Does anyone have access to your accounts?"

"I have to approve everything, but sure the team can submit vouchers, they know the charge codes. I must have overlooked something."

He ran his fingers through his thick head of hair. "Who have you talked to about this so far?"

"Nobody. I've been so busy getting ready for these meetings and trying to find the money, I haven't had time."

She drew a deep breath. "Plus, I didn't want to tell anyone. I'm not sure why I told you."

"Money doesn't have feet, so you just haven't found the right trail. When we get back, let me look at your documentation. Maybe I can help you."

"You'd do that for me? I didn't tell you because I expected something from you. I just needed to say it aloud to someone who might understand why my stomach has been in a constant knot since I found out."

"Sure, if I can. I'm not an accountant, but I'm good at seeing patterns and deciphering data. I'll do what I can, which might not be much."

She wagged her finger at him. The last of her inhibition gone with the wine. "You don't come off as the kind of person who steps out of his comfort zone for others."

"Wow. You don't think very highly of me, do you? I think you've insulted me several times during this meal."

"I'm a Sagittarius. I'm always very straightforward. I'm not one of those women who is afraid to say what's on her mind. I didn't mean to insult you, I'm just being honest."

"Then, you should have said something to Roxy."

"She is the last person I want to tell until I know what's going on. Roxy expects her teams to solve problems, not bring them to her to resolve. You and I don't know the same, Roxy. She's a wonderful person, but she'll look at this missing money as a personal affront. As if the money was coming right out of her pocket. She doesn't tolerate…"

"I know she can be tough, but she has to be to run a business in a man's world. I think she can be fair. She thinks highly of you."

"She does?" The news should have had her doing somersaults, but after twelve-hour days and constant dedication, Macy had expected no less. "Well, the next few weeks will tell."

After they settled the check, he stood. It didn't take long for the scowl on his lips to fade. Another good quality.

She gathered her purse and briefcase and walked ahead of him out of the restaurant.

"We can walk to the hotel from here," he said. "Are you okay with that?"

She hesitated for a moment. A walk after dinner sounded like something a couple would do. But this wouldn't be the first time she'd read too much into a simple request.

Outside the temperature had dropped and a cool breeze blew. It wasn't quite dark, more like that in-between time before the sun settled below the horizon and the day had taken on a calmness that only twilight brings. Foot traffic had picked up, but now, instead of business people hurrying from one appointment to the next, the pace was slower. Everyone seemed to be holding hands and enjoying private conversations.

"I'm a little turned around. How far is the hotel?" Her heart wouldn't stop hitting against her chest as if it was trying to tell her something she didn't want to hear.

"It's only a few blocks, three or four."

"Let's hope my heels hold up that far. They're cute for meetings, but they aren't meant for a lot of walking."

He glanced down at her feet. "I've offered to carry you, it still stands."

She huffed through her nose, an unattractive sound she hoped he didn't notice. The words from this morning's horoscope were branded on her brain and flashed like a neon sign.

Today's planetary alignment will have you feeling more emotional today. You will have more feelings for one person in particular. Don't try to rationalize your feelings away, you can't. Welcome this change in your life and perhaps let them know.

Earlier today those words were easy to dismiss, but doubt had parked itself in the middle of her chest, and she wasn't sure what to believe. Was her horoscope talking about Avery?

The faint scent of his cologne still clung to the fibers of his suit. He took long casual strides and swayed just a little with each step. His hand brushed against hers. She froze for half a second. She was being silly. It was an accident.

"I think the Watney contract was the most difficult. The others should be easier." She glanced up at him. If she kept the conversation on business, then she could regroup and reign in her emotions. No matter how friendly he was on this side of the pond, she couldn't consider him a friend. His last name was Malveaux, which meant he was a natural enemy, just like mosquitoes. Enjoying his company was betraying her mother. How could she think about liking him? What was wrong with her?

"I don't think we have anything to worry about on any of the future contracts. You're the English International secret weapon." He bumped her shoulder just as she caught a large crack in the sidewalk.

"Agh!" Her arms flailed. He grabbed her before she tumbled to the sidewalk. He saved her a skinned knee by catching her before she smacked the cement.

"I'm so sorry. I didn't mean to tap you that hard. Are you okay?" He held her by the waist.

"No, I should have been looking where I was walking." She caught her breath.

He picked up her briefcase from the sidewalk and looked her in the eyes. "Are you hurt?"

"I'm fine." She put weight on her left foot and squealed. "No, I'm not."

"Here let me help you. The hotel is just a block away. I can manage you and the briefcases." He tightened his hold on her, pulling her against his muscular body. His fingers slipped under her armpits, and she erupted into laughter.

"You're ticklish?"

"Very."

He nodded like a man let in on a big secret.

"And if you tell anyone, you'll be sorry."

"I wasn't planning to tell a soul. But it's good to know you have a weakness. After your performance here, I was beginning to think you were infallible."

She pointed to her ankle. "We both know that's not true."

"That's my fault." He repositioned his arm tighter around her waist. "I promise to be gentler around you."

Maybe, this time her horoscope was right.

Chapter Nineteen

Avery readjusted his hand around Macy's waist, making sure it didn't slip too low. His klutziness had worked to his advantage. He now had a valid reason to hold on to her without worry of a reprimand.

He wasn't shy or awkward with women, but with Macy, he needed to be careful. Sure, she was tough on the outside, but she couldn't hide her soft core. That part of her was wounded. That's the part he wanted to protect.

"I'll get you some ice for your ankle as soon as we get to the hotel. Then you'll need to elevate your foot."

"I'm sure I'll be fine in the morning. Stop worrying. I'm tougher than I look. Besides, how do you know so much about taking care of sprains?"

"College football. I had my share of sprains, tears, and broken bones. That's when I realized I wasn't meant to be a football player."

"You wanted to play professionally?"

"Of course. Me and one of my best buddies had our national football careers all planned. He pursued the dream. I decided to study something a lot less physical."

"You know a NFL player, personally?" She nodded. "My brother would be impressed."

"Well, he doesn't play anymore. Now he's a coach, sidelined by a torn patella. Does that mean I'm not cool now?"

"To my brother, probably. But he changes his opinion daily."

He helped her up the hotel stairs and into the lobby.

"I'm fine, Avery. I can walk from here." She put some weight on her foot. Her limp wasn't as pronounced, but she still winced.

He remained right beside her, just in case, wanting to be the hero for her. She was tough and certainly did a good job of taking care of herself, but he needed to be more than just some guy to her. Now and then a hint of insecurity flickered in her eyes. Sure, she tried to mask it, but he'd seen it the very first time he saw her. Maybe that was the moment the attraction started. Too bad his Y chromosome was in an overactive macho mood that night.

Linked together, they made their way to her hotel room. He'd never walked slower or enjoyed it more.

She pressed her weight against him and removed her room key card from her purse.

He helped her to the bed.

"I'll get some ice."

"No, no. I'm just going to go to bed. Ice isn't necessary." She waved him away without meeting his eyes.

He lifted the ice bucket in the air. "Be right back."

"Avery, come back here."

She called to him, but he was already out the door. No way was he going to go back inside and allow her to talk him out of this chance to do something nice for her. He located the ice machine in the alcove at the end of the hall. With the full bucket, he rushed back to her room. The door was still slightly open, so he stepped inside without knocking.

"It's starting to swell." She looked down at her ankle, her brow knitted together.

"This should take care of that." He tied a knot in the bag and held it at the base of her leg. "Are you in pain?"

"No. But we've got a lot of walking to do tomorrow."

"Don't worry. If you don't think you can walk through the airport, we'll get you home."

Her face relaxed, and she leaned closer to him. "Who is we?"

"I. I will make sure you get home, even if I have to charter a plane. This is my fault."

"It's not your fault. Stop saying that. Sometimes stuff happens, especially to me. And I can't allow you to do that."

"I wasn't asking your permission. I just need to do what I can to make this right."

She leaned back against the headboard. The fight in her seemed to ease out of her body. Her shoulders relaxed and so did the tension around her mouth. When she let her defenses down, she was a different person. Warm. Approachable.

His hand started to go numb. He adjusted the ice bag without letting go. Tonight, was one of those rare opportunities that he could get close to her without hearing an objection. She might have a slight injury, but he was having fun.

"Are you in pain?" he asked.

"No." Her lashes fluttered. "My leg is frozen though."

He removed the bag. "The bag has been on for twenty minutes. Maybe we should let it thaw for a moment, then reapply the ice." He positioned himself beside her against the headboard.

"You're very nice." She touched his leg.

The gesture was innocent, but his libido took a wild leap off the cliff. Was he finally making some progress with her?

"If you need to get back to your room, I'll understand. I can put the ice back on in a few minutes." She lifted her hand off his knee but the intimacy connecting them continued.

"I'm good right here."

"You know if word got back to the office that you were in my room this late at night all kinds of rumors would be started."

"You don't seem to be the kind of person who cares too much what people say behind your back."

"Then I'm putting on the performance of a life time. It's all a façade. Around Roxy, I feel like I'm always tiptoeing. Before I utter a word to her, I examine it ten different ways. The last few weeks has been a constant knot of trouble that is threatening to become permanent," she paused. "I need my job. I've worked hard to be recognized. I don't have the luxury of leaving because the atmosphere isn't to my liking. Not right now, anyway."

"I thought you were happy at English." He shifted his body to get a better look at her face.

"I'm talking too much. You don't want or need to hear my problems."

"We're sharing stories. Please keep talking."

"I'm happy enough at English. The money is good. But I don't think it's a job I want to do forever. I can't be myself there." She eased a little lower on the bed. The two of them were quiet for several moments. Reasons to stay were growing thin. In a moment she would tell him it was time for him to leave.

"I'd better get outta here," he said. "You're tired. We had a long day. Put the ice back on for a few more minutes when you can tolerate the cold again."

"You know, you're very different than I first imagined. Don't get me wrong, you have a stuffy side, but mostly you're easy to talk to."

He scratched his head. "Thanks, I think."

"Today is one of the best days I've had in a very long time. "

"How can that be? You twisted your ankle."

"That's nothing." She flipped her hand at the swollen ankle. "Watney signed the contract, Albabo signed their contract. These two accomplishments are a huge confirmation for me. I think I proved to you I know what I'm

doing. In the last year, this day is up there. One of my best."
She stared at him, holding his eyes. He was close enough to
kiss her, but there was a veil between them.

The lack of sound in the room made it impossible to
ignore the sound of his breathing. In the hours they'd spent
together, they'd crossed from co-workers into that magical
moment just before they took the next step. That's the story
that played in his head. That's the story he wanted to hear.

The electricity in the air connected the two of them, even
more than the gentle hand that had been on his thigh.

"Can you stay a little longer?"

The second she said the words, she knew there was no
way to retreat from the comment. Nor did she want to. Today
was one of those days she'd watched unfold on those
romantic movies she watched late at night. But she was still
safe, on home plate. She hadn't crossed the line or done
anything embarrassing like trying to kiss him or admitting
she liked him.

For a few moments, she wanted to live in the world where
she was the heroine and liked by everyone. Where everyone
wanted the best for her and rooted for her with sincerity.
Where some handsome guy happened along and decided he
couldn't live without her and he was willing to tell the world
how he felt. Where Roxy was thrilled with her work and
promoted her, where her mother and brother were doing fine
and didn't rely on her so much. Sure, that kind of stuff only
happened in make-believe, but didn't every woman want a
piece of that dream?

Even before he reached for her, she knew he would. With
his hand on her cheek, he turned her head a fraction of an
inch to brush her lips. The gesture was light, but her body
heated several degrees. He'd touched her face. The reaction
of her heart pointed at the significance of his action. The last
time she came this close to being bubbly and overjoyed was

in high school when she was foolish enough to think she and her boyfriend had a forever love. That was a long time ago, but with Avery, the feeling was one hundred times more intense. His tongue slipped into her mouth, and her soul opened, allowing him in. If this was foolish, then, for now, she was going to be witless.

Just for now.

Just for tonight.

Just this once.

He deepened the kiss. Pulling Macy down on top of him and enclosing his arms around her.

She leaned her body into his and fought off all the reasons why she should jump up and walk him to the door. How could something that felt so good, be wrong. Hadn't her horoscope said for her to take this chance to let him know?

The palm of his hand cupped the back of her neck. There was nothing rushed about his action. Everything he did seemed measured and aimed at pleasing her. When was the last time someone did something solely for her? It was too long ago to remember.

"I can't believe we're doing this." His voice was low and husky.

She pulled away a fraction and stared down at him. "You're right. We probably shouldn't be doing this.'

"I've been hoping for this for weeks..."

"But that doesn't make it okay. Besides, I can't forget..."

The big smile that took over his face was infectious. "Yes, we all know that I'm not as cool as I think I am. Now you know my kryptonite, when it comes to you, I'm a klutz."

"A relationship is not something I want right now."

"And why is that?"

"Because I have high expectations of the man I want in my life. I know what I want is impossible to get, so for now, I'm just going to stay on the sidelines." She spun around and sat up.

He pulled up to sit beside her and lifted his chin as if he was preparing for a blow. "Tell me what you want from a man."

She looked down at her hands. This wasn't the first time someone had asked her this question, and she was used to receiving snickers aimed at her reply. She didn't want to hear them from him.

"You'll laugh at me."

"I promise I won't." He made a poor attempt at crossing his heart. "I mean it. If I tell you what I want from a woman, then will you share?"

"Maybe."

"Okay." He rubbed his hands together. "I want a woman who sees me. Not the things I have, or the family I come from, but one who wants to know my heart. I want someone decisive and feisty, a woman with her own opinion and not afraid to share it. Honesty and a sense of humor are important, too," he paused. "I've never articulated that before. It sounds like a lot of wants. Maybe that's why I'm still single."

"No, it's not a lot. I get it." She sighed. "I want a man who is honest, loyal, and patient. A man who will put me first, at least half of the time. A man with a sense of humor and one who isn't afraid to show his feelings for me." She waited a moment. "Go ahead and laugh and tell me I'm not realistic. I already know that's why I'm alone."

"I don't think that unreasonable. Isn't that what everyone wants?"

"Maybe, but then they end up settling for so much less. I'm not willing to do that. I'm a child of divorce. I've seen how marriage can wreck your life."

"I've been in relationships. Bad relationships, so I agree with you. But…"

She held up her hand. "No. There are no buts. I want what I want, and I know it's not reasonable, and since no one can live up to my expectations, I'm not in a relationship."

Her words had stripped the air from the room. She should have expected his reaction. Every time she told someone what she wanted, they looked at her as if she'd just stepped off a spaceship.

"Can I tell you a secret about me?" She had one more confession that was sure to send him into orbit.

"There's another one? Okay, what is it?"

She paused for a long moment. "Do you believe in horoscopes?"

He sat up higher on the bed. "You mean like the stars and the planets align? Stuff like that?"

She nodded.

He scratched his temple. "I can't say that I do."

"Why not?"

"First of all because I'm a realist, and second of all the stars and the planet have nothing to do with what goes on day to day. We control our own destiny."

"My horoscope said we'd kiss today." She used the most matter-of-fact tone she could muster.

"Kiss, huh? I thought we'd do a lot more than that. What would you say if I told you when I climbed out of bed this morning I was determined I was going to kiss you."

"Don't get the wrong idea. I read my horoscope every day, but I'll be the first to admit there is no science behind them. But growing up, I needed something to hold on to, to believe in and this became my thing. Now reading them has become a habit and sometimes there is a little truth in the horoscope"

"I get that. For a while, I carried a rabbit's foot."

"In high school?"

"Kindergarten."

She studied his face, trying to interpret his words and his body language. The moment hit her full on, moving faster than she could keep up. The more time they spent together, the more she liked him. He might not be Mr. Perfect, but he was checking off so many boxes.

"My ankle is better, at least now it's numb." She eased away from him and stood up, stretching her arms over her head, hoping he'd think she was sleepy.

"I'd better be going then." He pushed off the bed. "I really enjoyed your company tonight. This trip turned out much better than I could have imagined. I know more about Macy Rollins and I hope you know more about me. He tilted his head as if he was going to say something more, but instead he picked up his briefcase and exited the room.

She flopped on the bed, her heart beating just as fast now as it did when he kissed her. She wanted to reach for him. Kiss him again. But she'd done the right thing. Her heart may not have believed it, but her head did.

Chapter Twenty

Macy gave a final glance around the hotel room. It was time to leave the magic behind. The business part of the trip was successful, her interest in Avery not a good idea. It was time to head home and say goodbye to all that. She reached for her phone and pulled up her horoscope.

Today you should have feelings of success and happiness with the things you're accomplishing in your life, Sagittarius. Your career is going well. Your personal life has reached stable ground but could use some attention on the romance side. Your stars are aligning for love, so choose well. This could be a relationship that lasts longer than any others.

All those beautiful words and this time she wasn't sure she could believe any of it. If everything was so grand, why was that money missing from her accounts? Why had Michelle quit? She'd hesitated when Macy asked her to pull the audit paperwork, but Michelle wasn't a thief.

Two signed contracts were super, but she couldn't rest until she had answers to those important questions. She gathered her things and left the hotel room.

The elevator touched down in the lobby. Her steps were so light, she could have been walking on clouds. Yesterday with Avery reminded her why people wanted to be in a relationship and why they were willing to make sacrifices to be with someone. The warm taste of his mouth against hers still lingered.

Avery turned away from the lobby window just as she stepped off the elevator. No expensive suit, today. His broad stretch of shoulders pushed against his T-shirt and his muscular thighs defined his jeans. He looked like a regular guy, who could be interested in an average working girl. He was the kind of man she imagined herself with whenever she allowed her thoughts to wander. Smart, thoughtful, considerate.

She reprimanded her heart for lusting after Avery when there were so many other problems that required her attention. When they were back at home, he would go back to his glitzy world, and she'd return to the apartment she shared with Gayle. He hobnobbed with the upper crust of Philadelphia society, she couldn't afford to hobnob. He had his pick of beautiful women, and there were so many in the city, she'd get lost in the crowd. If she didn't want her feelings hurt, she needed to remember to stay in the slow lane.

She straightened. Pushing away the intimacy they'd shared and the easy way they'd interacted while in Europe, now was the time to get back to normalcy.

"Good morning, Avery." She stepped beside him.

"You're walking without a limp. I guess that means I didn't cripple you."

"I'm as good as new. I iced it down again last night," she said. "Are you ready to head home?"

"Two contracts successfully negotiated, and I don't know how many more to go."

"The rest should be easier," she said.

"Sir, your car is here." The bellman picked up their bags and led them to the waiting vehicle.

Traffic near the airport slowed. While they inched ahead in the long line of cars waiting to unload, Avery cleared his throat. "I hope my behavior last night wasn't too far out of line."

"No. No. We had a few drinks. We were excited about the contract. We…"

He leaned towards her and his breath brushed her face. His lips pressed into hers, parting her mouth just enough to slip inside. This kiss was gentle, without the urgency of the night before. The tenderness made her dizzy. He pulled her closer, and she collapsed against his chest. Sooner than she wanted, he released her but continued to look at her. "I kissed you last night, but it had nothing to do with the wine at dinner or the success of the meeting. I kissed you last night, and this morning, because I wanted to. I couldn't resist."

She cleared her throat. "I don't know what to say."

"So, our feelings aren't mutual?"

"Yes, our feelings are mutual. But our feelings are secondary. We have a job to do, and we both have too much at stake to be careless."

"I can assure you this is no careless gesture." His eyes slid across her face.

The car pulled into the departure lane. Macy accepted his hand as he helped her out of the car. Now was not the time to shake up her life. Roxy might fire her if she found out they were involved. She wanted him for her sister. A man in her life would be another distraction. Something else to take her away from the things she needed to focus on, like the missing money.

Together they made their way through security and onto the plane. They were seated next to each other. At least she had a few more hours to enjoy his company.

She shoved the magazine in the seat pocket and snapped her seatbelt. The real challenge would happen when they were back in the office, passing each other in the hall, sitting across from him at a conference table. There was no way to put them back into neutral territory.

"Listen, this is crazy," she said.

He shifted in his seat. His dark eyes were intense, daring her to question what was blooming between them. "Why is it crazy?"

"We work together. You and Celeste are entangled, well at least Roxy thinks you are. You've got to clear the field. There are too many obstacles on it right now."

"If we're both consenting adults, we aren't violating any work ethics. And I am not entangled with Celeste."

Macy sat back in her seat. He was stubborn, but she needed to remain firm. But could she? She knew what it felt like to pursue someone, but never had anyone been so adamant about pursuing her, at least no one worthwhile. If there wasn't so much at stake, she could relish in the moment. But like always, there was no enjoying the moment.

"I need some time. I hope you'll give it to me," she said

"Why do you need time?"

"To consider how this will impact my job. If this is the right thing to do. If we're going to do this, I need to be level headed and not rush into it like a teenager with nothing to lose."

"How much time?"

"I don't know."

When the plane touched down at the Philadelphia International Airport, and the seatbelt light went out, Macy jumped from her seat. If Avery refused to behave, then she would be strong enough for both of them. It might take all her willpower, but she could handle Avery. She had to.

She walked beside him. Disappointed that she had to quash what was budding between them, but it was the right thing to do. Her focus needed to be work. Boys always just get in the way. Was he worth the sacrifice? Or did she just want to believe he was? The last time she thought she found Mr. Perfect, she was wrong.

"Have you talked to Roxy since the meeting with Watney?" He watched the baggage carousel. The sexy timbre of his voice sent a warm sensation washing over her. She had to listen to him through a filter, so that she wouldn't give in.

"Yes, I told her we signed the contract."

He directed his gaze at her. "It usually takes a few days of reiterations to iron out a contract. You've got skills."

He planted a kiss on her cheek before she could step back. "Let me carry that bag for you."

"Gayle should be outside waiting for me."

"Good, I'll get to meet your roommate." He collected their bags and let her lead the way out of the terminal. The humid air was oppressive. A welcomed reminder that the fantasy she'd been living in was over and it was time to get back to reality.

"Look, Macy, before you meet your friend, how about we get together tonight? I need to stop by the club and make sure my brother knows I haven't abandoned him. Why don't you come with me?"

She stopped before exiting the airport. "Do you think that's a good idea? I mean…"

"Look, there are no reasons why we can't be together. Besides, we'll only be there for a few hours."

She nodded her head before agreeing.

Gayle waved from the pick-up lane.

"You must be Avery." Gayle extended her hand.

"And you must be Gayle."

"Damn, you look even better in person. Do you have any available brothers?"

"Why thank you for the compliment, and yes I do." He placed her bags in the trunk.

"I think we better go." Macy closed the trunk and ushered Gayle into the car. Avery winked as they pulled away.

"Macy, he is yummy. Did you resist him?" Gayle licked her lips before pulling into traffic.

"It took all the willpower, I had. And Avery is far from the perfect man I'm looking for."

"There is no such thing as a perfect man. You're going to be alone forever unless you get more realistic."

"Alone is not bad. It beats having some man start off great and as you're all in love he knocks you off your feet and steals everything from you."

"Oh boy. Let's change the subject. How was your trip?"

"The customer was pleased with the offer. We only had to make a few changes to the contract before they signed."

"You know me well enough to know I don't give a shit about the customer part, tell me about the Avery part."

"There's not much to tell. He was pleasant." Macy refused to act like a giddy teenager over a few kisses.

"Do you like him?"

"Our working relationship survived his earlier comments."

"I don't mean work, Macy. And you know it."

"I don't want to lose my job. The last thing I need is to start a fling with someone in the office. Avery is off limits." Macy adjusted her position in the seat. If she said it repeatedly, she might believe it.

"I didn't say anything about a fling. Why did you mention a fling? What happened?"

"Nothing, forget it."

"You know I won't forget it, so you might as well tell me." Gayle took her eye off the road long enough to look at Macy. "What are you afraid of?"

"I'm not afraid of anything," Macy said. "Relationships are overrated. Look at what happened to my parents."

"Every time you want to run away from something, you use your parents' divorce as a reason. Lots of people get divorced. It's not the end of the world."

"My situation was different. My parents didn't just get divorced. My father…"

"Yeah, I know. Your father walked out, took all the money, disappeared, and it's all your fault, for being a kid and wanting things and demanding attention and being in the way. And on and on and on. Do you know how many times I've heard that lament? Child, it's time you put that woe-is-me song away."

"Can we change the subject?"

"Suit yourself. But don't come whining to me when Avery gets married and you're standing outside the church with huge tears in your eyes. Because you deserve happiness, too, Macy." Gayle maneuvered her way through traffic.

"Michelle quit. She up and quit and I didn't know anything about it." Her voice rose several octaves.

"Your assistant? Why? What did you do to her?"

"Nothing. I was in Europe." She rubbed her forehead. "But I don't get it. I told her about the missing money. She was supposed to help me find out what's going on and just like that she quits. Without warning."

Gayle took her eyes off the road, a little too long.

"Red light, Gayle." Macy reached for the steering wheel. The car stopped short.

"You think Michelle, is stealing from English?" Gayle said.

"She was living from paycheck to paycheck. Nobody would let her get away with coming in late, leaving early and all her other antics like I did. I treated her like a little sister. Trying to help her out, help her be more professional, so she could have a career and not just a job."

"Maybe that was the problem. Maybe Michelle was ready to step up her game."

Macy shook her head. "Let's stop by her place. I want to talk to her. I want to know why she quit."

"Now?"

"Yes, I need to know. Now."

"Can't you just call her?"

"She hasn't been picking up. Probably because she stole a hundred thousand dollars."

"Okay," Gayle said. "Which way?"

Macy pointed out the turns. In front of Michelle's apartment complex, she hesitated.

"Go ahead. Get out. You wanted to come here and confront her, right?"

"There is no way Michelle is going to confess to stealing the money. I'm not sure how to get the truth out of her."

"Don't mention the money. Just ask her why she quit. See if she has a brand-new sixty-two-inch television on the wall."

Macy pointed her finger at Gayle but decided to keep her mouth shut. She climbed the stairs to Michelle's third-floor apartment. The last time she was here the two of them were celebrating Christmas. This time Macy wasn't sure what to say. Maybe the words would come to her when she saw her assistant's face.

Outside of apartment 3Q, Macy pushed the bell and waited. When there was no answer after several seconds, she pressed the button again. The neighbor across the hall opened their door.

"You looking for the tall, black girl?"

"Yeah. Do you know Michelle?" Macy asked.

"She doesn't live there anymore. Thank, god. The place has been so much quieter without having her blast her techno-music at one in the morning."

"Do you know where she moved?"

"No clue. But I sure won't miss her. She's someone else's pain in the ass now." The neighbor hurried down the hall.

Macy followed him, but her pace was a whole lot slower. How could Michelle move out of her apartment in a matter of days? Didn't it take months and a ton of boxes for someone to relocate? With 100K almost anything was possible. How could she not know anything about this?

"That was fast." Gayle started the engine. "So, what did she say?"

"She doesn't live there anymore. She moved." Macy stared at Gayle.

"What do you think that means?"

"Nothing good, that's for sure."

"Oh, by the way, your brother called. He thought you were getting home this morning."

Macy plucked her phone from her purse and punched her brother's number.

"What's up?" she asked when he answered.

He didn't respond in his usual rapid manner. She said, "Brian, what's the matter? Why did you call? Is everything okay?"

"Whoa, sis," he said.

"Brian, you never call before noon unless something is wrong, or you need money. Which is it? If you're calling about the hot water heater, I already know about it."

"You think I care about the water heater?" He chuckled again, and Macy missed his infectious good mood. He was always easy going and happy.

"Okay then, what is it?"

"When are you coming home again? I need to talk to you about something. It's important."

"Did you get a cheerleader pregnant?"

"Ha, ha. No," he said with deadpan dryness.

"Tell me what it is. You're making me worry."

"It's a conversation I want to have to your face."

"Well, that's a new twist. When did seeing my face matter?"

"I'll tell you when you come home."

"How about the weekend? I've got something going on in the office that I can't delay."

"That works. Bye, sis and don't worry." He disconnected the call. Macy didn't know what to think. Her brother was calm and collected about everything. The house could burn down, and he wouldn't think it was important enough to tell her.

Macy stared at her phone. "Why is Brian so secretive?" she muttered.

"What's going on?" Gayle didn't take her eyes off the congestion as they snaked up the interstate.

"I don't know yet, but I hope it can wait until I find Michelle and that missing money."

Chapter Twenty-One

The plans he had of seducing Macy last night evaporated the moment she pushed off the bed. Until that point, she was as enamored as he was. That wasn't just a friendly peck, and she was the one who asked him to stay.

Avery pulled his car into his building garage and caught the elevator up to his loft. He closed the door and dropped his bags on the floor. He had enough time to shower and change before picking Macy up.

Keeping his promise to stay out of relationships was impossible to keep. Kissing her may not have been the smartest thing he'd done, but it sure felt right. There was something about her being off limits that made him want her even more.

In the kitchen, he pressed the button to retrieve his messages from the land-line and poured a glass of wine.

The first message was from his father. "Avery, give me a call. I tried to reach you on your cell phone. I don't understand how you can have an expensive phone, and nobody can reach you. Suppose your clients wanted to get in touch with you? It's important. Give me a call." Avery paced the kitchen as he listened to his remaining messages.

His brother, Austen, had also called and wanted to know when he could drop by the club. Avery saved that message without waiting for it to end. The other calls were from clients, he'd call them back tomorrow.

He swallowed the wine in one gulp before placing the glass on the coffee table and reaching for the remote to turn on the music. Jazz blared through the surround-sound in his loft. If he hadn't been a jerk that first night, maybe Macy would be stretched out in his bed this very minute. His body warmed to an image of her in her bed. He shook his pant leg, giving his erection plenty of room.

He cursed under his breath as he scrolled through the caller ID, looking for Celeste's number. There was no reason to wait another moment to straighten her out on the status of their non-existent relationship.

He sat on the end of the sofa. The music softened his edges of disappointment. He closed his eyes, hoping to relax, but his body revved for action. When he couldn't delay it any longer, he dialed Celeste's number.

"Hey, Celeste, it's Avery." He needed to resolve the lingering issue between them. The only way to do that was to remain calm. They small talked a bit. Celeste complained about Roxy being tough on her. Wanting her in the office every day like a grunt.

She sounded like she'd rather step forward for a root canal than talk to him.

"Listen," he said gently. "Your sister seems to think you and I are considering marriage."

"Yeah, I know," she muttered. "It's Roxy. You know how she is."

Avery released a long slow breath. How was Celeste able to be nonchalant about this, when she was overly dramatic about everything else? He tried to ignore the heat rising up his back.

"Can you talk to her today and get this straightened out?"

She hesitated. He knew it meant trouble. "Umm, I'd rather not do that right now."

Avery took another deep breath to modulate his voice. "Why not?"

"Look, Avery, I'll handle this my way. I would prefer you just keep your mouth shut for now because if Roxy stops writing me checks, you better believe Malveaux and

Malveaux won't see many more checks either. I'll make sure of that."

Avery snatched the phone away from his ear, ready to throw it across the room. The last of his resolve vanished in a poof of anger. "Celeste, please don't be foolish enough to think I'm some sucker. I am not intimidated by your whiny ways and if your sister believes anything that comes out of your mouth, then shame on her. Either you get this straightened out or I will. If I have to do it, it won't be pretty."

"Just do me a favor." She sniffed into the phone before beginning to cry. When her sobs grew louder, Avery held the phone away from his ear again. "I know this might be hard for you to do, but give me two weeks," she said. "I'll clear it all up. Either that or I'll make you wait until the baby gets here and do a paternity test."

"You're pregnant?" He couldn't keep the disbelief from taking over his voice. There was nonstop drama with this one. "The baby is not mine. I've never touched you. What are you trying to pull? You are one crazy..." Avery yelled into the receiver.

"Avery, you have no idea what it's like to try to live up to someone's expectations of you. To always fall short. Roxy is the big success. Our father left her the whole company because he thought I was a twit. In a few weeks, I turn twenty-five, and I can get my full inheritance. But if Roxy thinks I've screwed up again, she can delay it another year, she's the executor. Another whole year." Celeste cried uncontrollably now. Avery struggled to understand her.

Avery fell back against the chair. He knew exactly how she felt; always trying to prove yourself. The quest for the English account was his way of demonstrating to his father that he was competent. He dropped his head in his hands. He wanted to get Celeste out of his life, but if she started a rumor that he'd gotten her pregnant, it might take nine months before he could clear his name. In the business world nine months was long enough to kill her career, or waste too much time defending his name. He pictured another Saturday morning listening to his tirade about how he ruined his political chances and dragged the Malveaux family through another scandal. One week was a whole lot better than nine months.

"Celeste, listen, you have one week, not two. And if my name is not out of your little scheme to extort money from your sister, then I'm blowing the lid off your antics."

"You can't tell anyone, Avery, not anyone. Because if Roxy finds out the baby isn't yours, I know she'll delay my trust."

"Did you tell her I was the father?" He stood and paced to the windows.

"No, she just assumed like she does about everything."

"One. Week. If it takes longer, it's your problem. Not mine and I'll match you rumor for rumor. You can count on that."

Avery depressed the end button on the phone with so much force it fell from his hand. He picked up his glass and hurled it against the wall.

Chapter Twenty-Two

The smug sensation in Macy's chest blossomed. She was on a date with Avery. Her life was in two parts, her work life and her fledging love life. She pushed work aside. This moment was for enjoying.

Avery pulled his car into the valet line at the club. Based on the outside, the inside was packed. A crowd lingered outside, and the line waiting to get inside extended down the block.

"I don't think your brother needs to worry about you showing up. This crowd is crazy."

"Yeah, but in the beginning, clubs are always like this. It's two and three years in when you have trouble drawing a crowd." Avery climbed out and walked around to the passenger side. The valet had already opened her door, but she reached for Avery's hand.

Avery nodded to the attendants as they made their way inside. Being with him was like being with a rock star. There was no waiting in line or second-class treatment. Someone always wanted to take his picture and beautiful women couldn't wait to throw themselves at his feet.

They breezed across the first floor and made their way to the elevator to take them to the VIP lounge.

"You don't get here often?" Macy asked once they were inside.

He sighed, giving her the impression he didn't want to be here tonight. "Not as often as Austen would like. Clubs are not my thing, but for my youngest brother, why not?"

The doors parted, and they stepped out. Macy was relieved to be away from the pounding sound of the bass on the first floor.

"Oh, there you are. I thought you'd abandoned me." Austen gave his brother one of those man-hugs and chest bumps. "Macy it's good to see you again."

She nodded, unsure if she should hug him. At the moment she wasn't Avery's girlfriend, which made for an awkward few seconds.

"I just got back in town today. It looks like you haven't missed me." Avery tilted his head to the party going on downstairs.

"I do want to talk to you about something." Austen paused. "Macy if you don't mind?"

She waved her hand. "No, not at all."

Austen and Avery moved to the bar and started a whispered conversation. She took a seat on the extended lounge. The music soothed her weary body. The last few days had been an emotional ride. She needed time to sort out what was real and what was just make-believe. Never had she gone to dinner with a man several times, had cozy conversations on a bed and kissed without moving toward a relationship. In Avery's circles no one probably ever made an official proclamation, and she was hesitant to raise the question.

A server arrived with a glass of wine balanced on a silver tray. "Mr. Malveaux asked me to bring you something to drink."

She accepted the drink and settled into the cushion to relax for a moment. So much had happened in such a short period it was hard to keep things compartmentalized. What part of their relationship was work and what part was personal. The lines blurred. Instead of sitting in a nightclub while Avery handled his business, she should be at home combing through files to find out how Michelle stole that money and if she could get it back before the audit.

Why was she having such a hard time focusing? Before she could tease out an answer, Avery slid next to her on the sofa with a glass of wine in his hand.

"Thank you for waiting," he said.

"Is everything okay?" she asked.

Without answering he studied her face. His gaze was so intense she had to look away. "Why are you staring at me like that?"

"I guess I'm trying to figure you out. In so many ways you remind me of my mother."

She stiffened. "I've never met your mother, so I don't know if you just gave me a compliment or an insult."

He chuckled. "My mother is wonderful. And like you, she has a fiery personality. She's more of an observer than a talker, but when you have her attention, she makes you feel like you're the center of the universe."

"She sounds special. So thank you for the comparison."

He cupped her face. The passion in his eyes was so hot she struggled to take a breath. The moment he pressed his lips to hers, the ability to suppress her feeling for him evaporated. She met his intensity with her own searing affection.

Loud voices behind them made Avery break away, and turn around. Macy followed his glance to see Dennison Malveaux stroll into the lounge. She could almost see a sudden change in the atmosphere. Austen left the bar to greet his father.

"I'll be right back." Avery stood and shook his father's hand.

"Son, I didn't expect to see you here tonight'" Dennison spoke to Avery, but his eyes were locked on hers. "I thought you were still out of town."

"I got back earlier today."

Macy didn't want to shake his hand or greet him. This was as close as she'd ever been to Dennison Malveaux. His deep-set, narrow eyes bore through her.

"Dad, this is Macy Rollins."

His father stuck out his hand, and she shook it. His flesh was cold, just like his heart. The urge to leave was as forceful as her dislike of him. She took several short breaths, to calm her swirling stomach.

"Aren't you the girl who works at English?" he said.

The idea that he would call her a girl was enough for her to come back with something equally insulting, but she took another breath. "I've been with English for over five years."

"So what are the two of you up to?" Dennison directed his question to his son.

Avery placed his glass on the table. "Can I talk to you at the bar for a moment, Dad?"

Dennison followed his son across the room, but Macy didn't miss the icy stare he directed at her. The two men talked in harsh whispers, but above the hum of the music she could make out a few of Avery's angry phases, *his life, his business*.

She could only wonder if Avery's father's objection to her was as strong as her objection to him. The golden shine on the night vanished. She was too exhausted to interpret the body language on the other side of the room.

A moment later, Dennison made his way to the elevator and disappeared inside. Avery returned to the lounger and sat beside her.

"Sorry about that," he said before picking up his glass and finishing off the contents.

"Avery, it's late. It's been a long day. I'm ready to go home." Her head throbbed with the beginning of a tension headache.

"I had planned to take you out to dinner. Please don't let my father upset you."

She put her hand on his knee. "Another time, maybe." Tonight she needed to retreat and regroup. There was a reason she wanted to keep Avery at a distance. She just needed to remember it.

Chapter Twenty-Three

Monday morning, Macy rushed past the crowd in the lobby to get to her desk earlier than usual. Stopping for coffee or to read her horoscope were luxuries for people that didn't have any worries. She had dozens. In addition to returning calls and replying to messages, she needed the extra time to prepare for the audit.

At least last night her mother sounded fine when they talked. Whatever was going on at home didn't equate to 'Mom is sick, come home right away.' She sighed. Whatever her brother had to tell her would have to wait until after the audit.

"You're here early this morning." Avery's voice washed over her with a fragrance so crisp it woke her senses. Every time he came into her office, his scent and masculinity lingered long after he was gone. Was he even aware of his mystique and how his presence overpowered her?

"So are you. I've got a good reason for being here. What's your excuse?" She tilted her head, hoping her prettiest side showed. He probably didn't notice the lilt in her voice, but she heard her attempt to be playful and coy.

He slid into the chair. "Other than the night I nearly broke your ankle, I enjoyed our time in Geneva. Maybe I ought to apologize for kissing you, but I won't"

"I wasn't going to ask you to."

"What was your horoscope this morning? Did it say anything about a new relationship?"

"No way am I telling you. You're making fun of me." The post this morning mentioned the words soul mate and a business alliance. But he'd think she was making it all up.

"Did you read mine?"

"I don't know your birthday."

"How can you know my business by way of the tabloids and not know I was born on July fifteenth?"

"I focused on the big stuff." She tapped her pencil on the desk.

"Are you busy tonight?" He pulled his chair closer to her.

"Why? After our night at your club was cut short, I think you and I shouldn't…"

"My father was way out of line, if he didn't get the message at the club, he's gotten it now. That, I know for sure."

"Does he object to me or does he object to your dating in general?"

"Neither matters to me," he said.

She pulled back in her chair. Flirting with him had been fun. Taking things further was risky. "What about Celeste?"

He rubbed his chin. "I knew you were going to say that, and you have nothing to be concerned about. I've spoken to Celeste. She's straight."

Macy raised her eyebrows. "I doubt that." She mumbled.

"I owe you a dinner. What do you say?"

She teased the idea for a moment. Wanting to say yes, but knowing she should say no. "Okay, what do you have in mind?"

"I'll pick you up at seven. Dress casual." He stood. "Oh, yeah, and I'll need your address."

She scribbled her address on a piece of paper and handed it to him. He reached for it. His hand lingered against hers. Regardless of what her horoscope said, he was moving too fast. There were more reasons to say no to him then there were to say yes, but she wanted to say yes to everything he asked.

"Look, you need to get out of here so I can get some work done. That's the reason I came in early."

He paused for a moment, staring at her as if he was seeing something for the first time. Was he looking at her crooked eyebrows that she'd plucked this morning?

As soon as he was gone, she spun her chair around to the window and closed her eyes. This morning she had to read her horoscope twice, just to be sure she'd seen the words right. The words remained branded on her thoughts just like the sun was always in the sky.

Your planets have aligned to bring you something special like the arrival of a soul mate. You might meet someone worth dating or someone you can call an ally. The electricity between you two will be undeniable. So, jump in and enjoy.

She reached for her phone and pulled up his horoscope. She bit her lip hoping his projection matched hers.

There is harmony in the air. All your planets have aligned. Your relationships will be problem-free, and you deserve to enjoy yourself. If it's love you want, then you may meet someone who fulfills your needs.

Macy had double-checked the post to be sure she had the right zodiac sign. Good stuff like this didn't happen to her. She closed her eyes for a moment and tried to imagine the two of them together. The fantasy always had them laughing and happy. But, she knew better.

Macy opened her eyes at the sound of Roxy's heels tapping on the tile floor. Purpose sounded in every step. She stuck her head in the door. Her freshly curled, blond tresses bounced on her shoulders. "Good work in Europe, Macy. You have the contracts?" Roxy breezed into the office and took a seat.

Macy handed Roxy the requested paperwork. "It was easier than I expected, a serious adrenaline rush. Both customers were hesitant, but there was a moment when I knew I had them. It was almost as if the air in the room shifted."

"It looks like you and Avery make a good team. I had a few doubts in the beginning." She scanned the signatures on the last page. "We're lucky his schedule was open. For a moment I thought you might have to go alone. You know I wanted Celeste to fly over, hoping she and Avery could spend a little time together, but that girl..." She shook her head.

Macy smiled using the expression she saved for the office, which was polite and showed the right amount of interest. She had work to do and Roxy was ready to talk. She'd settled back in the chair and crossed her legs. Macy shifted in her seat. Hoping guilt wouldn't give her away. How could she entertain the idea of being with Avery when he was with the boss's sister? Obviously, Avery hadn't talked to Roxy about the situation between him and Celeste yet. The question was who was he deceiving and why?

She brushed her hand over the sleeve of her blouse. There was nothing extraordinary about her that he couldn't find in almost any girl, so why was Avery even pretending to be interested?

"Did you hear me, Macy?" Roxy sat forward.

"I'm sorry." Macy redirected her attention. "What did you say?"

"Are you ready for the audit?"

"Yes, just about." Macy's reply came out with a gush of air.

"The preliminary word is that everything is going great. Let's hope we can get it finished up in a day or two, so we can focus our attention back on the Dragon negotiations."

"Yeah, right. I'm meeting with them tomorrow." Macy looked down at the papers on her desk. Now would have been the perfect time to tell Roxy about the issue, but the words stuck in her throat. There was still a chance to come up with a reasonable explanation and what was the use in telling Roxy if there was nothing to worry about?

Roxy stood. "I'm off." She paused. "Are you sure you're alright? You look almost pale."

"I'm fine. Really." Macy forced her head up and produced a smile that had to be as counterfeit as her accounts.

Macy caught the elevator to the third floor. Celeste's office door was open, and Celeste was seated behind her desk. Macy walked in and closed the door.

"I still don't have access to the accounting system. I've had my access revoked before and it has never taken this long to reset."

"Welcome back, Macy. I heard you did a wonderful job as usual." Celeste smiled.

"Celeste, my access."

"Yes." She turned to her computer and began striking the keys. "This place has been a mess since you left. All kinds of things have gone wrong. Let me see what is going on." She continued to look at the computer.

"You're just now looking into this?"

Celeste turned to her. "Like I said. We've been swamped." Celeste's eyes narrowed and darkened.

"Whatever. Can we get it fixed now?"

"That's what I was doing." Celeste rolled her eyes, then turned back to her computer. She stroked several more keys. "I think you're all set now. Let me know if you have any more issues."

"It was that easy? Then why didn't someone do that last week?" Macy stood. "Celeste, did you purposely delete my access?"

"Now, Macy, why would I do that."

Macy held her gaze for moment. "Because you could."

Chapter Twenty-Four

From the moment Macy agreed to go out with Avery, she couldn't focus on any of the important things. Instead of pursuing Michelle, she thought about what to wear. Instead of rechecking the few audit documents she had, she was wondering what she and Avery would talk about. This was a real date. Everything up to now was only practice. Dating Avery was like playing with an open flame?

"Look at you. Don't you look nice? Don't tell me you're going out on a work night." Gayle placed her hand on her hip.

"Just so you know, I'm going out with Avery tonight."

"A date?"

"Yes. He asked me out, and I said yes."

"I know you checked your horoscopes to make sure the stars are all aligned." Gayle waved her hands in the air like one of those used car blow up balloons.

"Go ahead and make fun of me. Like I've said before, I'm not settling for mediocre so anything that gives me an advantage, I'm going to make good use of it." She stuck her nose up in the air.

"I hear you, girl." She strolled away, her slippers flopping against the floor. "Your cell phone is chirping."

Macy rushed into her bedroom and read the text message from her brother. "We need to talk. Now"

She sat on the edge of the bed and dialed her brother. "Brian, if we need to talk why didn't you call me?"

For several moments her brother said nothing. The only sound was his heavy breathing.

"Brian, what is it?" Her heartbeat ratcheted up a notch. "Did something happen to Mom?"

"Coach. I spoke with Coach today about the scholarship." He huffed. "He said he wasn't sure I was going to get it."

"I thought you said it was a sure thing. Did something happen?"

"I thought it was." He gulped. "Can we talk?"

"Sure." She sat on the edge of the bed. "I'm listening."

"No, Macy. Talk in person."

"I'll come home this weekend. I promise." Guilt pinched her heart.

"Tonight, Macy. Can't you make some time for me?" She heard the pain he was trying to hold back. "I need to talk to you, and it can't wait." He was agitated, any moment he'd burst with emotion like he'd done when she explained their father wasn't coming back.

"Okay, Brian. Tonight."

"Can we meet in Dover? We can have dinner at the Olive Garden." His breathing wasn't as heavy.

She looked down at her dress and matching heels. "Okay. I'll be there, but give me two hours. I'll leave now."

She hung up and stared at the ceiling. If everything happened for a reason, then there had to be a reason fate was keeping her and Avery apart. Before she could call him, the doorbell rang.

"I got it, Gayle." She hurried to the door, unzipping her dress. If she got out of the house in the next three minutes, she could make it to Dover in two hours.

"Avery, I need to cancel." She kicked off her sandals. "I've got to meet my brother. Something's come up."

He stepped over the threshold. The crisp scent of his cologne was as intoxicating as the cleft in his chin.

"You look flustered. What happened?"

"I've got to go to Dover. My brother has a problem with his coach, and I need to be there for him." She picked up her shoes and hurried to her bedroom. Forget changing. There was no time. She zipped her dress back up and slipped into a pair of bronze colored flip-flops and grabbed her purse. "I'm sorry. I couldn't tell you sooner. He just called."

Avery stood by the door as if he were waiting for something more to happen.

Macy shouldered her bag. "We'll have to do it another night." She looked back at Gayle's closed bedroom door. "Gayle, I need to borrow your car. I've got to see Brian. It's an emergency."

Gayle rushed out of the bedroom. "I've got a photo-shoot tonight. I was going to drive." Gayle's robe hung open exposing her bare breast. She looked up, spotted Avery, grabbed the top of her robe, clutching it so it closed. "I didn't know you had..." She pointed at Avery.

"He's leaving." Macy faced him.

"Actually, I'll give you a lift since there seems to be one car and two needs." His eyes sparkled like sun off the ocean, and his smile widened.

"I've got to go all the way to Dover," Macy said. "It's four hours round trip. I can't..."

"That means I'll have you all to myself for at least four uninterrupted hours."

"I can't." She looked back to Gayle for an answer.

"Yes, you can." Gayle adjusted the robe and tightened the belt. "I hope everything is okay."

Avery extended his elbow to her. "My car awaits."

Macy paused. No matter what, she couldn't disappoint her brother. Whatever was bothering him must be pretty serious, because Brian seldom made demands. She looped her arm through Avery's and closed the door behind them.

They were on 95 South when she said, "I'm going to have to buy a car. It won't be anything as fancy as this one, of course." The comment sounded ungrateful. "Thank you for doing this. I really mean it."

"I don't mind." He drove with his right hand high on the steering wheel. "How do you manage without a car?"

She straightened. Telling Avery the details of her financial status wasn't something she wanted to do. The only person who knew about her money situation was Gayle. Nobody wanted to hear her crying broke. "Cars come with payment, and they need insurance and gas and maintenance, and they need tires. Once we get my brother into college, I'll see what I can do." She shifted and pushed her chin a little higher. "I make out just fine, riding Septa, Amtrak, and taxi's, especially when someone else is picking up the tab. Gayle has a car, and usually, I can borrow it if something comes up."

"I'm sorry. I didn't mean to come off like that."

She brushed off his comment with a sweep of her hand. "As soon as my mom and I get Brian situated in college, and he gets a scholarship, things won't be so tight. Until then, I can't afford the expense."

"Do you know what the crisis is about?"

"He's a high school senior. It could be almost anything or everything. All he'd tell me was it had something to do with his coach and the scholarship."

"Have you been able to talk with your assistant?"

She pursed her lips. "No. I haven't been able to reach her and she's moved out of her apartment and left no forwarding address," she paused. "I talked to the building manager. Everyone seems to be glad she moved."

"You never really know people, do you?"

"Yeah, I think something's going on with her. I just don't know what, yet."

They arrived at the restaurant before Brian. The hostess placed them in a booth large enough for a family of five.

Macy scrolled through her phone when it pinged. "He just sent a text. He's just a few minutes away."

Avery moved closer to her. "Me being here isn't going to be a problem, is it? I can sit at the entrance and let the two of you talk if you want." He was being nice. Sitting with a porcupine would have been more fun for him right now since she was wound tighter than a spinning toy.

"No. I don't think Brian will mind. We'll see what he says when he gets here."

Avery ran his finger down the menu. "Let's order an appetizer while we're waiting."

"Fine, you decide." No matter what she ate, she wouldn't taste it.

Brian arrived before the appetizer. "Sis." He slid into the booth next to her.

"This is Avery. We were going out when you called."

Avery reached across the table and shook her brother's hand. "I've heard a lot about you, Brian."

"I've never heard your name. But that doesn't surprise me." He faced Macy. "Does that explain the sexy dress with the flip-flops?"

"You didn't give me time to change." She placed her hand over his. "What's going on, Brian? What happened? Did Mom get the check to replace the water heater?"

"I took a hot shower this morning. Does that answer your question?"

"Okay, I get it. What's up?"

He started to talk, then stopped and glanced across the table.

Avery pushed back. "If you'd like for me to give you two some privacy…"

Brian hesitated a moment. "No. You can stay." He cleared his throat. "Today the coach told me that no one from the University was going to come see me. How can I get that scholarship if no one visits the school?"

"Did something happen? The coach was so sure the University of Maryland wanted you."

Her brother shrugged his shoulders. This was just like Brian, to have only half of the information.

"What about the other schools?"

"I want to go to the University of Maryland. It's a bigger school. It has the major I want." He sounded like the little brother she always protected.

"Can I say something?" Avery said.

"Sure." Macy gave him her attention.

"I know the Defensive Coordinator there. We were college roommates, and he just signed on there a few years ago. I can give him a call." He directed his attention to her. "Remember, I told you about him."

"Yeah, but I can't let you do that. That's asking too much."

"You'd do that for me?" Brian perked up.

"Wait a minute. Wait a minute." Macy held her hand up toward him to stop him from saying anymore. "We can't ask him to do that."

"Why not? If he can help, why not?"

"Because, Brian, Avery is just a friend. We can find another way to work this out."

Brian looked at her for a moment, then across the table at Avery. "Man, if you can help by making a phone call, I'd really appreciate your help. Come on, Macy. How can making a phone call hurt anything?"

Avery held up his palms. "I do not promise anything will change, but I'll attempt it, if your sister is alright with that."

Both Avery and Brian focused on her. Either her brother was going to think she was blocking his path, or she was going to be indebted to Avery. Boxed in with no way out, she closed her eyes for a moment. The picture of her father walking away as if they were dime store trinkets was branded in her memory. Somehow, they'd managed her tuition, and now she had to do everything she could to make sure Brian had the same opportunity.

Brian poked her in the arm. "Come on, sis. It's just a phone call."

She looked into her brother's dark brown eyes and, just like she did when there was only one Pop Tart left, she gave in.

"Okay. But, Brian, please don't get too excited about this. Nothing might happen. We need to think about alternatives."

He released a deep breath. "Thank, you, Avery. How soon can you call him?"

"I'll do it tomorrow." He stared across the table at Macy and smiled as if he'd just accomplished something big. "Now, since this is supposed to be a date, let me treat the two of you to dinner." He turned to face Brian. "What position do you play?"

"Cornerback. You'll have to come see me play."

"I'll tell you what, if I can talk the coach into coming, I'll come watch you, too."

Brian held up his hand for a sophisticated high five. "That's a bet, man. Sure 'nough. Maybe you can drag my sister, too. She hasn't been to a game since the first one."

By the time the entrees were cleared from the table, Brian and Avery were chatting like they'd known each other for years.

"Will you all be having dessert?" the server asked as she cleared the table.

"Brian, it's getting late, you have school tomorrow. You'd better get down the road."

"She's always babying me," Brian said to Avery. "Oh yeah, there is one more thing I need to tell you."

"Oh boy, Brian. What else?"

The smile fell from his face. "I've talked to Dad. He wants to talk to you."

Brian could have poured his ice water down her back, and she wouldn't have felt any colder. Her mind refused to function. She fumbled for the right words.

"Brian." She shook her head. "When? How?"

"He showed up outside my school one day. He said he was sorry…"

"We already know he's sorry. I don't want to talk to him." She folded her arms over her chest.

"He just wants to talk, Macy. I've talked to him, and he say he's sorry. I gave him your cell number." Brian dropped his head and lowered his voice.

She closed her eyes and drew in a deep breath. All of her thoughts whirled around the hurt little girl her father left standing in the doorway. That was the 202 area code number that kept showing up on her phone. She sighed.

Brian had been too young to understand the destruction their father had caused. But she couldn't forget, and she couldn't forgive.

Chapter Twenty-Five

Avery kept his eyes on the darkened road, as they drove back to Philly. He stole glances at Macy every few miles. Her teeth held her bottom lip in place. She hunched in the passenger seat as if she was trying to shrink from sight.

"Are you upset I offered to make that call for your brother?"

She straightened and rubbed her hands together. "No. If you can help him, I was wrong to hesitate. I'm the one who usually saves him from disaster. It's kinda my thing." She made a sound that resembled a sniff, but her eyes were clear.

"If you hadn't accepted my ride then I couldn't have made the offer. So, you're still his big sis with all the answers. I just hope I can help. He walked out a lot happier than he walked in."

Avery entered the city limit and took the Broad Street exit off 95.

"Where are we going? This isn't my exit."

"We're still on a date, so I thought we'd stop and have a drink," Avery said.

"I can't go anywhere fancy. I have on flip-flops, remember." She looked down and wiggled her cherry red painted toenails.

"Okay, then I have another idea. How about we go back to my place for a drink? I figure it's the least we could do since our dates keep getting interrupted."

She stared at him for a long moment.

"Just a drink. That is, of course, unless you decided you'd like something else."

"Yeah. Let's do that."

The last thing he wanted was for her to see the look of relief on his face. Being turned down over and over again was damaging his game. He forced his face to remain neutral when he swung a left turn and took the fastest route to his high rise.

He pulled into his assigned parking space in the garage and turned off the car.

"I should have figured you'd live in a place like this," she said before stepping out of the car.

"Would you prefer I live in a box under one of the city bridges?"

"No. I was just making an observation, ignore me."

Together they made their way to the elevator. If only there was some way to get her upstairs without having to press the penthouse button. Any other time he would have liked to show off, but Macy wasn't impressed with his *things*. He hoped she was dazzled by his personality and everything he did to show her he cared.

The condo was dark. He turned on the entrance light and rushed ahead of her. He hadn't planned on bringing her back to his place, but sometimes the dating gods granted him favors. "What would you like to drink?" He strolled into the kitchen.

"I'll have a glass of wine." She moved beyond the kitchen to stare out of the wall of windows. The city's twinkling light reflected off her brown skin. They could be awesome together if only she'd disable the invisible protection surrounding her like the walls of Fort Knox.

From the wine fridge, he selected a bottle of white wine. In Europe, she'd always picked a Riesling. So he opened the bottle and poured two glasses.

"You've been exceptionally quiet. Care to talk about it." He handed her the glass.

She took a sip, staring at him over the rim. "I can't get over what Brian told me about my father. Why he wants to talk to any of us after all this time takes more balls than I thought he had." She gripped the glass so tight the veins in her hand bulged.

"How long has he been gone?"

"He left when I was thirteen. I remember hearing my mother crying from her bedroom for months. I didn't think she was ever going to stop."

"Did your mother tell you what was going on?"

"She didn't have to. I saw the late payment notices. I heard her begging for more time to pay the mortgage. I saw the look in her eyes when she placed our dinners on the table, then said she wasn't hungry because there wasn't enough."

"Maybe he wants to make amends now." The sadness in her eyes was even harder to accept than her words. Her pain was visible. Maybe this topic was too sensitive. He wrapped an arm around her shoulder and placed his chin on her forehead. "I'm sorry this happened to you."

"We don't need him now. We made it without him." She trembled, slushing wine over the rim of the glass.

He removed the glass from her hand and placed both of their glasses on the table. "I didn't mean to upset you." He cupped her shoulders with his palms, trying to still her body. "If you'd rather not talk about him, we don't have to."

"Let's talk about something else."

"I've got an idea. Let's talk about that kiss we shared in Europe that you ended while I was just getting started."

"That was a test. We were out of the country, heady about the success of our meetings and maybe a little too jovial to think straight. Tonight, I think we're both more levelheaded."

"If I'm feeling the same way about you tonight, what excuse will you come up with for me?"

She tilted her chin, her eyes fastened on his. "That you're feeling sorry for me and trying to make me forget about my father." Something in her eyes opened his heart and pulled her inside. Maybe it was his need for her or the want he couldn't deny, but he couldn't resist her for another moment.

His mouth covered hers, sinking into her soft lips. Her skintight dress wasn't forgiving enough to allow him to touch more than the flesh on her arms. The dress was like a protective coating. He could see every curve, he just couldn't touch them.

He released her mouth but continued to stare into her eyes. "What did your horoscope say today? Are our stars aligned?"

Her face glowed with a laugh. He could spend a lifetime looking into her bright brown eyes.

"Are you making fun of me?"

"Of course not. I want to know. I'm not saying I believe all that stuff about stars and planets, but if you do, then I want to know."

"Okay. Today is supposed to be a happy one for me. My horoscope said someone special was going to be in my life today."

He pointed to his chest. "That's me right, not your brother?"

"Maybe it was referring to the both of you."

"I'll take that and this." He pulled her close and pressed his mouth to hers again. Her body flattened against his. But when she wrapped her arms around his waist, his heart swelled.

She pulled back just enough to study his face, hoping he would continue to hold her. Whether he thought she was a nut for sharing her family drama on what was supposed to be a romantic evening, she couldn't tell. But he didn't release his hands from around her. Being held close to his chest was something she'd been afraid to imagine, but one she wanted to enjoy for a long time. "Either way, my horoscope was right, wasn't it?"

"Aren't we happy with the way things worked out?"

"Very. Thank you, again." She kissed his cheek.

Maybe she'd been wrong about him.

Maybe Avery was nothing like his father.

Maybe he had a heart, a big one. Offering to help her brother was beyond anything she could have expected from him.

The intoxicating expression on his face made her heart thump harder. There were good reasons to pull away from him. But she couldn't. As risky as being with Avery was, she couldn't walk away. She needed to forget about the past, to stop glancing backward and focus on the offerings of the future. Maybe now was the perfect time to open the lock on her heart.

Avery pulled her closer. His hands warmed her skin beneath the thin fabric of the dress. She needed to feel his skin, to enjoy every moment of what before had only been her imagination.

She pushed his jacket off his shoulders, allowing it to drop to the floor. She loosened his tie and kissed him at the same time. The weight of his tongue against hers let her know he was here, now, with her. He didn't hold back. The tender way he cradled her neck made her know it wasn't simply lust that percolated the air in the room.

With one hand he unzipped her dress, allowing the delicate garment to join his jacket on the floor. Avery released the hook on her bra, with the other, freeing her breasts. With his index finger, he circled one nipple, then the next. The sensation sent a jolt of pleasure through her body. How was this possible? How could he call her body to attention with a single touch?

"How about we remove your pants?" She tugged at his belt.

He placed his hand over hers and helped with the buckle. Then he released the button, unzipped his pants and stepped out of them along with his briefs, without breaking eye contact with her.

He pulled back and studied her. His eyes spoke a language her soul understood. She saw more than lust, or maybe that's what she wanted to believe, needed to believe, as the warmth between her legs bloomed.

His chest was exactly as she'd imagined. The hair was soft and dark just like the curls on top of his head. Every muscle in his abdomen was well defined. She ran her hand along each one, teasing his flesh the way he'd taunted her.

"I want you, Macy." His husky voice melted any resistance she pretended to have.

"I want you, too." She lifted her head to look into his eyes. The sincerity in his eyes touched her heart. Were they moving too fast? In college, she'd stuck to the three-month rule before having sex, but tonight, even sticking to three minutes would be like forever. Her horoscope had been right before but never like this.

He scooped her up in his arms. She closed her eyes and soaked in the moment. She planted kisses on his bare chest. This was the part she would dream about nights from now. The moment just before, when all she felt was her feelings for him.

In his bedroom, he placed her on the king bed. The soft cotton duvet against her burning skin made her arch up, just enough to catch his mouth. This kiss was deeper, longer, more powerful. In an instant he was on top of her, pressing her into the firm mattress. The heaviness of his body intensified her pleasure.

He walked his fingers along her thigh, hooking them inside her panties and pulling them down. With a slowness that made her claw at his back, he teased her pubic hair before slipping inside her fleshy core. His stroke was masterful, waking up every cell in her body. There was nothing rushed in his touch. He seemed content to spend his time driving her hips into the bed.

The only thing missing from the evening when she'd imagined it was the candlelight. But this was better. The light from the moon beamed through the open slats in the blinds and cast a striped pattern along his legs. The time she'd spent with Avery was more romantic than anything she could have imagined. She'd given up on fairy tales a long time ago. Avery had extended a hand inviting her into a world that she thought was far beyond her reach.

"Your skin is so soft." He ran his hand along her back. The heft of his penis throbbed against her thigh. There was no way to ignore what she wanted him to do to her. Instead of trying, she spread her legs.

He slipped on a condom and climbed on top of her. The heat coming off his body warmed her flesh. He pressed his tongue into her mouth and eased into her at the same time. The sensation brought her hips off the bed to meet him.

Together they found their rhythm, matching each other's thrusts. His smell, his touch, his taste filled all her senses. The intoxicating moment was beyond her grasp of words. Her mind whirled around every sensation until she was wound so tight she couldn't hold back another second. Her climax lifted her hips off the bed driving him deeper.

"Oh, Macy, this is it." He whispered in her ear, and his body stiffened. She jerked in time with his spasms until they were both too limp to move.

Chapter Twenty-Six

There was no way he could sleep. Macy's slender body was nestled against his, giving off enough heat to keep him awake. What he wanted was to take her again, and again. But there was no need to be greedy. Unlike dates with other women, this wasn't just a one-nighter. Macy was the woman who could change everything about him.

She had a sense of humor. She had integrity. She was outspoken, and she was gorgeous. His finger trailed along her arm. Her brown skin glowed like a new penny.

He rubbed the bridge of his nose. His obsession to be with her edged toward unfamiliar territory. Could this be love? Or was he infatuated with the novelty of a woman who didn't throw herself at him?

No. What he felt for Macy was deeper than infatuation. This feeling could stay with him forever and he'd never tire of it. Love hadn't been on his radar that night in the hotel when he met her. He'd thought he could postpone settling down until he turned forty, forty-five if he got lucky.

As long as Macy was willing to enjoy what they had right now, the two of them would be fine. If she started talking about diamonds and baby buggies and a house on the Main Line, he'd find a way to handle that, too.

He ran his finger along her jaw. She stirred but didn't wake up. He didn't recognize his behavior. Watching her sleep as if he were love struck. He eased out of bed and out of the room.

In the living area, he collected their wine glasses from the table. The wine was warm. In the kitchen, he poured the remains down the drain. Hunger rumbled in his stomach, reminding him that dinner had been more talking and not so much eating. He opened the refrigerator door and removed a pound of imported cheese and summer sausage from the door.

Within minutes he'd warmed the sausage, sliced the cheese, and arranged everything on a crystal tray.

"What smells so good?" Macy strolled into the room, wearing nothing but her panties. She must have found them mixed in the bed linen. Her hands covered her breasts. She picked up his shirt from the floor and pulled it on. "I didn't want to slip back into my dress. I hope you don't mind."

"Not at all. I should have pulled a t-shirt from my drawer for you."

She'd pulled back her sleep-tousled hair in a ponytail. At least she hadn't attempted to look like she'd just stepped off a photo set. She hadn't reapplied her make-up or lip gloss. Refreshing. A woman who was willing to be herself.

"I thought you might be hungry." He pointed to the dish. "I was going to serve you in bed. Would you like wine?"

She sat at the kitchen island. "No wine. I think wine is the reason why I'm sitting in your kitchen nearly naked and ogling you. How about soda?"

"I planned to fix us something to eat and come back to bed. I didn't think about dressing."

"I'm glad you didn't. Otherwise, I'd feel a little uncomfortable since my dress and bra are somewhere around here." She glanced over her shoulder. Her eyes lingered on the leather sectional for a moment. "Your place looks exactly the way I imagined."

"How so?"

She spun around on the stool, facing the living area. "Expensive. Everything in this place is decadent. How many people make a snack at two a.m. on a crystal platter? Is that Waterford or Baccarat?"

"If it makes you feel any better, I can see if I have paper plates and plastic tumblers."

"You know you don't, so don't pretend. While I'm here, I might as well see how the other side lives. I get plenty of paper and plastic dinnerware at home."

He found a two-liter bottle of ginger ale in the bar. "Okay, soda for you and a glass of wine for me. You carry the dish, and I'll bring the drinks."

"Can we eat in here?"

No, was his immediate answer. He wanted her back in his bed. But he didn't say that. He said, "Sure." He took the seat next to her at the kitchen island.

"After we eat I need to get home."

"Are you sure? I was hoping you'd stay the night. I can drive you home in the morning."

She reached for a slice of cheese and placed it on the crackers he'd pulled from the cabinet. "No. I don't think that's a good idea. We're on our first date, and even it's a little late to think about impressions, I don't think I should sleep over on our first date. I don't want you to think I'm easy."

"I have a lot of thoughts about you, but I'd never call you easy."

"After we enjoy this delicious snack, you'll take me home?"

"Only if you promise to let me take you out on a proper date tomorrow."

Her infectious smile warmed every layer of him. Who was he fooling? She was getting to him.

"One other thing before you go." He rubbed his knee against her leg.

"I know what you have in mind." Sincerity marked her face.

He cupped her face, slipping his tongue into her warm mouth. She gave him as much as he gave her. Going to battle

163

with his tongue only stirred him more. "Let's shower before I take you home."

"What else do you have on your mind?"

"You'll see." He led her to the bathroom. When the water temperature was perfect, he opened the door and allowed her to step inside in front of him.

"I don't think you have any intention of behaving yourself."

"You're right. None what-so-ever." He grabbed the soap and ran it along her shoulders, between her breasts and then along her back. Pressing against her soft skin.

She reached for his hardened erection. With deft strokes, she drew him closer.

He cupped her soapy breast and pressed his erection against her thigh. He planted slow kisses along her neck and shoulder before he slipped his finger into her moist center.

She shuddered. "Okay, but you have to promise to get me across town sometime tonight." She sought his lips and wrapped her legs around his waist.

Macy curled around the pillow in her apartment, in her bed. Nothing felt better than being in Avery's apartment, in his bed, but she had standards, she at least had she had to pretend to live up to them. None of which included staying overnight at his place on their first official date.

They were going on another date, in a few hours and with any luck, there wouldn't be any calls or emergencies or family matters to interfere.

Gayle knocked on the door before sticking her head into the room. "I didn't hear you come in last night."

Macy sat up in the bed. "That's because I didn't get home until early this morning."

"Oh, my, my. Dish please." Gayle flopped on the edge of the bed and curled her legs in a yoga pose. "Is everything okay with your brother?"

"Yes. Avery even offered to make some calls to the college on his behalf."

"Great. You guys are getting along." The syrupy sweet sound of her voice said she already had them knee deep in love.

Macy held up her palm. "Whoa, horsey. We had one date, and we're going on another one today." She shrugged a shoulder. "I like him."

"You like him a lot. I know you. I can tell by that silly little smile on your face. You haven't dated in months. I was beginning to worry about you. And I might be wrong, but that glow must mean something too. Did something happen that you're not telling me."

Macy pulled the sheet up over her head. "I'm not saying anything." She giggled. "Now get out of here and close my door. I need a few more minutes of sleep."

Gayle pulled the sheet away. "Wait a minute, lady. What about all that talk about him being a Malveaux? One minute all you do is work, work, work. Now you're swooning and doing other things that you can't talk about with your mother. Girl, you're either cold as ice or hot as hell. You have no medium dial setting do you?"

"Gayle, give me a break. I'm a big girl. I've got my eyes wide open."

Her cell phone rang. She patted the night table until her hand landed on the phone. She pulled it under the sheet and looked at the screen. The 202 number. Her father. Her finger hovered over the accept button. She kicked away the sheet and sat up to gawk at the phone. There were countless nights when she'd wished she could talk to him, hear his voice. Now that the moment was here her heart pounded so hard she couldn't move. If she wanted, she could talk to him, or yell at him, or confront him. This was the opportunity she thought she wanted. She'd rehearsed the spiel so much, she had it memorized. But she was supposed to catch him off guard, when he was having lunch at an outside café, or walking the aisle of a grocery store, not the other way around. She declined his call.

Chapter Twenty-Seven

In the morning, Macy rolled a pencil across her office desk with her index finger. Somehow, she was supposed to get through the day when all she wanted to do was think about the glorious weekend with Avery. Her priorities were getting mixed up.

He could be the perfect man if there were any such thing. Sleeping with him several times last night hadn't alleviated her common sense, only put it into question. Their situation was so imperfect. They worked together.

He was crystal, and she was a paper plate.

He was wine, and she was beer.

He was couture, and she was a sample sale.

He lived in a penthouse, and even though he'd tried to hide the elevator panel from her, she knew. She lived in a pen with an underachieving roommate. But most of all, there was no way she would be able to look at his father without wanting to wrap her fingers around his neck and squeeze until his eyes popped out. Avery's father had used every tool available to him to make sure her mother didn't get much from the divorce. Virgil Rollins had paid for the high price experience of Dennison Malveaux and the gamble had worked in his favor. There was no fifty-fifty split of assets because Dennison had helped Virgil shift them long before her mother even filed. All of her mother's appeals had ended with the same result. She couldn't prove there was more money, so she couldn't get more money. And all these years later, Macy still held on to the resentment of both men.

Enough with the wandering thoughts. Monday morning meant time to continue the digging. She reached into her drawer and removed the account files. She needed to make another attempt at finding that money. The more information she could provide the auditors, the less painful her meeting would be.

She glanced at the clock. After lunch, she had her first meeting with the auditors without being any closer to finding the missing money than she had been two weeks ago. Instead of sticking her head in the clouds with Avery all weekend she should have been trying to track down Michelle. Or at least going through the numbers, again and again. Without some solid answers, the meeting wouldn't go well. Her horoscope hinted at problems today. She scrolled through her phone to find the post.

You are on the brink of something big, but don't expect it to be easy or breezy. Your next move will be a big one. You are close to a life changing event. You will have a breakthrough soon.

She picked up the pencil and tapped the eraser on the desk. The breakthrough had to mean answers to the questions she'd been researching for weeks. It had to. That's where she needed a revelation. For once, luck, or good fortune, or the gods, or Mother Nature or whoever was strumming her life's strings might grant her a favor.

Her phone rang, and she picked up the receiver without checking the caller I.D.

"I've got good news." Avery sounded excited.

"I could use some."

"Cal, my college roommate, returned my call this morning."

Macy closed her eyes and held her breath.

"He's going to take a look at your brother. He promises to get there before the season is over. Isn't that great news?"

She exhaled. "Yes. Wow. I don't know what to say. Brian will be over the moon. Thank you so much. Do I need to do anything?"

"No, he's going to reach out to the high school coach. If you text me the name of his school and his coach's name, I'll send it to Cal."

She reached for her cell. "I'm sending the information now."

Was he burrowing his way into her heart? "You're a lifesaver. How can I thank you?"

"Have lunch with me today?"

"Is that all? You're so easy. I'd love to, but I can't. I need to spend some time looking over my accounts before my meeting this afternoon."

"Then let me take you out tonight. Someplace special."

"That sounds like a wonderful idea." She said the words slowly, measuring each one because she wanted to answer the question with an operating brain and not a malfunctioning heart.

"Okay. How 'bout I pick you up about seven?"

"Great," she paused. "Did you mean it when you said you'd look at my sales account?"

"Of course. I got all the information you sent. I've already started on it."

She released the air hung up in her lungs. Avery sounded confident. Together they'd find the glitch. "Oh, good. There has got to be an explanation, but I do not see it. I've never had a problem like this before. Never." She took a quick breath, pushing down the anxiety building in her chest. "I don't know what I'm going to say to the auditors. The last thing they want to hear is 'I don't know.'"

"It's okay. We've got a few hours. Let me do some digging. I'll get back with you."

"I can't manage calm. I might be able to manage a step away from hysterical, but only if I close my eyes and pretend I'm on a beach in the Caribbean."

He chuckled. "Okay, ten minutes with your eyes closed then get back to it. There is an explanation. We just have to find it. And we will."

"I can't believe Michelle would steal the money and leave me on the hook for it. I thought I knew her."

"Let's not jump to conclusions. Let's go where the data takes us. If she took it, we'll find out soon enough. Stay calm."

She exhaled. "Okay. I can do this," she said more to herself than to him.

She placed the phone back in the cradle, put her head back and closed her eyes. Stress weaved its way through her stomach but talking to Avery had lessened the intensity. His tone never faltered. There was something comforting about talking to a man who could face down anything without worry. He was so confident. How could she doubt him?

Before she could bury herself in the files piled on her desk, she called her brother. Brian squealed so loudly when she gave him the news she had to pull the phone away from her ear. He must have knocked something over because there was a clatter as loud as his squeal.

"Are you okay?"

"Yeah. I just dropped my tablet. Macy, you are the best."

"Hey, Brian. Do you like him? Dad. Do you like him?" She hesitated, wanting him to say no.

He didn't say anything for several moments. "I don't know." His words sounded hollow, like he didn't want to be honest with her. "I've only talked to him twice. I guess he's okay. Are you going to talk to him?"

"No. I don't think I want to talk to him or see him."

"Your choice."

She imagined him shrugging his shoulders like he always did when he finished with a topic of conversation.

How could Macy have made such a large miscalculation? Avery glared at the numbers in front of him on the computer screen. Her account wasn't short one hundred thousand dollars. The figure was closer to two hundred thousand dollars. He ran his finger down the screen. Several huge charges hit just last week, but there was no corresponding documentation to support the expenditures. All of the discrepancies were in the selling expense accounts.

He reached for the phone to call Macy, but Roxy breezed into his office without knocking.

"I see you're getting settled. And already you've got two successful negotiations to brag about. How is it going?" Her claw-like nails matched her glitzy top. She sparkled like someone in a Broadway show.

"Good morning, Roxy." He sat back in his chair and folded his arms in front of him on the desk. "I was going to find you today, so we could have a little talk."

"What about?"

"Your sister."

Roxy's brows drew closer together. "This doesn't sound good."

"I get the impression you think I'm about to propose to your sister." He chose his words with care.

Roxy tucked a band of curls behind her ear. The thoughtful expression on her face told him she was measuring her words too. "Maybe I've been a bit premature, but the way Celeste gushes about you and how well the two of you are getting along, it seemed only natural. I know my sister, and she never gets heady about anyone." She pursed her lips. "I guess I was just excited that for once my sister is interested in someone who can sit at the family dinner table without being a major embarrassment. The last guy she brought to dinner had tattoos on the side of his face and dropped F-bombs throughout the meal."

"I know you care about your sister, but maybe you're a little too hard on her. Living up to your expectations may be harder for her than you think."

Roxy pushed out of the chair. "Celeste doesn't have to live up to my expectations. She just needs to have some expectations." Roxy's hard tone let him know this line of discussion was over. They were sisters, they'd survive without his input.

He nodded.

"Tell me, what did you think of Macy during the meetings? Does the board have anything to worry about? She's handled herself well, even under pressure with that near Bunting fiasco. That should be enough to win approval from the senior staff, but I'd like to have a little more ammunition to hit them with when we meet. A recommendation from you could seal the deal. "

He dropped his head. How could he have forgotten Roxy had asked him to spy on Macy? Sweat peppered his back. His fiduciary duty to English prevented him from lying, but exposing Macy's account discrepancies felt like a betrayal. There was no way to hide the discrepancies in her accounts. The moment auditing found the incidents, they'd have to put it in the report. His mind swirled around the facts, looking for a way out.

"She was brilliant in Asturias and Geneva. The way she handled those customers through that negotiation was skillful. You're lucky to have her on your team."

"That sounds like an endorsement. What about her weaknesses? I need to know so I know what I'm up against. If she has some big problem down the road, I don't want to look like the idiot who promoted her. Don't hold back anything."

He'd just made progress with Macy, now this. Her trust was as fragile as crystal. Would she see this as a betrayal?

"You hesitated, Avery. Is there something you're not telling me? I hired your firm to help me run mine. To help us get to the details so things run smoother around here. If you don't think you can do that, let me know. Macy is a nice girl, but if you know something you're not telling me then maybe it's your ability I need to question. Your allegiance is to English."

He cleared his throat. "There is a problem with her selling expense account. She's unable to reconcile it, so far. She's looking into the accounts and feels confident she'll straighten it out before the audit is finalized."

"How much are we talking about?"

"Almost two hundred thousand dollars."

Roxy's face flushed. "That's not chump change." She placed her palms down on his desk. "Is it possible she's stealing from me?"

"Of course not." He smacked the desk harder than he intended. "You know she's not that kind of person. Why would you jump to that conclusion? Her assistant quit quite unexpectedly. Macy thinks she might have something to do with this missing money."

Roxy straightened, but the pained look on her face didn't go away. "I won't tolerate malfeasance. She is the last person I would suspect of something like this. We pay our managers well, and in return, they are supposed to follow the money. All the time." The tone of Roxy's voice was icy. She sounded like Macy had walked in with a gun and held the company up.

Avery stood too. "Please don't jump to conclusions. I don't believe she's done anything wrong and she just needs a little time to get it sorted out."

"How does $200K get lost? That's huge. And pretty irresponsible, I might add." She was almost yelling. "There are few things that get me this angry. The accounts are under Macy's control. She should have kept a closer eye on her assistant. Don't make excuses for her."

"I'm not. But she's innocent until we have more facts. You've accused her and now you're ready to convict her. Calm down a moment and give her time to do the research."

"We may have just run out of time." Roxy strolled out of his office, her face stiff.

Chapter Twenty-Eight

If Macy sat perfectly still, she could hear each tick of the wall clock as the second hand swept past each number and every black dot that represented the minutes. No matter how hard she tried, she couldn't slow down the second hand or the minute hand. In just ten minutes she had to go up upstairs, sit with a team of auditors, and try to explain something that she didn't understand.

Hearing Avery's upbeat voice would have no doubt reassured her, but he hadn't called. When she told him about the missing money, he hadn't given her the suspicious eye. He believed her. And even more important, he believed there was an explanation that would explain everything, and they just needed to find it.

She swiped her palms on her pants. From Roxy's comments, no one else had issues with their accounts, so any idea that this was a company-wide problem evaporated.

She reached for the phone and dialed Avery. When the call went to his voicemail she hung up and stood. Outside her office door, Celeste walked toward her. "Well, Macy how are you this afternoon?"

"Hey, Celeste. I don't have time to talk I'm on my way to a meeting." Macy tried to step around her.

"With the auditors, right? You don't have anything to hide from them, do you?"

A cold chill spread across Macy's back. She stopped. "Why would you say that?"

"I know my sister thinks you're the next Mary Poppins, but you don't have me fooled. You've been getting cozy with Avery and you're always buttering-up Roxy. I don't trust you."

"And I don't have time for your nonsense."

"Rumor has it, you're up to something." Celeste pursed her lips.

"I'm up to something? What does that mean?" What have you been up to?"

"I meant up to something else. Something no good."

"Did Michelle say something to you?"

"Who's Michelle?"

"I've got to go." Macy continued down the hall. The more distance she put between her and Celeste the better she felt. She'd already asked around the office about Michelle. Nobody knew anything.

The sooner she got this over with, the better. She made her way to the bank of elevators. Each step was like wading through quicksand. She was certain this mystery would have unraveled well before she had to sit down with the auditors. Two weeks of studying the numbers until they blurred, and still no answers. Her suspicion around Michelle grew. Her missing assistant, the missing money were more than a coincident.

The elevator doors parted, and she almost collided with Roxy.

Macy tightened her grip on her envelope and tried to step aside. "Oh, Roxy, I'm so sorry."

Roxy paused for a moment. She started to speak but waved her hand in dismissal before walking away. Was she angry? Did she know about the missing money?

Macy rode the elevator up three floors without taking her eyes off the button panel. As long as she could focus her attention on something physical, her mind quieted a little. The constant worry about her job and money and rent and what might happen tomorrow made up a heavy load to carry. She released air through her mouth. All she had to do was get through this meeting. It was tough, but she'd find out what was going on. Now that the trip was over, she had the time needed to sort through every aspect of the selling expense account.

Before opening the door of the conference room, she squared her shoulders and reached for the door handle.

Four auditors were on one side of the conference table. The human resources director sat at the far end of the table. He didn't look up when she walked in the room.

"Please take a seat, Macy." The head auditor indicated the only empty seat in the room.

Macy nodded. Her heart zoomed into overdrive. This wasn't the meeting she'd expected. If HR was here, something else was going on. She closed her eyes and tried to slow her breathing. *Stay calm, Macy. Stay calm, Macy*, she repeated in her head.

"We're going to jump right in, Macy. We've been reviewing your accounts in advance of this meeting, and we've found several large expenditures that don't match the receipts. I'm sure you're aware of them. Is there a reason you didn't bring them to our attention?" The lead auditor spoke without taking his eyes off the paper in front of him. He pushed his glasses up the bridge of his nose.

"I had hoped to figure out what was going on before this meeting today." Her voice was barely audible.

"Do you have any explanations for these charges in the amount of $187,000?"

Macy tried to control her shaking hands, but the effort was useless. Papers scattered across the table when she attempted to examine her documentation. All the composure she had mustered evaporated with the stony stares of everyone across the table from her. "There must be some mistake. I've been looking into my selling expense account, and I know there are only charges for $100,000 that I can't account for. But…"

"This last report has a much higher total." The lead auditor pushed a spreadsheet across the table. His skinny index finger was as intimidating as his tone. "Can you explain the charges?"

Macy stared at the paperwork. She closed her eyes, hoping when she opened them she'd be back in Neverland. She opened her eyes and stared at the piece of paper in front of her. They didn't believe her. They thought she was stealing from the company. She could read the accusation in the stiff way they held their bodies. "No, right now I don't. But I'm looking into it. I should have some answers by the end of the week."

"Ms. Rollins, we've already given this situation quite a bit of discussion. Under the current circumstances, we are in agreement that until this is thoroughly investigated English International is putting you on a leave of absence. Unpaid."

Macy blinked several times. "What are you saying? Am I fired?"

"No." The HR Director coughed into his closed hand. "You'll be on leave while we investigate. We should have some resolution in two weeks. If you know something you're not telling us, now would be the time."

She couldn't accuse Michelle without evidence. Smearing her name wouldn't help her. Since Michelle reported to her they would probably think the two of them were in on this capper together. "I've done nothing wrong. I'm sure there is a reasonable explanation for this. My assistant just recently quit. I'm trying to locate her to talk with her. She might know something that can get this all settled." She pointed to the papers spread out in front of her. "If I can stay, I'm sure I can figure out what is going on."

"We can't allow you to stay while we investigate. We need to separate you from the issue. Then we will determine what is going on." None of the auditors made eye contact with her. Their decision was made before she walked in the door.

"I have some vacation. Could I take my vacation and be paid while you complete your investigation?"

The HR Director shook his head. "That's not a possibility."

For a moment the room was quiet. There had to be something she could say to make this right. "How soon…"

"Immediately. We'd like you to gather anything personal from your office that you'd like to take home with you and exit the building."

She sat up straighter in the chair. "It sounds like you're firing me."

"Until we have finished our investigation, please do not return to the building." He stood. The meeting was over.

Chapter Twenty-Nine

Macy made it home without breaking down in the taxi. She fumbled with the key at the door, but once inside she threw herself on the sofa and curled her body around the pillow. She squeezed her eyes tight, fighting back tears. Why did this happen? How could she work so hard for a company that would accuse her of stealing? She didn't know what hurt more, the embarrassment of being ushered out of the building like a common thief or the knowledge that English thought she was stealing.

Betrayal was the only word that came to mind. English had betrayed her. After giving up weekends and evenings and holidays and her social life, they had thought no more of her than to send her home.

She bolted upright when she heard Gayle's key in the lock. What she wanted was a little more time to wallow in her blanket of unhappiness. What she needed was to get her job back. She curled her feet under her and placed her hands in her lap.

She ran her index finger under her eyes before Gayle saw her. Black mascara smudged her finger.

"Hey, what are you doing home so early?" Gayle glanced at her watch. "It's not even six yet. Are you sick?" Gayle perched on the edge of the chair nearest the sofa.

Macy bit her lip. "They sent me home."

"Why? Are you contagious?" Gayle pushed off the chair and made her way to the kitchen. "Whatever you've got, don't give it to me. I've got a final call back for a shoot later this week, and I don't want to be sick."

"No. I'm not sick," Macy spoke loud enough for Gayle to hear her. "The company is investigating my accounts. They sent me home. Without pay."

Gayle rushed back in the room. "Wait a minute." She shook her head as if she was trying to clear out old information to make room for something new. "You mean, like you might be fired or arrested for stealing?"

Macy looked down at her hands. "Pretty much."

"How much money are you talking about?"

"One-hundred-eighty-seven thousand dollars."

Gayle's eyes grew bigger. "Did you say thousand dollars? Holy.crap. That's...that's a lot of money. And they think you stole it?"

"Stole it. Spent it. Lost it. I'm not sure what they think. But the head of HR told me to stay away from the offices until they finished their investigation. So now I can't even help uncover this mystery. The only information I have is what I was able to smuggle out in my purse and the copies of the documents I had been looking through."

"What do you think happened? You must have some clues."

"I know Michelle quit for no reason. I know Celeste has it in for me. But I didn't think either of them would go this low. And I thought I was so smart, always checking and double-checking everything. Working late to stay on top of everything and look what it got me. Nothing. A big fat nothing." She clenched her fist. "I can't help but think Michelle's quitting has something to do with what's going on. Avery says I shouldn't jump to that conclusion."

Gayle moved beside her on the sofa and embraced her. "He's probably right. She could have quit for a whole lot of reasons."

"Then why isn't she returning my calls and why did she move?"

181

Gayle shrugged a shoulder. "We're tough, honey. English International ain't the only company in Philly. You'll find something else."

"If I don't find out what happened to that money, can you imagine what kind of reference English will give me? That's if they don't decide to prosecute me. The only job I'll be able to get is a dog walker."

"Don't laugh at that. I hear dog walkers make good money."

"This is serious, please don't joke."

"I'm sorry. I was trying to cheer you up. Maybe the auditors will find it. Isn't that what they're supposed to do?"

"They didn't look like they were in a hurry to exonerate me."

Gayle sat beside her. "I'm going out tonight. Want to come. At least you can forget about your troubles for a few hours."

Macy shook her head. "I wouldn't be any fun."

Gayle gave her a long look before going into her bedroom and closing the door.

A new fear started blossoming. Until she said the words to Gayle, she hadn't thought about references. Leaving the outcome of this mess in some stuffy old HR Director's hand would be like kissing her whole career goodbye. They thought she was guilty, and wouldn't work too hard to clear her name?

She reached for her phone and dialed Michelle's number again. Without ringing, her call went to voice mail with the standard, leave a message. "Hey Michelle, this is Macy again. I really would like to talk with you. Please give me a call as soon as possible. It's important." She hoped she sounded casual. If Michelle heard the hysteria festering in her chest, she wouldn't call back.

Next, she dialed Avery's number. She'd be about as good company as a snail.

"How did it go?" His voice was smooth and it calmed her. Maybe he'd be willing to stop by. They could stay in and just have a drink.

She told him what happened without leaving out any details. "I even ran into Roxy just before my meeting, and I should have known something was wrong. As talkative as she usually is, she didn't say a word. She just looked at me like I was an oddity."

The line went quiet for several moments.

"Macy." There was hesitation in his voice. "I told Roxy about the missing money."

She uncurled her feet, placing them on the floor. The temperature in the room seemed to rise twenty degrees within an instant. "You what?" She enunciated the words, not trying to hide the incredulous sound of her voice. If being sent home was unbelievable then this was downright unimaginable. She'd trusted a Malveaux and again one of them had upended her life.

"She…she…stopped by my office late this morning, and I told her. I had to disclose." He could have been singing the National Anthem for all she cared or heard. The moment he said he told Roxy about the missing money everything else skidded to a stop.

"I asked you to keep it to yourself."

"You asked me to keep your addiction to horoscopes to myself. Which I have. But you never said anything about the accounts. Those are company accounts. I would never have promised to keep information from the company. The information was going to come out sooner or later. The auditors were going to find out, they would have told her."

"But I was supposed to be the one to tell her. Not you. If you hadn't told her, I doubt if the auditors would have found out about the screw up so quickly. I could have had a few more days to investigate. The minute you told her she probably went straight to HR. All evening I've been feeling betrayed by English, and now you've betrayed me. I trusted you." Her voice raised three octaves. She was squeaking. "How could you do this to me? You had no right, or at the very least you should have told me you were going to tell Roxy."

"Macy, calm down."

"Don't tell me what to do."

"Look we're supposed to get together tonight. We can talk this through over dinner."

"I'm not going to dinner with you. I'm not one of your bimbos that will accept anything you dish to me. Forget my number. Forget my name. Forget me. You are no better than your father," she was yelling now.

"What does my father have to do with this?"

Just hearing Avery's voice was too much. She ended the call. She marched to her bedroom door then back to the sofa. With her fists clenched at her sides, she yelled something inaudible. Everything was red. She closed her eyes and massaged the lids. This is what she got for thinking she could trust a Malveaux.

Chapter Thirty

In the morning, Macy pulled up to the small kitchen table and spread all the papers she'd managed to smuggle out of the office across the surface. She stifled a yawn before flipping through her phone to find today's horoscope.

Gayle shuffled into the room. "Don't tell me you still look at that crap." She reached for the coffee press and started her morning ritual of making an espresso shot.

"Say what you want, but it was dead-on yesterday. I just thought when it said I was on the brink of something big I was going to find the answers I was looking for about my accounts, not that I might lose my job. It's all about the interpretation."

Gayle nodded toward the phone. "What does today's message from the stars say?"

Macy found the post.

Make the most of today. Ask for what you want, a promotion, a favor from a co-worker. If a new job is on your list of things to pursue, today is the day you will wow them. Get going.

"Are you kidding me?" Gayle's hand was on her nonexistent hip. "You're making that up."

"Nope. That's what it says. And doesn't it sound like it was written especially for me?"

"Are you looking for a new job?"

Macy put her phone down and stared at the papers spread out the table. "I'm not sure I can go back to English. Not after what's happened. Roxy knows me. She should know I wouldn't steal from the company. But Brian is getting ready to go to college. I have to help my mother cover those expenses. The last thing Brian needs is to be swamped in college loans, the way I am."

Gayle sat down across from her with her coffee cupped between her palms. "But you're good at that job. And what if they find out what happened? Then everything would be okay, right?"

"I don't think so. I don't want to work with Avery. I don't ever want to see him again. I'm done. I'd rather be a dog walker."

Macy's cell phone rang. She glanced at the screen.

"Aren't you going to answer that?"

"No. It's Avery. That's the third time he's called me this morning. The man is a traitor. He's just like his father."

"I knew you were moving too fast. But maybe he's really sorry."

"Yeah, and maybe I'll forgive him when hell freezes over. Do you want to wait around and see that?"

"No, I don't." Gayle pushed away from the table and stood. "Can I help you with this stuff?"

"No. I've got all day. No place to go." Macy shrugged her shoulder. "So I might as well take my time and go through all this stuff again. Get outta here and let me figure out my future or whatever this is."

Macy stared at the table. There was only one person to blame for the lump sitting in the middle of her chest like Mount Everest, and that was Macy Denise Rollins. The only thing she was supposed to focus on was work. The moment she gave Avery Malveaux a second look, that's when things fell apart. Better than anyone, she knew men couldn't be trusted. They all had a self-absorbed streak that put their needs above anyone else's. She'd betrayed herself, and that was the main reason she was so disgusted.

The doorbell rang. Macy glanced at the clock on the microwave. It was only eight in the morning. Who would be visiting so early? She made her way to the door and peered through the peephole. Avery stared back at her.

"I know you're there, Macy. Open the door."

She pressed her back against the door. No way was he getting in. "Go to hell. I don't want to talk to you. You should have gotten my message when I didn't take your calls."

"I came all the way across town. The least you could do is let me in." His voice sounded strained.

"The least you could have done was be honest."

He pounded on the door. "Let me in so we can talk."

Gayle came out of her bedroom. "What is going on? What's all the yelling about?"

Macy walked away from the door and plopped on the sofa. "Avery is at the door. Don't answer him and he'll go away."

Gayle pushed beside her. "Are you sure this is what you want to do? He might be able to help you get your job back."

"He might be the reason I lost it." She fought back tears.

Avery rapped on the door again. "Macy, are you going to open the door?"

"No." she shouted from the sofa. "Go away."

She sat in silence with Gayle until she heard his footsteps retreating. "I'm going back to what I was doing. If anyone is going to fix this mess, it's going to be me."

"I've got an audition. Are you going to be okay while I'm gone?"

Macy waved her hand. "I'm fine. You don't need to sit around here to keep me company. I'm a big girl."

"That's what you think," Gayle tried to whisper.

"I heard that," Macy yelled.

"Good. Then I won't have to repeat myself." Gayle opened the door a few inches and peeked before stepping out and closing the door.

Five hours later, Gayle strolled into the kitchen. "You're still in the same place and still in your pajamas. Please tell me you haven't spent the whole day huddled over those papers."

Macy placed the stack of papers she'd been holding back on the table. "I have. And the numbers have blurred into one big, blob of black. I've compared every customer invoice against last year's invoices for the Dragon Negotiations and there are no glaring differences. There are a few new customer accounts, but that's expected. We're growing the business. I just don't get what's going on here. I don't. I've set those new customer invoices aside and I plan to investigate each one of them"

"Too bad you didn't take a shower and put on real clothes, because I just saw Avery pulling into the parking lot."

Avery got out of the car. He took a deep breath. The evening air was crisp and cool, quite different from the temperature earlier today. He loosened his tie. This wasn't going to be easy. Nothing about Macy was easy. Calling her hadn't worked. Coming to her apartment hadn't worked. But he wasn't leaving until she talked to him face-to-face. She might dismiss him after he had his say, but he had to try.

He made his way inside the building and into the elevator. If she wanted to be stubborn, he could play that game too.

At her door, he squared his shoulders and waited a moment before knocking. From inside he heard voices but couldn't make out the words. He watched the peephole, and the moment it darkened he said, "Macy, open up. I want to talk to you."

"I told you earlier, I don't want to talk to you. Why can't you understand that?"

"Either you open this door and talk to me, or I'll cancel the call to the coach. Your brother's opportunity will swirl down the drain, just like your job." He forced his voice to sound firm. He'd never go back on a promise, but she didn't know that.

"You wouldn't." The bravado in her tone was gone.

"Do you want to test me and find out?" He swallowed. His ultimatum sounded like something his father would do to get his way, but she left him without any other alternatives.

She was quiet. He waited, knowing she'd open the door. She'd do anything for her brother.

He waited several moments. Was she going take the risk? Maybe his threat was too much? He opened his mouth. "Macy…"

She yanked open the door. If her eyes had been daggers, she would have sliced him into a million little pieces. "You bastard."

He stepped over the threshold before she changed her mind. The apartment looked the same way it did the first time he saw it. There was no view of the city, no large windows, but the place was decorated with modern pieces.

Macy stood just inside the door in a pair of pink pajamas, and her hair stood up in places as if she'd been pulling at it. There was even a smudge on her cheek that looked a lot like grape jelly. Her feet were bare, and her toes were still the same shade of red that she'd sported at his place. She looked perfect.

He braced her shoulders with his hands. She yanked away from him and gave him a stare cold enough to freeze the sun.

"I just needed to talk to you."

"So, you think you've got me."

He walked past her, deeper into the room. "I've outmaneuvered you."

189

She spun on him, ready to pounce. "Just like a lawyer, twisting everyone's words to get what you want." She crossed her arms over her chest and made fists of her hands.

"And what does it say about you that you thought I would betray you? Don't try to pretend that you're the only wounded party in this mess." His voice grew louder.

"Did you lose your job? Have you been called a thief?" She stabbed his chest with her finger.

"I tried to call you all afternoon, right after my conversation with Roxy."

"After they told me to leave the building, I didn't feel much like talking."

"I was doing my job. That's all I was doing. I have a fiduciary responsibility to English International. I had to tell them what I knew."

"What do you want? You did your job. Should I clap for you?" She smacked her hands together, slow but loud.

He stepped toward her, but her eyes warned him not to get any closer.

"I believe you. I know you wouldn't take anything that doesn't belong to you. I want to work with you to get this cleared up."

She stared at him without speaking. After a minute, her breathing seemed less labored.

"I don't need any help. I'll figure out what's going on." She moved to the door. He blocked her path. She wasn't going to dismiss him like he was in kindergarten.

"I'm not asking you to let me help. I'm telling you."

Her head snapped back. "You're blackmailing me?" Her face darkened. She was ready to do battle.

"I'm going to help you."

"I don't want another thing from you. Nothing." She spat out the words. How was she able to be gorgeous and angry at the same time? The fire burning in her eyes only made her more attractive. No way was he giving up on them just because she hated him right now.

"Well, we have a problem, don't we? Because I'm not leaving until you agree." He positioned himself on the sofa, loosened his tie and crossed his ankle over his knee.

Chapter Thirty-One

Macy planted her feet wider. The smug look on Avery's face angered her. He was propped up on her sofa, looking more comfortable than she'd ever been on the cheap fabric. If she could put her outrage into a few well-structured sentences, he would slink out the door like the worm he was.

He was asking to help her, but if he had let her explain things to the auditors, she would have been given some time. She was positive she could have convinced the auditors and HR she could unravel this mystery.

She sat on the opposite side of the room in the only chair available and exhaled through her mouth. "I don't understand how we can work on this together. I don't trust you to look out for my interest. You work for English, and no matter what happens or what you find out, that's where your loyalty is going to be. You just said it." She sounded calmer than she was.

"We need to find out where the money went. You have the same questions that English has. There is only one answer to that question. I want to help you find it." His words sounded rehearsed.

Now she had an inkling of how her mother felt when her father strutted off. Loving her father and hating him at the same time. Today, Avery looked as if he'd taken extra effort on his appearance to visit her. Every hair slicked into place with perfection, the cleft in his chin didn't sport one dark hair, and even though his tie hung loose, she still thought he was as handsome as ever.

"Why are you doing this?"

"I'm helping you. Why are you fighting me on this?"

She studied his face. Her stomach bubbled with anger, but her heart wanted to reach out to him.

Gayle stuck her head out of her bedroom door. "Macy, can I talk to you?"

She glanced at her roommate. "Now?"

"Yeah. Right now." Gayle beckoned her with her hand.

She gave Avery another hard look before walking away. Maybe he'd get the hint and leave before she came back. There had to be something more interesting he could destroy.

Gayle closed the door and sat on the edge of the bed. "What are you doing?"

"What are you talking about? He barged in here." Macy pulled her hair back and tied it with the band that was lying on Gayle's bed.

"He's offering to help you. Why wouldn't you want his help? You haven't had any luck on your own."

"Are you eavesdropping on us?"

"No. You're talking so loud I can hear you over the television. The neighbors probably can hear you."

Macy dug her toes into the thick carpet. "You don't understand, Gayle. If he's offering to help me, there must be a reason. He's a Malveaux."

"Listen to yourself. You're not making any sense. If he was out to get you, why would he keep coming here? I get it, your father was a jerk and maybe Avery's father is a jerk, too. But that doesn't mean all men are jerks or that all men suck." She paused. "And what did your horoscope say today about asking a co-worker for help? You read that bull every day, so why don't you take the advice? He's a co-worker, and he's offering his help."

Macy eased onto the bed beside Gayle. "You have no idea what I'm going through."

Gayle pressed her lips together. The skeptical look on her friend's face said she had a whole lot more to say.

"Are you kidding me? I know exactly what you're going through. We've been friends since junior high school. You have complained about your father since the day I met you. You have found something wrong with every man you've ever met. But I saw you the other night, or morning, when you came home from Avery's place. You were glowing like the morning sun. You like him. Maybe you love him. Honey don't go messing this up just because you can't get over being mad at your daddy." She squeezed Macy's leg. "You get me?"

Macy stared down at her hands. Things had to be getting pretty bad if Gayle was the levelheaded one. "I don't love him."

"Yeah, sure, go with that."

"I'm not saying everything you said was true. But maybe I could let him help me." Macy stood.

"One more thing honey?"

She didn't want any more advice tonight. Gayle had given her too much to think about already. She exhaled through her nose loud enough for Gayle to hear. "What?"

"Please comb your hair and put on some clothes before you go back out there. A man doesn't need to see how bad you can look until he's put a ring on that finger."

She shook her finger at Gayle. Oh, what the hell. She spun around and stormed into her bedroom. Who did Gayle think she was saying all those things about her? Sure, Gayle could be carefree and careless. With a mother and a father who thought everything she did was the most wonderful thing in the world, her self-esteem was high. There probably has never been a day when Gayle stared back at her image in the mirror and wondered if tomorrow was going to be the day when her world fell apart.

Macy picked up her brush, ran the bristles through her hair and examined her face in the mirror. There was even something sticky on her face. She swiped it with her finger.

"Jelly. No wonder he thinks I'm a pushover. I'm not putting on makeup," she muttered. In the closet, she stepped out of her pajamas then pulled on a pair of jeans and a tank top.

Without checking her appearance again, she went back into the living room. Avery was still in the same position. But now his face was expressionless.

"I was wondering if you were coming back. You changed?"

"Yeah, so what?"

He held up his hands as if he'd never had to surrender to something before.

"Look, this is how it's going to be. You can help me untangle my accounts. But that's it. We can start tomorrow. Stop by when you've finished work for the day."

"I'll be here at nine."

"In the morning?"

"The sooner we get started, the sooner we'll get some answers."

She nodded without showing excitement. "You're going to give me the whole day?"

He nodded.

She pointed her finger at him. "I'm calling the shots. Okay? Don't show up until ten." Nine would have been okay, but with him, she needed to be tough or at least pretend to be.

He stood. Working with him was going to be harder than she imagined. She needed a plan where he did his investigating at his place, across town.

Chapter Thirty-Two

Macy smacked the alarm clock off the nightstand. Trying to sleep last night was like trying to sleep on a bed of rocks. She couldn't get comfortable with her mind racing from one thought to the next and her body aching for a man that wasn't good for her. The baggage between them kept piling up.

With no job, she didn't need to wake up early, but setting the alarm was part of her ritual. Right now, she needed the structure in her life.

Today, she wanted to know her horoscope before putting her feet on the floor. Any guidance that could get her through the day would help manage her emotions. How else could she spend time alone with Avery? She held her breath while punching the keys on her phone to find the post.

Today it is pivotal that you put on your game face. Things will happen that will throw you off balance. Be prepared for the unexpected, or you'll be knocked off your feet.

With her hand over her mouth, she read the words a second time. Was this good news or bad? The last time she was balanced was before she ran into Celeste in the hall. First Celeste, then Roxy and finally being sent home from work. She drew a deep breath. "Come on, girl, pull yourself together," she whispered.

By the time Avery rang her doorbell, she had dressed, her face was clean, and she had managed to put on a pair of shoes.

"You're early."

"I brought coffee and bagels." He balanced a bag on top of two large paper cups. His computer bag hung from his shoulder. "Skinny caramel latte, no whip cream, right?"

How could he remember something so trivial? "Right. I scrambled some eggs. That's the only thing we have here to eat."

"Sounds like we've got all the essentials to a good breakfast."

She closed the door behind him before following him into the small kitchen. His jeans and a black button-down shirt were the most casual she'd ever seen him.

He glanced at the kitchen table. "Wow, you've been busy."

"I started last night. I can't let this go. The whole idea that almost $200,000 has gone missing under my watch is making me neurotic. I think about it all day and all night. And I can't let go of the thought that Michelle might know something about what's going on."

"Well, that's what we're going to find out." He cleared a corner of the table and set the cups down. He dropped his computer bag on the floor beside the chair. "Let's eat first, discuss strategy, then we'll get started."

"Is there ever a time in your world when you are not in control?"

"That's right. I forgot. You're calling the shots. What do you want to do first?" His face opened into a big smile.

She waited several moments with her hands on her hips. There was a reason he was sitting at her kitchen table, smiling like an emoji. He was helping her. Without answering, she opened the bag, pulled out the bagels and popped them in the toaster. There was no way to get the work done if she continued to be hostile.

Focus.

Focus.

Focus.

For a few minutes, they ate without talking.

Avery took the last bite of his bagel and wiped his hands on the napkin. He opened his bag, removed his computer and placed it on the table. "Where would you like to start?"

"I've gone over the invoices several times. I've segregated the accounts I know well, where the charges look reasonable." She picked the tallest stack of paper. "These accounts are new to me. The team is big, so I don't know every single account by name. I don't recognize the names, but we've had this big drive to increase business, so I need to check them out. I haven't found anything blaring about them. Without my office computer or access to English files and the accounting system, I've had no way of drilling any deeper to see which salesperson they belong to."

"That's what I'm here for. Give me the names, with the accounts numbers, and we'll check each one." He booted up his computer, processed all his security log-ons, and then looked up at her.

"There are over fifty of them." She hoped the task wasn't too daunting for him.

"We've got all day. What we don't get done today, we can do tomorrow."

She placed her chin in the palm of her hand. "Tomorrow. You're willing to give me another day? What will Roxy have to say about you being out of the office?"

His face softened. "I'm not required to show up at English every day. Since you're not there, it's more fun to work out of my office."

She cleared her throat. There was no use getting emotional just because Avery gave her a cute puppy dog kind of look. He was only offering her more time, not a kidney. Besides, players always had bags full of those kinds of responses to use anytime they needed one. All the bumbling around in the beginning was probably part of his routine. He probably even had an act that would make her want to take off her panties, again.

"Okay. Let's get started."

By one o'clock, they were halfway through the pile. She tried to rub moisture back into her dry eyes. The work was tedious. "We need to take a break. We've looked at over two-hundred accounts." She pushed back from the table and stretched her back.

"I was going to suggest that an hour ago, but then I remembered you're calling the shots."

"Ha. Ha." She pressed her hands over her head, to help loosen the tightness in her shoulders. She picked up five invoices that they hadn't been able to find any activity on, in the company system. "What do you think this means?"

"Hard to tell. If you've got courier charges and no information, it could mean the account numbers on the invoices are wrong, the account has multiple names, the billing data was entered incorrectly, or who knows what else."

She found her calculator under a stack of papers. "Let's see what these invoices total." She punched in the number. When she finished, she glared at the total. "Just these five total close to one-hundred-thousand dollars. I'm going to call Pepper, the temporary assistant who is filling in until they replace Michelle. Maybe she'll do me a favor." She reached for her cell phone.

"What are you going to ask her?"

"To check with the sales team to see who these accounts belong to."

"Let me ask my assistant at English to run that check. We don't want to get Pepper into any kind of trouble, since she's not working for you while you're out. Besides, she might have been told not to take any direction from you."

She exhaled. "How quickly I've forgotten."

Avery placed his elbow on the table. The whole time he talked, he stared. She turned the chair away from his Jedi mind tricks.

"What did she say?" She asked as soon as he hung up.

"She only checked two. They're in the system, but the sales field is blank on both. She's going to do some more research. According to her you can't set up a customer in the system without identifying the salesperson, so she thinks there may be a system glitch. She promised to do more checking and get back to me. I trust her. She won't tell anyone what I'm asking." Avery stood. "I'm starved. Let's get outta here, grab some lunch. We can talk about our next steps."

Lunch with Avery under other circumstances wouldn't have required major thought. But everything was different now. She couldn't slip up and fall back into his bed.

"Yeah, let's do that. My treat," she said. There was a total of five hundred dollars and change in her checking account and this time next week she could be jobless. But she wanted nothing from him.

Avery ignored the odd look she gave him. One thing he'd realized about Macy was that she could be as infuriating as she could be loving. She had to come to things on her own. No amount of pushing or persuasion could convince her until she was ready. Their first dinner together was a corporate expense on each of their company credit cards. She wouldn't allow him to pick up the tab, even though he wanted to treat her. She claimed it was because they were on company business, but now he understood the reason ran deeper than that.

Traffic in the city was thick. He turned onto Chestnut Street. Maybe he'd never met a woman like Macy before, but he knew how to get his way. And at least once today, he was going to have his way.

"Where are we going?"

"To lunch," he said without looking at her.

"Where."

"My favorite Asian restaurant. I figured since you were paying I might as well pick a good place. It's not often a woman treats me to lunch."

"I was going to buy us some sandwiches and a couple of drinks."

"Well I'm driving, and you can't jump out, so I guess I win." He pulled into a parking lot. "We're just late enough to miss the lunch crowd and well ahead of the dinner crowd, so not having a reservation shouldn't be an issue."

If her lips could stick out any further, she would probably trip over them. Manipulating her wasn't any fun, but nobody called all the shots with him.

By the time the server handed them the menu, Macy looked as if her seat was on fire.

He stared across the table at her. With her head down, he couldn't make out her expression, but that didn't stop him from wanting to tease her. "Are you ever going to forgive me?"

"There is nothing to forgive, is there? You did your job." There was a thread of ice mixed with her words.

He nodded. For now, they'd do things her way. No way was she going to pay for lunch and order him around. He wasn't pussy-whipped. At least not yet.

"Are you ready to order?" the server asked.

"For starters, I'll have the chicken and ginger dumpling and an order of king crab summer rolls. For my entrée, I'll have wasabi tuna tataki. Macy, what would you like?" By the time he added dessert the bill would be over a hundred dollars. Well over what she wanted to pay, for sure.

She glared at him across the table. "I'll just have an entrée. Garlic shrimp stir-fry." She handed her menu to the server, then hunched across the table. "Are you trying to break me, Avery? Is that why you picked one of the most expensive Asian restaurants in the city and ordered like you've got ditches to dig this afternoon?"

Now he had her. There was fire in her eyes. At least now she was paying attention instead of trying to be nonchalant. He sat back in his chair. "Yes. I'm trying to get your attention."

"You've had my attention all day. Haven't we been working together?"

"You've been tolerating me. Treating me like your man-servant. That's not the kind of attention I'm talking about. Don't pretend to be obtuse."

The sag in her shoulders indicated that for a moment she'd let down her guard, exposing her vulnerability.

"We're going to figure this whole mess out. You'll keep your job. We've already made progress today." He reached for her hand across the table. She pulled away.

"You think this is all about my job?" She crossed her arms. "I thought, however incorrectly, that we were heading in one direction. I now know that I was wrong. I've been wrong before, so I know how to get over these types of things. You orbit in an atmosphere that I can't even imagine, now that I'm grounded in reality, I realize what a big mistake we were."

If she meant to pierce him with those words, then she'd done an excellent job. Here he thought they had stumbled upon something different. Different from all the other average relationships out there. A mistake. She had pegged everything between them as a mistake. This woman knew how to strike a blow. Monica had used him for money, slept around on him, but never once had she punched a hole in his heart. "What mistake?"

She waved her hand. "Doesn't matter now."

"The other day you said I was no better than my father. What did you mean by that? You don't really know my father."

Maybe his tone alerted her to the seriousness of his question because she looked across the table, locking eyes with him. Her face hardened. A storm brewed behind her features. Maybe he didn't want to hear the answer to his question.

"I know enough about your father. The incident in the club, I'm sure he wasn't giving me his blessing. And your father represented my father when he divorced my mother. Thanks to your father's excellent legal skills, my father managed to hang on to all his money except the small child support payment he had to pay each month. We were so poor. Sometimes our mother didn't eat just to make sure there was enough food for Brian and me. Something was always broken in our house that my mother had no money to get fixed." Her eyes were glassy. She was on the verge of tears. "I blame your father and my father. Maybe I blame all men. What kind of man leaves a woman and two children so defenseless? My father was scum, but I didn't think lawyers helped their clients cheat."

"Are you referring to your father or mine?" He wanted to reach across the table and put his arms around her or stroke her back until the pain in her eyes went away. He couldn't erase that time in her life, no matter how much he wanted to.

Her mouth tightened. "Both."

"My father prides himself on winning. Winning no matter what. Sometimes I think he would have mowed down his own mother to get to where he wanted to be. But let me make this clear. Very clear." He had to push down the anger boiling in his stomach. "*I am not my father.* I didn't sell you out. I was only doing my job. You might not like the way I handled things, but I would do everything the same way again if I had to. You need to understand what's required of me. I'm a principled man, and I'm always going to do the right thing. You can count on that."

The server placed the appetizers on the table, ending that conversation.

"We came here to discuss strategy. I think we need to stop by the courier's office after lunch to see if they have any information they can provide on those new customers. The invoices are in my purse. Let's get back to our purpose. Our only purpose. And since you ordered all of this food, you can pick up the check."

"I intended to."

"So, this was all a set-up."

"This was about me caring about you. Wanting to do something nice for you."

She almost smiled. He could tell because her lips weren't as tight.

Chapter Thirty-Three

Macy poked at her lunch without enthusiasm. After her outburst, she remained immersed in her version of the story and she was just as certain Avery was waist deep in his side.

"After lunch, I'd like to see if we can find Michelle. I don't know where she lives now, but I know a few of her after work hangouts. Let's swing by and see if she strolls in. I should have done this before, but I thought I had time. I had no idea English would put me on leave." She shook her head. "I guess I thought they'd help me solve this riddle. Silly right?"

"No. I wasn't expecting such severe action either." He glanced at his watch. "Don't you think it's a little early?" He glanced at his watch. "It's not even six yet."

Michelle never worked until six p.m., and I don't think she's going to start now. Besides if she pocketed that money, she's probably not working anywhere. She won't need to work for a long time."

He nodded. "Okay," he said the word slow, not fully in agreement. "You're calling the shots, so which way?"

"There's a small bar on South Street that she liked to stop in after work. According to her, it had the hottest men and the cheapest drinks."

"How often did she go there?"

"Several times a week. Otherwise, I wouldn't have suggested we go there. This might not pan out, but I'm getting desperate."

"No need to get snippy with me. Do you think that could be a reason for Michelle to quit?"

She closed her eyes. "I'm sorry. I'm stressed. Not just a little. I'm stressed by yards. I feel like I'm going to pop at the seams."

"You don't have to apologize. I understand this is difficult for you. Just don't take your anxieties out on the person who has the most faith in you."

For a moment she had a sliver of hope that he wasn't like his father. That her judgement about him was right. He could be trusted and he was someone she could depend on. But the moment she softened toward him, she would open herself up again and being vulnerable came with consequences. Avery pulled into a parking garage. They walked down the stairs and onto South Street. She pointed out the bar.

"I'm not sure if we should wait inside or outside."

"Inside. Definitely, inside. Let me buy you a drink."

"I...I..."

"That wasn't a question." He held the door open for her. It was too early for the regulars to fill every inch of the taproom. Inside was dark, the space was tight, but at least it wasn't crowded. They were able to get two stools at the bar close to the door. She ordered a glass of wine, and he had a dirty martini, with four olives.

"It seems strange drinking this early in the day," she said, relaxing a bit. "I could get used to this kind of living."

"Well, you just might be back to work real soon, so don't get too used to drinking this early." Avery pulled an olive from the toothpick in his drink and chewed it.

A band of light fell across the room when someone opened the door. Macy turned around and for a moment she locked eyes with Michelle.

"That's her." She grabbed Avery's arm. The startled look on Michelle's face said she wasn't going to saunter over and have a little talk. Her eyes were so wide, she looked like she'd been smacked in the face with a bat. Even though

Macy couldn't hear her, she saw Michelle's lips form the words *oh shit*.

Before Avery could place twenty dollars on the bar, Michelle took off. Macy rushed out the door in front of him. She spotted Michelle running, already a block away. "There she is." Macy pointed to Avery when he came out.

Avery sprinted ahead. Even with her flats on, Macy couldn't keep up with him, and Michelle had a head start. Macy slowed. Her lungs burned. Sitting behind a desk all day had turned her muscles into mush. She stopped and placed her hands on her knees.

She tried to keep up with Avery, to keep an eye on him. She couldn't run fast enough. Sprinting wasn't her thing. Avery disappeared around a corner. She stopped at the intersection to rest against the building.

Several minutes later Avery walked up behind her. "She took off down some side street, and I lost sight of her."

"Now what?"

"Don't worry." He was panting.

"If she ran like that, she must have stolen the money, right." Macy tried to catch her breath.

"Innocent people don't run like that. We'll hire an investigator. I know someone who can find her, and we'll get some answers."

"I can't afford your 'someone' I couldn't pay for lunch today."

He stopped. His face was stern. "I didn't ask you to pay."

"I won't take money from you, Avery."

"I'm not offering you money, Macy. I'm offering you help." He reached for her hand.

She pulled away and walked just ahead of him back to the parking garage. "Let's ride around, maybe we'll spot her."

Chapter Thirty-Four

Macy climbed the stairs alongside Avery. He was trying too hard. Which meant he had a reason.

"So, are you mad at me for not catching up to Michelle?" Avery backed out of the parking space and headed to the exit.

She faced him. "No. Of course not. I didn't catch her either."

"Then why did you storm off like that?"

She swallowed the hurt that she disguised as anger. "I don't want you holding my hand or being superficial nice. We're looking for the money missing from the English account. That's it."

His face flushed, the solemn nod was his only reaction to her comment.

They rode several minutes without talking. Driving slow through center city was easy because of all the traffic. Trying to pick up Michelle in the crowd of people was not.

Macy stared out the window.

"Let's stop by the courier's office and see what information they have on those two accounts with no sales lead." Avery spoke without looking at her. He gripped the steering wheel with both hands.

"Yeah, that's a good idea."

Outside of the courier's building they sat in the car while she dug the documents from her purse. "Maybe I shouldn't go in there. I'm suspended so this might be a violation of some company policy. I can't walk in there with English documents, demanding information."

"I'll go in."

"What will you say?"

"Don't worry. I question people for a living. I'm a lawyer, remember?" He took the papers from her hands. There was a chill that wasn't coming from the air-conditioner.

"Why am I so nervous about this?" She closed her eyes.

"Because this ordeal may be coming to an end for you."

"Don't you find it odd that these ten invoices have consecutive numbers? The probability that they were generated back-to-back has to be one in a million. That would have to mean these contracts were sent out on the same day, at the same time, probably by the same salesperson." She pushed her fingers through her hair.

He shuffled through the papers examining each one. "Let me go get some answers." He patted the seat next to her leg and climbed out of the car. The image of Avery taking long strides to the door was like watching a movie with the volume turned down.

Sure, as soon as this was over she could get her life back on track. There would be no Avery to talk with, to laugh with, or to hold on to. Without his distraction, she could focus on her job, if she still had one when this was over. Or, maybe she could find a better job, one without Celeste and one where she didn't have to worry about running into Avery.

She glanced at her watch. He'd only been gone five minutes. If the place was as slow as usual, then he'd have to wait twenty minutes before anyone even noticed him standing at the counter. If she got her job back, she'd have to convince the purchasing department to go with a national courier company. If English wanted to grow, they needed a world-class courier, not this small charity case that she assumed Roxy felt she needed to save from bankruptcy.

Thirty minutes later, Avery opened the door and strolled across the parking lot. She couldn't read his expression with his sunglasses in place.

When he climbed into the car, she waited for half a second for him to start talking.

"What happened? What did you find out?"

"That place is crazy. Why does English use this courier?"

"Long story, now tell me what happened." She almost bounced in the seat.

"First of all, it took a long time before anyone even noticed I was standing at the counter. When a guy that looked like he was just released from central lock-up finally shuffled over to help me, he was no help at all. He couldn't find their copies of the invoices. I asked him to double-check, and he claimed he did but found nothing." Avery stared at the invoices in his hand.

"What do you think that means?"

He shook his head. "I'm not sure, but my instincts say this just got a whole lot deeper. Between Michelle and this chicken shop, almost anything could have gone wrong."

"Look." She pointed across the parking lot. "What's Celeste doing here? She couldn't be dropping anything off. Coming down here is beneath her, or at least she thinks it is. If she wanted to mail something, she would have sent her assistant."

"I wonder how long they will take to wait on her" He sat up straighter, craning his neck for a better look.

Within minutes, Celeste exited the business with the slacker that had waited on Macy weeks ago. Celeste's arm was looped through the slacker's arm, leaving no question about their relationship.

"Well, our little investigation just got a whole lot more interesting. I can't imagine Celeste would look at slacker guy, much less touch him."

As if Celeste heard the statement, she pressed up on her toes and kissed slacker on the mouth.

"What did you call him?"

"That's my name for him, now. Slacker guy. He has about as much ambition as a sloth. I'm sure he's the dope that lost the Bunting contract."

"Do you have a name for me?"

"Several. But I'm not telling you any of them."

"I have ways of making you talk."

"Not anymore. I'm barely speaking to you at all. When we've uncovered some answers, you go live your life, I get to live mine, and my brother gets a shot at a scholarship. Isn't that our deal?"

He smirked.

"Now what are we going to do?"

Avery started the car. "We'll follow them." He eased out of the space.

"What about my invoices?" She drew back to stare at him. "Why has the color drained from your face?" Her high-pitched questions echoed in the car.

"We're going to follow them because something is not right here. I didn't get any answers when I went inside, but maybe I can get answers through Celeste. The more I know about her, the more I'll have to leverage with."

"Why do you need leverage against Celeste? Is this about the missing money or are you interested in something else?"

"Both."

"Oh." She sat back. "She's got her claws in you, too."

Avery eased into traffic two cars behind Celeste's red Lexus. This mystery kept growing. Every time he thought he had an answer, another question popped up.

"What's your plan?" Macy asked.

"I'm not sure I have one yet. I agree with you, Celeste wouldn't come down here because she needed something couriered, so we've got to figure out what she's up to. Maybe this guy is the father of her baby."

Macy gasped. "Celeste is pregnant?"

"That's supposed to be a secret. She wants her sister to think I'm the father. Now I think I know why."

"Two questions. Can you actually keep a secret? And the second question, why does she want Roxy to think you're the father? The whole situation is crazy."

"I told you I had to tell Roxy about the money. I'm not sure why you're not getting that," he said with clipped words. "And, second, if the father of her baby is the guy she just deep-throat kissed a moment ago, with his big pants halfway down his ass, the tats covering his arms and the high price sneakers, that might push her sister over the limit. I think Roxy is threatening to cut off Celeste's line of cash."

Macy held up her hand. "Is that why she's been all over you?"

"Yes. Now I can put the pieces together."

Celeste's car turned on Second Street across from the beer distributor.

"Look, Slacker guy is getting out. You think she was just giving him a lift to buy beer?" she asked.

"No. I think he's picking up something to set the mood. I'll bet you he buys a forty. Maybe two."

"You're probably right. He doesn't look like a Cabernet Sauvignon kind of man."

Minutes later, Slacker guy came out with his purchase in a brown paper bag, clutched close to his chest. Celeste eased back into traffic.

"It looks like they're heading to her place." Macy pointed.

The traffic light turned red, leaving them trapped while Celeste turned and disappeared down the narrow street. "Good thing you know where she lives because I don't want to follow to close and have her spot me."

"Don't you know where she lives?"

"No. I've never been to her place. Like I've said, there is nothing between us."

"I've had to drop stuff off at her place several times," Macy said. "Turn here and turn again on Fourth Street. She lives in the cute little row of houses with the flower boxes out front."

"I don't plan to spy through the window. Based on how much time the two of them spend inside, I think we'll get a good idea what's going on."

He found a parking space across the street from Celeste's place and parallel parked.

"The heart wants, what the heart wants," he said. He knew that better than anyone.

Macy's eyes darkened. The set of her lips grew tighter.

"How about we listen to some music." He reached for the knob. "I think after thirty minutes we'll have our answer and can get out of here. I know the work we did this morning was tedious, but I think we need to finish with that stack today. I can't help but think Michelle, Celeste, and the courier's office are tied to this somehow."

"I have the same impression. I just need to figure out how." She snapped her fingers. "I have an idea. Tomorrow we'll call the courier, pretend we want to ship something to one of those nonexistent customers. We'll tell them they should have all the information on file. Then let's see what happens."

"That might work. Especially if we can get Celeste's beau to pick up when we call. If he's involved, he must have some way of identifying the phony accounts. At least we'll have more information, then we'll have something to talk to the owner about."

"But I still don't understand how the money transfers from your account to whoever is connected with this."

"Oh, that part's, easy. We're always sending something to our customers, product samples, accessories, documentation, training materials. With a bunch of phony accounts, the courier can invoice English for thousands of dollars. That line item along can be over a hundred thousand dollars a month. While we are doing Dragon negotiations it goes up more.

He nodded and glanced at the clock in the car. "We're done here. They're having sex, not sharing recipes." He turned the ignition. "Let's grab some take-out before we head back to your place, so we don't have to stop what we're doing to go for dinner…that's if you don't mind I call this shot."

She was slow to answer, but her face glowed with hope. That alone was enough to give him reason to believe they had a lifeline.

Chapter Thirty-Five

The moment Macy walked through the apartment door, with Avery behind her, Gayle scooted off the sofa.

"I'll leave you two to your detective work," she said, then closed her bedroom door.

Macy headed back to the kitchen and sat at the table. She looked across the table at him. His chin sported a five-o'clock shadow that made his appearance even more striking. He was so intent on what he was doing he didn't even notice her staring. For a moment she lingered on how natural it was to have him sitting across the table from her at her place. His presence didn't appear out of place in the tiny box she and Gayle called home.

"What do you think is going on?"

He lifted his head. Their eyes locked for a moment, just enough time to impact her heartbeat. "I'm not sure, yet. I just have a bunch of theories. Do you have any ideas you want to put out there?"

"When I first identified the discrepancy, I thought it was just some kind of mix-up, charges that should have gone to another account ending up in mine. Now I know it's more than that. Something criminal is going on and a lot more people are involved than I thought. I think proving my innocence is going to take more than you and me hunched over the kitchen table."

"Yeah. I started out thinking the same thing. But I believe we can find out who took the money. The list of people who had opportunity and access to your account information isn't that long. How many unverified customers do we have now?"

"Well." She shuffled through the papers, taking her time. "Counting the twenty we found this morning, we now have a total of forty." She placed her hand on top of the pile.

"What's next?"

She thought for a few seconds, "I want to put all these invoices in order by date to see if there is any correlation. Then when the courier opens in the morning, we'll give them a call. We'll need to work out a script on what we want to say." She glanced at the microwave clock. "It's after midnight. We've done enough for today. Besides, my brain is refusing to process anymore details tonight." She rubbed her eyes. "Let's start again tomorrow. You must be tired."

He pushed away from the table. "I'm not. I think we should continue while all this stuff is fresh. Let me pour you a glass of wine, then we can sort through all this and try to figure things out."

"Okay. The only thing I have is a Moscato. Not your favorite."

He found the bottle of her favorite wine in the refrigerator. From the cabinet she pointed out, he pulled two glasses and filled them before returning to the table.

By the time they'd sorted and discussed the invoices, the bottle of wine was empty, and they'd started on a second.

"Macy," he said her name like a question.

One glance at him told her something was bothering him. "Did you find something?"

"No. I just want to say I would never have called the coach or done anything to hamper your brother's chances at that scholarship. You know that, don't you? I just wanted the opportunity to talk to you."

"No, I didn't know that," she said, shaking her head. "I believed you."

Sadness filled his eyes.

"How was I supposed to know your threat was empty?"

"You've been around me long enough to know what kind of person I am. I am not vindictive."

"See, that's the thing. We don't know each other. We might think we do, but we don't. I don't know your favorite color. I don't know if you've had chickenpox as a child. I don't know if you prefer spinach or collard greens."

"Collard greens, of course."

"You're only saying that because you think that's my preference. I can tell by the way you lifted your eyebrow before you answered."

"See you do know more about me than you think. And you should have known I keep my word."

"And you should have known the moment you told Roxy about the money, I was going to be pissed."

He sighed. "I did. But I thought you would understand. I'm sorry, it was a judgment call. Maybe you will never understand why I told Roxy, but I try to live my life without secrets and without lying. If I'm open and honest, then I can sleep at night without worries. I know you don't trust many people, maybe no one, and that's your right. But I've never lied to you and I never will."

Neither of them spoke for several moments. There was nothing more to say. The topic of telling Roxy had been addressed and laid to rest.

She pressed her back against the hard chair. "I can't go on. Everything is starting to blur. Either I've had too much wine, or I looked at too many numbers." She stood.

"I agree. We're at a good stopping place. We can pick up here tomorrow, same time."

If his knees were half as wobbly as hers, he couldn't drive. The thought of him, on her sofa all night knotted her stomach. Keeping a distance between them was getting harder.

"How about I call you a service to get you home?" she said. "You can't drive."

"I don't have an account. I usually drive myself."

"Well, you can't tonight. So I guess that means you'll have to catch my sofa. I've never slept there, so I hope you'll be comfortable."

"I could sleep in the bed with you." His smile was an invitation. Too bad she couldn't accept.

"No, you won't. And don't think about stumbling into my room during the night with some lame excuse about trying to find the bathroom or seeing a monster in the closet."

"How about if I say I just want to sleep with you again."

"No. That won't work either." Her voice was stern. But she wasn't so sure she could ignore a request like that.

Chapter Thirty-Six

In the morning Macy went through her typical routine of stumbling out of bed, washing her face, brushing her teeth then climbing into the shower. She took extra time combing her hair and picking out her favorite jeans to wear. Avery had already seen her with jelly smeared on her face. There was no need to scare the man again. She sucked her tongue. What he thought didn't matter. Pretty soon he would be with someone else, and she could have as much jelly on her face as she wanted.

By the time she walked out of her bedroom, her casual, I don't care, but I really do, look was perfected.

The sofa was empty. The blanket and pillow she'd given Avery were at the end of the sofa, folded into a neat square. Instead of trying to slip into her bedroom, he'd slipped out sometime during the night or early this morning. Every time she thought she had him figured out, he did something to prove she didn't know him at all.

She released the heavy sigh sitting on her chest. "Get over him. He might be the perfect man for someone, just not me," she muttered before going into the kitchen.

The kitchen clutter seemed to have multiplied. The paperwork, his computer, and the calculators were where they'd left them last night. Even though she'd never tell anyone, she was pleased. He'd have to come back for his stuff. She shook her head. How could she find the answers she needed without getting more entangled with Avery? From the outside he possessed the qualities she wanted in a man, but together they had too much baggage for either of them to carry. Maybe she'd never find anyone to fill the void in her life, and she'd have to find a way to accept that.

She peered in the refrigerator. The only thing in it was the leftovers from last night's takeout. She pulled out the chicken. The congealed grease and lump of meat were not appealing.

"Where is Mr. Good-looking?" Gayle shuffled into the kitchen in her bare feet. At least she was wearing her bathrobe. For someone who slept in the nude, that was a huge step.

"I don't know. Isn't it your turn to do grocery shopping? We don't have any food in this place."

"Did the two of you…"

"No, Gayle. I slept alone, and he was alone until he left. After we find the money, I'll say goodbye to him. He'll go back to his life. I'll return to mine."

Gayle strolled across the kitchen. "One day your prince will come. Let's just hope you're not ninety-years-old by then and gumming your food at the home."

"Get off my case, Gayle. Don't you have some photoshoot to go to?"

"I'm hanging around all morning. After I have my coffee, I'll leave the kitchen to you, so the two of you better be on your best behavior. No screwing on the kitchen table." She reached for the coffee press and started the intricate process.

Macy shook her head. "Just promise to buy some food today. We're living like vagrants."

"Yeah, yeah. I will. You're so uptight. I hope your 'soulmate' comes along soon." She put the word soulmate in finger quotes.

Macy swatted at Gayle before collapsing in the chair at the table.

The doorbell rang.

"I'll get it," Gayle called out.

"No. I'll get it." Macy rushed toward the door, but Gayle had already opened it.

"I know this might not be any of my business, but can you please hurry up and solve this caper, because my grouchy roommate is getting harder to live with. If you know what I mean." Even though Gayle tried to hide her mouth behind her hand, Macy heard every word.

Macy placed her hands on her hips. "Weren't you leaving?"

Gayle ducked her head. "I'm gone."

Avery balanced coffee and a bag in his hand. How was he more handsome today than yesterday? His hair was still damp. He hadn't shaved, so his chin was a shade darker with stubble that made him look more rugged.

Her heart ballooned in her chest. Being with him was getting harder. He was being nicer than anyone had been in a long time. After today, no matter what happened, she needed to let him go. Send him away.

"I went home to change clothes. You didn't want to see me in yesterday's wrinkled clothes. I'm not sure I would have smelled so good by the end of the day. Besides, I had to pick up breakfast. So we could jump back into things this morning."

"Whatever is in that bag smells delicious." Almost as delicious as the scent of his cologne. Under any other circumstances, she would have told him so. "Gayle is going to do some food shopping today, so I should be able to feed you if we don't resolve our mystery today."

"Tell you what, if we don't resolve this quagmire today, I'll do your grocery shopping tonight."

They settled at the kitchen table, in the same place where they sat the day before as if they had already claimed their territory. He booted up his computer while she unwrapped the breakfast sandwiches.

"I spent a lot of time thinking about what we uncovered yesterday. I think I've come up with an idea to find out what's going on," Macy said.

"You've got my attention."

"This might sound crazy, but it's crazy enough to work. We send someone in there who pretends to work for English, demanding to see the manager for more details on these invoices. What was shipped, who at English processed the shipping request, that kind of stuff. That way we get past Slacker guy and get some real answers. All we need is the tracking information."

"That might work. There is just one problem with your plan. I was there yesterday, so they know me. Slacker guy will definitely remember you."

"I thought about that too."

"Did you get any sleep last night? It sounds like you spent the whole night looking for a fix to this." He pointed to the stacks of paper on the table.

Of course, she didn't. He was just a few feet away, and that's where she wanted to be. How was she going to get any sleep? "A little. Anyway." She fanned her hand, dismissing the look in his eyes that was more than concerned. "Gayle. We'll get Gayle to do it. She wants to be an actress. This can be her first impromptu part." She darted out of the chair before he could respond.

Without knocking she slipped into Gayle's bedroom and closed the door.

"What's wrong? Did something happen?" She jumped out of bed.

"I need your help with a plan I've cooked up with Avery." She leaned against the door, sucking in air like there was going to be a shortage soon.

"Does it entail drinking or sex?"

"No, Gayle."

"Will I get hurt?"

"Come on. I'm serious." She stood straighter.

"Your list of favors is adding up. You're already buying groceries for six months. What will this favor get me?"

She scratched her head. "Let's see. I don't have a job, and I'm broke. How about I give you a huge hug."

Gayle screwed up her face. "What is it this time?"

"I still don't know why I let you talk me into working with him. Do you know how hard it is to spend another whole day with him? He gawks at me with so much sincerity I want to believe he did cost me my job on purpose. How am I supposed to remember not to like him?"

Gayle slumped back on the bed. "I wish I had your worries. You know what your problem is?"

"Yeah, I do." She held up her hand, halting Gayle from saying the same thing she always did. "Please don't tell me again. Just help me out so I can get him out of here and get on with my life."

"What can I do?"

Avery kept his eyes on the road. The longer the trip to the courier took, the more time they had to work out what was supposed to happen when they arrived. Macy's plan sounded solid enough to get some results. But since leaving the kitchen to talk to Gayle, she hadn't looked him in the eye. An invisible wall was going up between them. If he'd made two steps forward yesterday, then today he was back where he started.

Macy spun around in the passenger seat. "You've been texting all morning," she told Gayle. "Do you remember what you're supposed to say?"

"Are you sure this isn't dangerous or illegal? What you've described sounds like a scheme somebody cooked up on a reality show."

"We think the accounts are phony, so you aren't asking for real information. Just pretend you're the assistant and you're looking for answers for your boss." He looked in the rearview mirror as he talked to her. "You've got the copies of the invoices, just ask them to give you some tracking history or some names or anything tangible."

He pulled into the lot, parking as far away from the building as he could.

"What am I going to get out of this?"

"You'll save my ass if you get some information. Which means I might be able to pay my half of the rent next month. Isn't that enough?" The edge in Macy's voice stoked the tension in the car.

Gayle took a deep breath before stepping out of the car. "I was only joking. Calm down Macy."

They watched her until she disappeared into the building.

"Are you going to tell me what's wrong with you?" He asked Macy.

She pulled her phone from her purse, scrolled through several screens before answering. "I haven't checked my horoscope yet. I was preoccupied this morning."

"Read it aloud. I'd like to know what's in store for you today.

She gave him a glance. "Okay.'

Tempers might fly today, yours and others. Those who you counted on yesterday may not be there for you today. Be careful which buttons you push today, things could backfire on you.

"That doesn't sound good. I'm glad I'm not you. What does mine say?"

"Your birthday is July fifteenth right. That makes you a Cancer." She scrolled down the screen.

Today you can be the adventurous one. Your bravery will take you further than you've ever been. Let your faith lead you. Be fearless, and you will get what you've been looking for. You are the one with the ideas, so go for it.

"Is that what it really says?"

"Yes. Mine reads like crap. Yours is fabulous. I should have guessed."

He nodded in agreement. "I like my horoscope. That post sounds just like me. Now I must live up to those words," he said, mimicking a superhero.

She kept her head down, eyes on her phone.

"You still haven't answered my original question. You've been quiet this morning. Is something bothering you?"

"I want Gayle to come out with the answers so I can defend my name. I want this to be over, my name cleared." She huffed.

"Aren't you enjoying our time together?"

"You think this is all fun and games, don't you? When this is all over, you get to go back to your deluxe apartment in the sky. People at work won't give you jaded stares thinking you just might be a thief. You don't have to worry if your roommate will actually buy the groceries you need. I'm dealing with real stuff. This is my life. Even if we figure this out, and they let me come back to work, will they ever really trust me?"

He reached for her hand, squeezing her fingers. "I was only trying to add a little levity to alleviate some of the tension. I'm taking this very seriously because I feel like I've had a hand in the way the company treated you."

She eased her hand out of his. "I don't need you to protect me."

"I'm doing this as much for myself, as I am for you. I want to be your hero."

Before she could respond, Gayle opened the back passenger side door and slid into the seat. "Let's get out of here. This place gives me the creeps."

"What did you find out?" he and Macy asked in unison.

"That place is awful. What a mess. I'm not surprised they can't find anything. I didn't get much. I made such a ruckus they let me talk to the owner and his assistant. I should get an Academy Award for my performance in there. I guess I got a little…"

"Gayle. *What* happened?" Macy shouted, glaring at her roommate.

"Okay. Okay." She pulled the papers from her tote. "The owner said these accounts were legitimate, meaning he clicked a few computer keys and found them in his system. He said Roxy English requested the shipments. He admitted he thought the charges to English were a little inflated, but without tracking information he couldn't validate if that was the case for sure. He kept scratching and shaking his head. The owner didn't have a clue."

"Why would Roxy be stealing from her own company? That doesn't make any sense," Macy said. "And if she wanted to, why would she use my account."

Silence filled the car. Of course, no one had the answer to her question. Nothing here was making any sense.

Macy half turned in her seat to get a look at both Gayle and Avery. "I'm going to put this out there. You guys tell me if you think I'm wrong. After what I saw yesterday, I think Celeste and Michelle are knee-deep in this mess."

"Michelle. Why would you think Michelle is involved?" Gayle scooted to the edge of her seat.

Macy started filling her in on what happened at the bar. Gayle's eyes widened and by the time Macy finished her mouth was in the shape of an O.

"Okay, so this isn't some little office mishap. What the hell is going on over there at English?"

"There is no secret that Celeste doesn't like me." Macy paused. "But I had no idea about Michelle. We've had lunches together. We've gone out to happy hour. Nobody would have let her get away with the stuff that I did. I feel so betrayed. I thought we were friends." When this was over she needed a complete reevaluation of life. Her personal radar might be broken.

Avery placed his hand on her leg. She didn't have the strength to pull away. "I think I can get to the bottom of this."

"How?" Gayle placed an elbow on the top of the driver's seat. "Can I help? I'm enjoying role-playing."

"Gayle, don't you have a shoot later today? If anyone is going to help Avery, it's going to be me. I'm the one muddied in this mess. What is the plan, Avery?"

"I don't have a plan yet. But I think I should meet with Celeste."

Macy folded her arms tight. "Should I go with you?"

"No. I'll have to do it alone. Just me and Celeste."

"I want to know what's going on," Macy said.

He started the car before turning his attention to her. "You're just going to have to trust me." His authoritative tone ended all discussions.

"Macy, I'll help you find Michelle," Gayle said.

"How? We don't know where she lives. She probably won't go back to the bar." Macy stared at her roommate.

"You know where her Mama lives."

Macy nodded slowly. A plan formed in her head. "We might have to stoop that low."

Chapter Thirty-Seven

Macy marched from one end of the apartment to the other. Her bare feet were noiseless on the worn carpet. Even though she was bone weary, she repeated the loop, hoping the constant movement would alleviate the anxiety percolating in her stomach.

Nothing. She hadn't heard from Avery all day. He'd said he had a plan and she hadn't challenged him. First, because the expression on his face left her no room to question, but also because she still trusted him, and that troubled her. She smacked her forehead and repeated the pace.

Lately she worried she was becoming an empty-headed bimbo who would buy the Brooklyn Bridge from any well-dressed, good-looking man.

A quick glance at the cluttered kitchen table was the reminder she needed that whatever happened now was beyond her control. Whatever Avery decided to do, had to work. She needed to come up with some strategies of her own.

She flopped on the sofa and dropped her head in her hands. An image of her walking through the doors of English International and back into her office wasn't as vivid as it was days ago. The edges of that happy day were faded, like decades-old paper. She couldn't go back to the place that had treated her with so much callousness. She'd given so much to English, but when she needed someone to stand up for her, there wasn't a soul. Instead a security guard escorted her to the door. The embarrassment was as raw now as it was the day it happened. There was no way to walk back into the office and hold her head up. No way.

"Are you going to keep walking back and forth until Avery calls you?" Gayle sat on the couch.

"I can't sit still." She wrung her hands. "I thought I'd hear something by now."

"Okay, what's the plan for talking to Michelle?" Gayle rubbed her hands together.

"Well, I can't just walk up to her mother's door and ask to see her. I'm sure she's told her family she doesn't want to see me."

"Girl, I can get a wig for every occasion. Tomorrow, we can go up to the door and pretend we're some of Michelle's old friends dropping by for a visit. Her family won't recognize you, and I don't even know if any of them know me."

Macy shook her head. "Gayle, your idea might be fine if we were still in junior high school and were having a little tiff with Michelle. But, this is serious. The next time I see Michelle, I've got to get her to talk. She has to tell me what she knows and how she's involved." Macy buried her face in her hands. She continued to take deep breaths.

"We can become two lady private investigators." There was a hint of joviality in Gayle's voice. The whole day had become an adventure for her.

"It can't be hard. I just want to talk to her. I want to know why she quit and why she's running from me." Macy looked up. "I need to walk up on her when she isn't expecting me, pin her down so she can't get away."

"You do know kidnapping is against the law, even if you think you have a good reason."

"I'm not going to kidnap her. Just trick her," Macy said. "And I need to do this alone."

Gayle's face fell. "Okay, I get it. You need to save yourself and all that crap."

229

"It's not that I don't appreciate your offer. I'm just not sure your plan will work, and I have this big clock ticking in my ear."

"Do it your way." Gayle jumped up, ready to tackle the obstacle. "Now let's go out for dinner. My treat."

"I can't. Suppose Avery drops by with some news."

Gayle pushed off the sofa. "Okay, I'll order something in. I'll choose."

Macy could hear Gayle shuffling through the take-out menu drawer. Whatever Gayle picked would be fine since her appetite had disappeared hours ago.

"I'm thinking about formally quitting my job," she called to her roommate. "This whole ordeal has taught me a lot of things about myself. I was so dependent on English I was willing to give up almost everything. I was living to work, instead of working to live." She made her way into the kitchen. "Roxy treated me like a puppet and the first time, the very first time something happens, she didn't even talk to me to get my side of the story, she didn't stand up for me. And now I'm finding out she might have been the one to set me up." Macy knew she was whining, but she didn't have the strength to be stoic.

"What will you do?"

"I don't know yet. But I know what I don't want to do. I'm not going to put my life on hold for another big company."

"What about Avery?"

She shrugged her shoulders. Whatever she said to Gayle, her roommate would twist her words to make her sound immature, insensitive, or downright loony for not giving him another chance in this male shortage world. The less she said the less ammunition she'd give Gayle.

Avery stood outside Celeste's condo door. The last place he wanted to be. But the moment Macy mentioned her hunch about what was going on with the courier, he could almost see all the pieces coming together. This whole caper had to be orchestrated by Celeste. It had her stink all over it.

He adjusted his tie before ringing her doorbell. He'd called her that morning, and Celeste thought this was a date, which proved how delusional she was. Poor thing.

She opened the door. The signature tight dresses and her ridiculous high-heeled shoes made her look like a caricature of herself. Her bright red lipstick was like a siren call. If she'd stop trying so hard, she could be an attractive woman.

"Well hello, Avery. I was so surprised to get your call." She pressed up on her toes to kiss him. He turned his cheek to her.

"Aren't you afraid you'll fall off those heels? In your condition that could hurt the baby."

"Look at you. Worrying about me." She led him into the house. "I'm glad you called me. I still think you and I would make a perfect couple. Are you reconsidering my offer?" She moved to a beverage cart. With a highball glass cushioned in her palm and held in place with her well-manicured fingers, she held the glass in the air. "What can I fix for you?"

He took a seat on the closest chair. "I don't want anything to drink right now. Why don't we sit and talk for a moment?"

"Talk? Sound serious," she said with a laugh.

"Take a seat, Celeste. I won't take up too much of your time." He relaxed into the sofa, leaving plenty of room for her to sit beside him.

"Aren't we going somewhere? How about Ambience? I haven't been there in a few days." She sat beside him, a little too close. Her dress rode up her thighs, exposing her tanning booth glow.

Questioning people wasn't difficult. Questioning someone who would rather opt for a lie than the truth required skill. He coaxed her into chatting, starting with the mundane. After they'd covered her health, his trip to Europe and her sister, the pleasantries were over.

"Did you know Macy was sent home a few days ago because of an audit issue?"

Celeste drew back. Her mouth opened just enough to see lipstick on her two front teeth. "She was sent home for stealing. Why are you being so delicate? Don't tell me you have a thing for Miss Suck-Up-To-The-Boss."

"You don't think she's capable of stealing, do you?" Avery asked in a normal tone.

"Of course, I do. You know her mother lives from one paycheck to the next and calls Macy all the time asking for money. I'm not surprised at all that she was stealing from English. She was probably doing a whole lot more than we know." Celeste crossed her arms over her chest after the self-righteous speech.

"Only you would think because someone isn't affluent than they must be a thief. Why don't you like Macy, Celeste?"

She jumped up from the sofa. "Do we have to talk about Macy? I thought we were going out."

From his breast pocket, he pulled a few invoices. He spread them out on the coffee table, end to end.

"What's all this?" she said.

"Go ahead. Take a look at them."

She hesitated without taking her eyes off of him. "You're so boring. I don't want to look at your papers today. I want to go out." She repeated.

He pointed to the papers on the table.

She picked up the invoice nearest her. Her eyes scanned the document for a moment before she put it back.

"Are you going to tell me why you brought English invoices here for me to see? Are we going out or not?" She tugged at her dress. Her eyes narrowed on him as if she dared him to ask another question.

He picked up two more invoices and held them out to her. Instead of taking them from him, she turned up her nose.

She batted her long fake lashes at him several times. "Why are you here, Avery?"

"I'm looking for some answers. The more I look at these invoices, the more I smell your hand in this."

"Why are you looking at Macy's accounts?" There was no mistaking the condescension in her voice.

"You haven't answered my question."

"I don't know what these invoices have to do with anything." She pushed the papers off the table, scattering them across the floor. "If we're not going out, then I think you can leave now."

"Are you sure this is how you want to play this? If you don't want to answer my questions, I'll find another way to get them." He stood up.

"What is it about Macy that turns you on? You're doing all this for her, aren't you? From the moment you laid eyes on her, she's had your nose wide open. You could do so much better."

"I'd be lucky if Macy would have me. Tell me about the thug guy at Pipeline Courier. Does he have your nose wide open?"

Her mouth dropped open. Her face turned red. She pointed her long, lacquered index finger at him. "You made me a promise, and you had better keep it. What I do in my private life is none of your business. Macy is a thief. She stole the money. She was fired. She got what she deserved. Get over it."

He stared at Celeste. A woman who could have almost anything in the world and she wasn't happy. Nothing was ever going to please her because she was the kind of woman that had to keep clawing at something.

Chapter Thirty-Eight

Macy parked Gayle's car across the street from the row home in Northern Liberties. The day was just beginning. If Michelle had a new job, she wouldn't leave the house before seven in the morning. Michelle wasn't an early riser. She was one of those people that came to life after lunch and could keep going well after midnight.

She slouched down in the driver seat, but she doubted that Michelle would recognize Gayle's car or even suspect Macy would be spying on her.

At seven-thirty a light came on in what Macy guessed was the living room. The windows upstairs were still dark. Then the front door opened. Macy couldn't tell if the person in the doorway was a man or a woman. They reached out and picked up the newspaper without stepping onto the porch.

Maybe this whole idea was as crazy as all the other ones she'd had, like tracking her down in the bar, or sending Gayle into the courier. Thinking she could solve this mystery was about as insane as thinking having a relationship with Avery was possible. Sex had a way of making her forget reality, sucking her into a make-believe world where red slippers could transport her anywhere she wanted to go.

The front door opened again, and Michelle stepped onto the porch. She looked up and down the street before venturing toward the steps. Michelle's steps were tentative. Was she waiting for someone?

After a moment, Michelle descended the stairs and headed up the street. Macy hadn't planned on following Michelle by foot, but she grabbed her purse and jumped out of the car.

She stayed far enough back and on the opposite side of the street so that Michelle wouldn't notice her.

Michelle reached Spring Garden Avenue and made her way to the Septa stop. Macy grew hopeful. Trapped on a train, there was nowhere for Michelle to run.

Within minutes Michelle slipped into a window seat and pulled out her phone. Macy made her way down the aisle, toward her former assistant.

She slipped into the seat next to Michelle. Michelle was so intent on scrolling her Instagram page she didn't look up.

Macy cleared her throat. "Why have you been avoiding me?"

Michelle looked up. Her first reaction was to bolt out of the seat. But Macy used her arms to block her exit. "You might as well sit. We're going to have this conversation. I've gone through too much not to."

Michelle flopped in the seat and exhaled. "What do you want, Macy?"

Before replying Macy swallowed. Should she just ask the direct questions or should she ask the questions pressing on her heart? "How could you quit and not tell me? And why are you avoiding me?"

"Look, Macy, I don't want any trouble. If you give me a couple of months, I'll pay for the supplies."

Macy shook her head rapidly. "What are you talking about?"

"The audit. You were going to find out I ordered over a hundred dollars of office supplies for my niece. I know it was wrong and the way you were going through the account you were going to find out."

"So why didn't you just come talk to me? I thought we had a relationship."

"Yeah, right. You're management." Michelle narrowed her eyes and pressed her lips into a thin line. "You gonna tell

235

me you wouldn't have fired me? The last couple of weeks you've been coming down on me about everything."

"So why did you move? Why haven't you returned my calls? And why did you run out of the bar like that?"

"Aren't you going to press charges? I can't pay the money back yet. Maybe in a few months, but right now, I'm living with my parents, which I wouldn't be doing if I had any extra cash."

They rode in silence for a few minutes. Evaluating Michelle's comments took more energy than it should have. Should she feel empathy for Michelle, or anger? For days she'd been wondering what was going on with her assistant and the answer was some pens, pencils, and notebook paper. Macy pinched the bridge of her nose. Shame on her for thinking everyone was like her or did things the way she would.

"What do you know about the missing money from my accounts? Did you take it?"

Michelle stared at her for several seconds without speaking. Indignation was the only way to describe the expression on her face. "You're not going to put that on me. I bought a few office supplies on your account without your approval. If I had done it six months ago, you would have never known anything about it."

"Then who did it...stole the money?"

"Well don't look at me. Two hundred dollars, I can pay back as soon as I get a job. Anything more than that is way out of my bandwidth," she paused. "So you haven't found the money yet."

"No. And HR sent me home while they investigate."

"So, you came looking for me because you thought I took it. Really, Macy?"

"You didn't return my calls. You moved without telling anyone and you tore out of that bar like you had something to hide. Why did you run from me?"

"You came for me with a lawyer. What was I supposed to think? For all I knew you were ready to press charges."

"You should have come talk to me. We could have worked something out."

"It looks like you couldn't work out your own situation."

"I'm trying. I've been going through the files that you never help me with."

"I had my issues. You were going to find out what I did. Anyway, you should just talk to Celeste English."

"Why would I want to talk to her if I didn't have to?"

Michelle tilted her head up, looking down her nose at Macy. "If you left your office long enough to hang out in the break room, you'd know what kind of shit is going on there."

Macy turned to face Michelle. "Tell me about Celeste."

Michelle glanced out the window before she said, "I don't have all the details, but according to the assistant pool, she hates her sister and is robbing her blind. And she's not too fond of you either."

Chapter Thirty-Nine

Macy eased her key into the lock of her apartment. Her shoulders slumped. She should have been happier. Michelle hadn't stolen the money from the account. That would have been an insurmountable betrayal, but at least she'd have an answer. Instead, the nightmare into the missing money continued.

Without a job to go to, there was nothing to anchor Macy in place. At any minute, she could have spun off into space and gotten lost in orbit. Pacing from room to room accomplished nothing. There was nothing else she could do with the files she had smuggled out of English, but that didn't mean she could sit on her hands and pray Avery was able to get somewhere with Celeste.

She dropped her bag on the kitchen table and flopped into the chair. The stack of papers was just as daunting now as they were before, and the answers were still as elusive. From her phone, she reread her horoscope.

Your thoughts are twirling like a summer storm. To stay focused you must ignore gossip and useless information, focus on the facts. If you don't find the proper balance, something else in your life might sputter out of control.

The words always seemed so right, but the stars hadn't led her to any answers yet. She sighed. Today she needed something upbeat. A post telling her the fairy godmothers had stepped in last night to work their magic on the mass of confusion surrounding her.

Avery had called last night. His meeting with Celeste was so late; he said he'd share it with her today. She checked her phone. No message from Avery yet. Her mind had come up with all kinds of outcomes on his meeting with Celeste. None of them worked in her favor. She gathered the documents into two stacks. One pile had revealed more questions than answers. The other pile was everything she had expected from the regular course of business.

When the files had been paper clipped and placed into her briefcase, she glanced at the microwave clock. Why hadn't Avery called? Had he given up on helping her already? Maybe real work had come calling with customers that had money to pay him for his time. But at least he could have updated her on his visit with Celeste.

She reached for her phone. Avery's number was in her memory now. After two rings he picked up.

"I couldn't wait another moment. What happened when you met with Celeste?" Her words rushed out.

"Haven't you heard, Macy?"

"Heard what?" Her heart sped up to match her tone. Was this ordeal finally over?

"Pipeline Courier caught fire this morning. There is nothing left of the place."

Silence stretched out between them. All the words in her head evaporated. Life had taken another turn down a dark alley.

"Are you still there, Macy?"

"Yeah. I don't know what to say. This wasn't a coincidence. I feel trapped in a horror movie, and every door I open is worse than the last one. How do you know this?"

"I drove by there this morning with the intention of talking to the owner. The fire engines were already there."

"Was the fire intentional?"

"I don't know yet. Everyone is tight-lipped until they pin down a cause."

"Where are you right now?" She picked up her purse.

"I'm still here at Pipeline. Maybe I'll get some information."

"I'm on my way. Stay there please." She ran to the door.

"There is nothing you can do here that I can't. I think you're wasting your time."

"Then it's a good thing I didn't ask you what you thought." She disconnected the call.

Outside the apartment, she walked three blocks to hail a taxi. Taking Gayle's car would have been faster, but her roommate had a photo shoot in New Jersey later in the evening.

The morning rush was over which made hailing a cab easier. Once in the backseat, she gave the driver the address.

Avery couldn't rescue her nor did she want him to. If he unraveled this riddle, she'd owe him. She didn't want to owe anyone, least of all a Malveaux. Forgiving him for telling Roxy about the missing money was one thing. Resuming their relationship was something totally different. What she needed to do was find out who took the money and why. Then she could start to excise Avery out of her life, her heart and mind.

She neared the courier, but police had rerouted traffic several blocks out of the way. She paid the cab fare and made her way down the three blocks on foot.

Avery stood on the opposite corner in his suit and tie, his hands deep in his pockets. His sunglasses made it impossible to know what he was thinking. But his posture was rigid. Something bothered him.

"What's going on?" she asked when she came up behind him.

He slid his glasses down his nose. "You didn't need to come down here. There is nothing you can do."

"This is *my* problem. I have every right to be here." Maybe if she thumped her finger against his chest, he'd get the point she was trying to make. "Was anyone hurt?"

"I'm just trying to save you some of this…this nonsense." He rubbed the bridge of his nose before sliding his sunglasses back into place. "The offices hadn't opened yet, so the building was empty. Look at that place. It looks like a bomb exploded in the center of it."

She shielded her eyes. There was nothing left of Pipeline Delivery. The buildings on either side were just as bad. The fire was out, but smoke continued to rise from the ashes. A crowd stood on the opposite side of the street, gawkers just like her and Avery.

"What happened with Celeste?"

He didn't answer right away, nor did he look at her. "She claimed she didn't know anything about the missing money."

"Do you believe her?"

"No."

"I staked out Michelle this morning." She said with pride.

He looked at her, now, a slight curve tugged at his lips. "Well, well, well. You've got a little sleuth in you. How did it go?"

"She stole from English, but only about two hundred dollars in office supplies, not my two hundred thousand. She thought I was hunting her down because I wanted to press charges."

Avery shook his head. "Do you believe her?"

"I do." She wasn't willing to tell him what Michelle said about Celeste. First, it was gossip. And second, what would he do with the knowledge, run and tell Roxy because it was his judiciary duty? She pushed her sneakered toe into ashes that had landed at her feet. "Is that Slacker Dude in the back of that crowd? The guy with the baseball cap." She stepped close to Avery and motioned with her shoulder.

He turned his head half an inch. The move was so slight she wasn't sure he was even looking in the right direction.

Before he could answer, she was across the street. If Avery could talk to Celeste, maybe she could get some answers out of Slacker. He turned to see her just as she approached. The glint in his eye said he was going to dash down the street.

She reached out and grabbed hold of his T-shirt. "You're going to talk to me." There was no mistaking her intention.

He tried to yank away, but she balled her fist around the thin fabric. Avery came up behind her.

"What are you doing, Macy?" he asked.

"We're just going to talk," she said without taking her eyes off the lanky guy. "Let's move over there." She nodded to an area away from the crowd.

"I don't have anything to say to you. Get off me." The angry skull tattoo on his forearm bulged.

"Man, you might as well talk to her now. She won't let you go until you do, and with the police just over there, you don't want to draw attention." Avery spoke with authority.

Slacker eyed them both. He seemed to exhale, and the hunch of his shoulders relaxed.

"You know what's going on with the English International accounts, don't you?" Macy asked as soon as they were away from the crowd.

"I don't know what you're talking about." Slacker looked at his unscuffed high-top Timberland boots, his hands shoved deep in his low-slung jeans.

"I hope you're smart enough to know Celeste will give you up in an instant. You've got to be smart enough to know she's using you."

He raised his head. His eyes narrowed. She had his attention now.

"It took me a while to figure out what was going on, but now I know. I'm planning to go to English with the information and you should know that you'll be the first one under the bus." She was lying, but Slacker didn't know that.

He tried again to jerk away from her. But with Avery just a few inches away, the attempt was half-hearted.

"You better tell me your side before I go to English later today. The minute Celeste gives you up, you'll be arrested for theft."

He stared at her for several seconds. She had to keep her face neutral.

"Look lady."

"My name is Macy. Macy Rollins. What's yours?"

"Anthony Davis." He returned his attention to his shoes. "This was all Celeste's idea. I didn't do anything. She said the money belonged to her anyway. The only thing I did was give her that package you were looking for."

"The Bunting contract? Why did you give it to her?" She let go of his T-shirt.

"She called and told me there were issues with it and to hold on to it. She picked it up." He shrugged. "If you have questions, you should get them from her. I ain't done a thing, and I'm not messing up my parole for a piece of…"

"Who was setting up all the phony accounts?" Avery shoved his finger into Anthony's chest.

Anthony's eyes were wide. "Look, she brought me the information on the accounts. I set 'em up. She told me how much to charge English. She made all the decisions. When the money came in, I worked with my girl here and we skimmed it off…we kept a little and gave the bulk of it to Celeste. This was all her idea. This month she kicked it up, a lot. It used to be chump-change, a couple hundred here and there, but the last two months she wanted thousands." He shrugged his shoulders.

Avery stepped a closer. "You're no idiot. You knew this wasn't right?"

Anthony dropped his head.

"Did you set that fire?" Macy asked.

"Hell no. Can I go now?"

"I think this is a story the police would like to hear. Don't you, Avery?"

Chapter Forty

Avery clamped down on his tongue. One thing he learned in law school was to let people talk when they thought they had something to say.

"Look, you have to believe me. I'm keeping my nose clean. I promised my Mom I would. The only thing I did was give Celeste an envelope. The one you brought in here a few weeks back. She works for the company so I figured it was okay. I thought those accounts were real, until you guys and that woman came in asking a lot of questions."

"Why should we believe you?" Macy glared at Anthony.

He offered to take a lie detector test as if that would solve everything.

"Where do you live, Anthony?" Avery asked.

He gave his address, and then pulled out his license to prove he was telling the truth.

"I needed that job." He nodded to the burned-out shell of Pipeline Delivery. "Ain't nobody gonna hire an ex-con. I needed that job for my recovery. So what was I supposed to do?"

"Are you the father of Celeste's baby?"

"Baby. She ain't having no baby," Anthony paused. "At least not by me. I was always using protection. I got three kids already, and I don't want no more."

"You do know protection doesn't work all the time, right?"

Anthony backed away. "Can I go now?"

"Yeah, go ahead. If I need to talk to you again, I know where to find you," Avery said.

"Hey, Anthony, thank you," Macy added before he took off. She turned her attention to Avery. "Now what?"

He pinched the bridge of his nose. "I think you cracked this case. Now you just need to tell this story to Roxy."

"She'll never believe me. Celeste is her sister. She thinks her sister is perfect except for a few misguided decisions. Besides, I'm not even sure if I care about all this stuff anymore." She threw up her hands.

"Are you serious? After all the work you've done, you're willing to walk away?"

"I wanted to clear my name, to make sure that English doesn't prosecute me. I think we have enough info to prove Celeste is behind this whole debacle. Right? You can tell Roxy this whole sordid story. As a lawyer, isn't that your duty?"

He grabbed her by the hand. "You're going to tell your own story. After that, you can do whatever you want."

He pulled his cell from his pocket.

"Who are you calling?"

"I'm seeing if Roxy is free. Let's get this over with."

"Today. Now?" The panic in her eyes made him feel bad for what he was doing.

He wrapped his arm around her and pulled her into his chest. "I'll be beside you. We'll do it together."

Roxy accepted his call. He talked without releasing Macy. No way was he going to let her go while she shook with fear or the rush of adrenaline.

"Roxy, do you have some free time this afternoon? I'd like to talk to you."

"Ah. I'm not sure," she said quickly. "How much time do you need? I think I've got a few minutes around three?"

He agreed and ended the call.

Macy peeled herself away from him. "What time?"

"Three. That gives us some time to talk about how we want to present this information to her."

"Should we try to talk to Celeste first? Maybe she'll admit to everything and tell her sister." Macy spoke using her hands to emphasize her words.

"Celeste wouldn't admit to anything even if we tracked the money right into her account. I think you've been through enough, let's tell Roxy everything we know and leave this mess in her lap. She helped create that monster of a sister. Now she can figure out what to do with her."

"I'm exhausted. I didn't think I'd ever say this, but I want to take the easiest route." Her shoulders slumped.

He planted a kiss on her forehead.

She flinched. "Don't do that. Don't kiss me."

Macy sat at the conference room table at English International. She tugged at the neckline of her dress. She tried to push her shoulders back to sit up straighter, but the weight of the last few days made it impossible. Even the air at English smelled foreign to her now. How could she have wanted to work for a company that abandoned her when she needed it most? Hadn't she had enough of that in her life?

From the moment Anthony made his confession, her stomach knotted, and now it was even tighter. All she needed was to get this meeting over so she could move on to a real life.

Avery took the seat beside her, but his presence brought little comfort. What she needed was to say goodbye to English International and Avery Malveaux. Only then would she be able to gather up the strings of her life and put them back in recognizable order.

Nothing had changed between them. If Avery hadn't shown up at English, maybe none of this would have happened. No matter what the outcome of this meeting today, he could go back to his solid gold world, and she would find her way around in her gold-plated one.

"You're shaking," he whispered to her.

"I know. I can't stop. I just want this to be over. It's after three, where is Roxy?"

"She'll be here. I'm sure she's bringing someone from personnel."

Macy forced her hands into her lap. A whole new life was waiting for her beyond this meeting. All she had to do was hold her emotions together for a few minutes. Then she could wave goodbye to English. Waving goodbye to Avery wasn't going to be easy, but it was necessary. They could fool themselves into thinking they could be a couple, but one day the rosy colored glasses would slip off, and they'd have to face the ugly reality.

Maybe she'd never learn to trust anyone, but at least she knew her shortcomings.

Roxy breezed into the room. As always, she looked as if she was rushing from some other emergency. The HR Director strolled in behind her, looking put out at having to be at the meeting. Roxy managed to look at Avery without acknowledging Macy.

Roxy took the seat on the opposite side of the table. The HR Director sat beside her.

"What is this all about?" Roxy directed her attention to Avery.

Macy cleared her throat. "Roxy, I wanted to share some information with you. Avery and I have been investigating the missing money in my selling expense account."

Roxy placed her right hand on the table and covered it with her left hand. She pressed her ample bosom forward. "No one asked you to do that." The ice in her voice chilled Macy.

"I did it to prove to the company and to you that I did not steal from the company. I had to find out for myself." She pulled the papers from her bag. Once they were spread out on the table, she talked Roxy through everything they'd found.

Thirty minutes later, Roxy's face was frozen. There was no color left in her cheeks. She glanced at the papers in front of her, but she hadn't touched a single document. "You want me to believe my sister was stealing from the company? My sister." She shook her head. "That has got to be the most preposterous thing I've ever heard. Macy, I was flabbergasted when I found out money was missing from your account, but I never thought you'd stoop so low as to blame Celeste for this." Roxy's hands hadn't moved. They remained locked in place on the table. For a woman as animated as she was, her stoic position could only mean she was holding back her fury. She directed her attention to Avery, leveling her gaze at him for several moments. "Avery, what the hell is going on here? Why would you allow Macy to waste my time like this?"

"Roxy," he started, using a tone she hadn't heard before. If Macy never heard it again, she'd be just fine. Maybe this was the way he spoke when he was in a courtroom. "Let me assure you, we didn't come here today to waste your time. The information Macy has shared with you is factual. She's done her homework. I stand behind it without a doubt. It may be hard for you to look at this objectively because we're talking about your sister. But data doesn't lie."

The four of them sat in silence for a moment. The tight draw of Roxy's jaw didn't relax. Macy watched as she grinded her teeth. The HR Director adjusted his tie. He cleared his throat several times without looking up. The only sound in the room was the large office clock, ticking off the seconds.

Macy refused to look away from Roxy's glaring stare. Macy could almost see her brain churning out a way to blame her for this entire debacle.

Macy pushed away from the table. "There is one more thing." She reached into her bag and removed her resignation letter. There was no use in giving it to Roxy since she refused to examine any of the paperwork. Instead, she placed it closer to the HR Director. "This is my resignation. After everything that's happened, I think this is a good time for us to part ways." Without waiting for Roxy to lob another insult across the table, she walked out of the conference room.

At the elevator, Avery caught up with her. "Good job in there. How about we do something tonight to celebrate?"

Her heartbeat outpaced her breathing. Talking to Roxy was difficult. Telling Avery this was goodbye seemed impossible. But she couldn't fool herself another day. He deserved better and so did she. "Can we talk in the coffee shop on the first floor?"

This late in the afternoon they had their choice of seating. Macy selected a small round table near the door, hoping to make an easy exit.

"Would you like a coffee?" He was poised to get what she wanted.

"No. I have something to say. The sooner I tell you what's on my mind, the better." She patted the table, hoping he'd sit and make this easier for her

Telling Avery, they weren't going to be a couple would have been easier if she'd done it in the elevator or, the cold hardened halls of English. Sitting this close, looking into his dark eyes, the task seemed insurmountable. After everything he did to help her, she needed to act like an adult. Stare him in the face. Tell him her truth.

She had years of twisted interest in the Malveaux family, a few months with him wasn't about to change anything.

"How do you think the meeting went?" Avery asked.

"About the way I expected. Roxy indulges her sister. No matter what, she wasn't going to take that news very well. The company will probably write off the missing money and pretend it never even happened," she said. "I can't imagine Roxy will prosecute her sister. I don't care what they do. It's not my problem anymore."

"But why did Celeste think she had to steal the money? Roxy probably would have given her what she needed."

"Roxy's husband was getting tired of funding the money train. She told me he was going to put a stop to it." Macy tapped her index finger on the table.

"I didn't know you were going to resign. I mean you mentioned you might, but I didn't think you were going to do it today. Are you sure you want to quit?"

She nodded her head. "After that meeting, I'm sure I did the right thing. Did you see the way Roxy looked at me? She made me feel like scum. I never want to feel that way again." She paused. "That's also why I wanted to talk to you in private. Now."

The small talk eased the lump that pressed on her chest. Sometimes the best way to handle a difficult task was just to do it. Was this how her father felt when he contemplated leaving his family for his mistress? Had he been torn between what was right and what his heart wanted to do? He had taken the easy way and followed his heart. She was going to follow her head and do what was right.

"Avery, this is goodbye for us. We had some fun, but if we're both honest, really honest, then we know a relationship isn't possible."

"I thought we were in a better place. You understood why I had to tell Roxy."

"I do. You're an honorable person. And without your help, I don't think I would have solved this whole thing. But, we're so different…"

"We're probably more alike than you're willing to admit. I have a few more zero behind the amount in my bank account, that's our only difference." His eyes were wide and the disappointment she saw challenged her decision.

"I need to focus on finding a job and my family." She leaned across the table. The kiss she planted on his cheek would have to last her a lifetime.

Jacki Kelly

Chapter Forty-One

The living room sofa, with the television in front of it, became Macy's favorite spot. Her butt had made an impression in the cushions that would last a long time.

The hole in her heart grew bigger every day. One day she would get over Avery and move on. That was the hope that got her out of bed in the morning and onto the couch. But that hope hadn't been strong enough to get her on the computer to look for a job yet. Her mind and heart had to reconcile soon. She only had enough money in her account to last another month. Being poor had a way of bringing her to her senses.

Today's horoscope came at her like a warning. She'd almost memorized the words.

Money is your biggest worry today. Your nerves will be on edge until financial matters are resolved. Focus on the things you can control and leave the rest alone. Stop the self-torture concerning what could have been. Those opportunities are gone. You're smart so put that brain to use. Concentrate on what you can control, and you'll find your way.

Avery might not believe in horoscopes, but this one had been written for her. Today's advice sounded good. But right now, sitting upright was an effort. Looking for a job would have been easier if she had some idea what she wanted to do. The thought of starting over again at a new company was too daunting to contemplate. The first week after kissing Avery goodbye she only got out of bed to eat peanut butter and crackers. This week she'd added chocolate covered raisins to her menu, along with making it to the sofa. She was making progress, even if it was slow. Any day now she planned to re-introduce her hair to the comb. For the first time in her life, she had seriously checked out. She'd stepped off the treadmill of life, and it felt good to slow down.

She heard Gayle's key in the lock and straightened up.

"Oh, look at you, trying to pretend you've had a productive day. I bet you didn't even brush your teeth today." Gayle carried a brown paper bag in one hand, her purse in the other.

"Then you'd lose."

"Well, you didn't comb your hair. If you don't start using a comb soon, your hair is going to get matted. I'm just telling you because that's what friends do." She dropped her purse in the chair before continuing to the kitchen. "I brought Chinese food for dinner. You get chicken and broccoli because you haven't eaten anything nutritious in days. Get your butt up. We're eating in the kitchen. I think it's time we had a serious talk."

Macy didn't move. Her appetite left the moment she'd said goodbye to Avery.

"I'm not hungry. Maybe I'll eat later."

Gayle stood in the kitchen doorway, eating from the carton with chopsticks. "Why don't you at least talk to him?"

"Because I don't want to."

"See, that's the thing. You do want to. You're being stubborn. Did he call today?"

"No. I think he's finally gotten the message."

Gayle shoved some noodles in her mouth. "Honey, I don't want to be a buzzkill, but you've got to pull yourself together. You've quit your job and gotten rid of the best boyfriend you ever had. You're only taking a shower every few days. I don't even know this person." She pointed a chopstick. "I want my best friend back. The one who was the rock in our relationship. I'm tired of being the responsible one. I want you to do the grocery shopping next week."

Macy climbed off the sofa with the blanket still draped over her shoulders. "Did my mother ask you to talk to me?"

"No. But if you think she could say something to help move the mourning process along, then let me know."

In the kitchen, Macy tore the paper off a pair of chopsticks. She removed the last container from the paper bag and grabbed a piece of chicken. "I'm going to start looking for a job tomorrow."

"You don't have to. I think I've found the perfect job for you."

"How can you find a job for me? I can't model. I don't want to be a model."

"The agency I work for is looking for an office manager. You'd be perfect with all your organizational skills and stuff."

"Are you serious?"

"The pay is good too. Can you go in for an interview tomorrow?"

"This is why you brought home dinner. You were just trying to get me in a good mood. Being the responsible one is hard work, isn't it?"

"Yeah, you can have it back right now." She nodded toward the living room. "I think your phone is ringing."

Macy rushed to her cell phone. Before accepting the call, she performed her precheck. Avery's number illuminated the screen. Blocking his calls was the logical thing to do, but something kept her from doing it. Knowing he was still making an effort made the pain of sending him away a little more bearable. He wanted her.

Back in the kitchen, Gayle had finished her carton of noodles. "Who was it?"

Macy settled at the table. "Tell me about the job. Will I get to go to some of the exotic places you do and wear fancy clothes?"

The music in the club thumped against his bones, but Avery didn't move with the beat. Macy wasn't his first break-up. It hardly seemed fitting to call what he and Macy did a break-up at all. But she had managed to take the full stage in his life. Now she was gone, and there was a gaping hole that wasn't repairable. At least not any time soon. The little caper they'd shared had been fun, even though she wouldn't have classified it that way. He just liked having a reason to be with her every day.

He nodded to the music. Showing up at the club, sitting in solace while sipping Vodka straight up was the best way to numb the emotions he didn't want to feel. Most nights the music drowned out all the questions he couldn't answer.

Austen strolled into their private lounge. "You're here again tonight, bubby?"

Avery lifted his glass to his lips to discourage the small talk.

"This isn't a good look for you. Playboys bounce back. Chicks aren't supposed to open our nose like that. If you want her back, buy a dozen roses and show up at her door." He poured a shot of Vodka before taking the seat next to Avery on the lounge.

"I don't want to talk about Macy, Austen." His tone was flat.

"There has got to be at least two dozen girls downstairs that can take your mind off of her. Tell me what you want; blond, brunette, blue eyes, gray eyes, big busted, flat asses or big asses and flat chested, you can have your pick."

"What I want is to be left alone. I'm fine drinking my sorrows."

"As your brother and business partner, I have to tell you two weeks is a long time to mourn over a girl. Have you even gone back to work yet?"

Avery sat up straighter. "Look, Austen. If I wanted your words of wisdom, I'd ask for them. I'm doing just fine. Why don't you focus on the club?" He slammed his glass down on the table. "I'm sorry, man. If me hanging out here is an issue for you, I can leave." He stood.

Austen grabbed him by the arm, pulling him back down to the lounge. "Geez, bro. I'm just worried about you. You weren't even this bad when you found out about Monica."

"Yeah, well, Macy was nothing like Monica."

"She won't talk to you. You've handled difficult cases before, approach this situation the same way. Pour on some of that Malveaux charm."

Avery snickered. "Macy is immune to charm, flashy displays of affection and anything material. She's working from a standard I don't understand. She never let me see the playbook."

Austen gave him a hardy back slap. "I can't recall a time when not seeing the playbook ever stopped you." He stood. "I better get back downstairs. As you said, someone has to look after the club." Austen exited the room with long strides.

Left to his thoughts, Avery settled back on the lounger. From the moment Macy said goodbye, his body was numb except for the few hangovers from the over-consumption of Vodka. For someone used to fixing other people's problems, there was no easy solution for him. He emptied the contents of his glass but continued to hold on to it.

"Can I come in? Your partner said it was okay." Roxy stood at the entrance of the private room. He hadn't seen her since that meeting where Macy resigned. He didn't want to see her now. She'd had a hand in everything that went wrong. Instead of running English like an International business, she allowed it to be a playground for her sister.

He glanced at her for a moment before returning his gaze to his glass. "What can I do for you?"

"You haven't been in your office in a few weeks. I thought…"

"I've asked my brother Austen to show up every day to handle any questions or concerns that may come up. Isn't he working out?"

She stepped further into the room, teetering on the highest heels he'd ever seen her in. She looked like a middle age woman trying to outrun middle age. "May I sit down?" She pointed to the chair opposite him.

He nodded.

"Your brother is working out just fine. I wanted to apologize to you. I guess I owe Macy an apology too."

He waved his glass around the room. "Macy isn't here as you can see, so you'll have to apologize to her somewhere else." There was a slur to his words, but hiding his condition from her wasn't a concern. He poured more Vodka into his glass.

Roxy looked down at her hands in her lap. Neither of them spoke. Instead, the constant beat of the music pounded in his heart.

Finally, she said, "I spoke with Celeste."

"Did you now?" He drained his glasses. Maybe he shouldn't have another. He was already beyond the ability to drive and sleeping in the club another night didn't appeal to him either.

"She admitted everything." She twirled her large diamond around her finger. "Everything Macy said was true."

He set the empty glass on the table. Throttling Roxy would have been easier than listening to her tell him things he already knew. "If you're looking for absolution, then I grant you peace." He fumbled with making the sign of the cross.

"I'd like for you to help me talk Macy into coming back to English. She won't take my calls. I even stopped by her place a few times, and no is ever home, or she's refusing to answer the door. Our Dragon negotiations aren't going well. We've lost three contracts since she's quit."

He stood. For the first time in weeks, he felt in control of his life. Maybe instead of granting Roxy absolution, what he'd done was granted it for himself. He walked over to the chair where Roxy was seated. Looking down on her, he said, "I wish I could help you."

Chapter Forty-Two

Macy made her way down 2nd Street against a stiff wind. It was colder than usual for mid-October. If she weren't so needy to have everyone like her, she would have said no to this meeting and hung up the phone.

The last few weeks blurred together. A few months ago, she thought she could do it all. Get a promotion at English, help her brother with college expenses, fall in love. None of those things had happened.

Outside of the café, she wiped her hands against her jeans. She could control this meeting. The minute she had enough she could walk out. She didn't owe anyone anything.

She opened the door and stepped inside. The heat warmed her face. She spotted Roxy at a high-top table and made her way across the room.

Roxy jumped up the moment she saw Macy. "I'm so glad you agreed to meet with me."

Macy nodded.

"Please sit down." Roxy pointed at the chair opposite her.

Macy slid into the seat and unbuttoned her jacket.

"Would you like to order something, coffee or a muffin. They have the best in the city. My treat." For once Roxy wasn't bubbling over with enthusiasm.

"No, I'm fine." Macy sat back in the chair.

The smile on Roxy's face disappeared. "Okay. Well. First, I want to apologize. I was wrong in thinking you would steal from the company. You were a loyal employee and a benefit to the organization. I was under a lot of stress. I know that's not an excuse,' she paused. "I'd like to offer your job back, with the promotion of course. You'd be a member of the leadership team and it comes with a twenty percent pay increase We'd like to have you back at English."

Macy leaned toward Roxy. Her former manager didn't seem as intimidating as before. Now it was impossible to remember why she thought Roxy held so much power over her.

"Celeste told me the whole story," Roxy blurted. "I had no idea my sister was capable of that kind of behavior. It won't make you feel any better, but she was skimming from several accounts, not just yours. We're getting her some help."

"You know, Roxy," Macy started. "what Celeste did was awful, But, she's not the reason I'm not coming back to English." Macy swung her leg back and forth. "I gave English everything I had. I put my life on hold, to make sure I was giving more than one-hundred percent to the company and in the end, it didn't matter. Nothing mattered. I was escorted out of the building like a criminal. Maybe all businesses would have treated me the same way, but what I learned was, I need to work to live, not live to work."

The color disappeared from Roxy's face. "Macy, please reconsider. I'm sure we can find a balance."

Macy pushed her chair back and stood. "I already have. I wish the best for you and Celeste." She placed her hand on Roxy's shoulder before walking out.

On the street, Macy didn't bother buttoning her coat. The chill felt good. She walked several blocks, organizing her thoughts along the way. Out of all the commuters she passed on the street none of them seemed as happy as she felt. The opportunity to talk with Roxy was cleansing. Now she could let go of all English anger.

Her cell phone rang. She pulled it from the outside pocket of her purse. After making sure it wasn't her father, she accepted the call.

"Macy, this is Lou, from Epson Model and Talent Agency. I have what I think is good news for you."

Chapter Forty-Three

Macy waited by the front door for Gayle. Her first week at Epson and she wanted to make a good impression. A quick glance at her watch let her know they had plenty of time, but Gayle was habitually late. For her, arriving late was an art form. She knew how tardy to be for private parties, grand openings, cookouts and yes, even work.

"Gayle, I don't want to be late. Hurry up." Macy called to her friend.

Gayle hurried toward the door. "I'm not sure the two of us riding together is going to work," Gayle said as she bent down to slip on her shoe. "I have an image to keep up. Being the first one in the office is setting the wrong tone for me."

Macy picked up her bags. "Oh, stop complaining. You don't even go into the office every day. As the new office manager, I can't be late. It doesn't set the right example."

Gayle looked down her nose. "I'm still not sure why you are getting a company car. I'm their top model, why don't I get one?"

"I have to get around the city to check on photoshoots. I can't do that riding Septa or taking a taxi. Besides you have a car."

"Yeah, but I also have a car payment. Wanna trade?"

"The car won't be mine. I'll just get to use it. Now, come on, girl." She pushed Gayle through the front door.

Gayle slipped behind the wheel. Within minutes they were in the thick of rush hour traffic, inching toward the small suite of offices occupied by Epson Model and Talent Agency.

"Remember, I'm going to be in Italy for several months, shooting for some new designers." Gayle changed lanes without signaling. "Please don't sit in the apartment every day moping about Avery. There's a party in Manayunk. I'll leave the address for you. You have to go and tell me everything I'm missing."

"I've got your trip written down in my planner." She patted the thick planner in her lap. "I'll have the whole place to myself, nobody there to bug me about what I'm eating."

"The party, Macy. The party."

"I'm not promising you I'm going to a party. Give me a little time. I like my new job, and I'll decide what I want to do with my private life."

"When are you going to get over that job?" Gayle shifted lanes. "The next time Roxy calls, can I answer your phone and cuss her out?"

"No Gayle. I just want to forget about English International and everything associated with it. Goodbye and good riddance to everything over there."

"You sure you're going to be all right while I'm gone? You'll remember to eat, right?"

"I'll be fine, Gayle."

Gayle glanced at her with an 'I'm not so sure' look.

"Haven't I been eating right and bathing every day and combing my hair and handling the office like a pro?"

"Yes, but that's all you're doing. You've thrown yourself right back into a new job and once again put your personal life on hiatus. One day you're going to look up, and you're going to be an old shriveled up woman and wonder what happened to your life."

"That's a choice I'm making with my eyes wide open." Macy stared straight ahead. Her feelings had been coated over with wax. Frozen in place. This mode of life suited her just fine. No more calls from Avery or Roxy or the HR department at English. All of that was in her past. Each day she put a little more distance between the hurt and her heart.

The ring from her cell phone filled the car. She fished it from her purse and accepted the call after checking the screen.

"Hey, Brian, what's up?"

"The coaches are coming this weekend. To the game." He was almost yelling.

"That's great. I'm so happy for you."

"I know, right. Let's hope I can intercept some balls and run them in." She could hear his smile through the phone. "I would like to thank your friend, Avery. He helped make this happen."

Her heart constricted. "Oh, we aren't really friends anymore. But I can give you his number, so you can call him."

"No. I want to thank him in person. He said he'd come to my game, to see me play, and you're coming too, right?"

She was going to be sick. Breakfast wasn't going to stay down. "Brian, I was there last weekend. Mom and I stayed for the whole game even though we were freezing."

"But the coaches will be here this time. You have to come, and make sure Avery comes too."

"Things have changed. I can't make him come, Avery and I…"

"Macy, the man did me a big favor. Huge. You think calling him to offer a thank-you is enough? That don't even sound right to me. Give me his number. But even if he decides to pass, you had better be in the stands on Friday night."

"I'll be there." She ended the call.

"Oh boy. That didn't sound good." Gayle pulled into the parking lot adjacent to the offices.

"He wants to thank Avery."

"So, what does that have to do with you?"

"He wants to invite him to the game, and he's insisting that I need to come to this particular game, too."

"Well, you knew you were going to run into Avery sooner or later. You might as well prepare for the collision."

"There are some things in life you just can't prepare for ahead of time. I may never run into him again, but Avery is going to be my Achilles heels, forever."

Chapter Forty-Two

Macy removed her jacket. It was one of those warm late October evenings that made her forget in a few short weeks ice and snow would be on the ground, leaving her yearning for the heat of the sun again.

The stadium was packed with revelers voicing their last bit of excitement for the final regular season game. According to Brian, if they won this game, they could compete in the playoffs. Why he wanted to run head-on into someone as big as him seemed silly, but it made him happy.

"You sure are quiet today," Macy said to her mother.

"You know I'm always nervous at his games. I'm fine." The reassuring squeeze her mother gave her thigh signaled everything was all right.

"I hope he has a good game. His whole college career is riding on this game, which doesn't seem fair. He's an excellent athlete. Maryland would be lucky to have him." Macy believed every word, but a scholarship would help.

"Brian told me your relationship didn't work out. I'm sorry, honey."

She shrugged. "We were just having fun. It's not even fair to call it a relationship."

Her mother stared for several moments. She could see through the bravado, but she wouldn't interfere. She never had.

By the time the game was over, the temperature had dropped. Macy put on her jacket, closing every button. She shoved her hands in the pockets of her jeans to warm them.

"Instead of running down on the field, we might as well wait here for a few minutes. He won't come out until after he's showered." Her mother turned her attention to the thinning crowd. "I know Brian told you about your father. I'm surprised you haven't mentioned him to me."

"What's there to say?" She followed her mother's gaze to the field. "If Brian wants to talk to him, then he should. I put all those feelings into a box a long time ago. There is no way I want to take the lid off now to let all that crazy out again. I'm just fine."

"Honey, you might think you're fine, but you are wound so tight I think you just might pop like a balloon. Something is bothering you. If you won't tell me what's bothering you, I hope you find a way to handle it." She took Macy by the arm. "Now let's get down there so we can congratulate your brother on the win."

Macy was slow to stand. Her legs were cramped, but even more, she wanted to get out of the stadium without seeing Avery. With this many people packed in the bleachers that was a good possibility. She crossed her fingers in the hope that Avery didn't feel the need to wait on the field after the game to greet her brother. Maybe they'd had a moment together before the game.

By the time they reached the fifty-yard-line, their designated waiting place for Brian, there were still several die-hard fans and family members of the ballplayers. Macy surveyed the crowd. Avery was nowhere in sight. She eased air out of her lungs.

Her mother pointed across the field. "Here comes Brian." She hurried toward him.

Brian was headed toward them flanked by Avery Malveaux and another man who could have been Avery's brother. He must have been the coach from Maryland. The wind had picked up just enough to blow Avery's hair. If it was possible, he looked even more handsome, and taller, than she remembered. One day she'd be able to look at him and handle her emotions like a real adult. Her heart fluttered as if a thousand butterfly wings flapped against it.

Macy sucked in a breath. "Girl, you can do this. You've had to handle a lot worse." She caught up to her mother with a plastered-on smile. All she had to do was inhale air through her nose, then release it through her mouth.

Brian hugged them both. "Mom, Macy, this is Calvin Bowe. He's a defensive coach at the University."

Calvin stuck out his hand. "Your son should be an asset to our sport organization. I can't believe we almost missed the opportunity to see him. Thanks again Avery for keying me in."

"This is Avery Malveaux. The man who made all of this possible." Brian beamed with more enthusiasm than he'd displayed in years.

Avery's eyes were glued to her during all the introductions. She kept her gaze on Calvin, her mother, her brother, and her well-worn sneakers with the lime green shoelaces.

"Mrs. Rollins, I feel pretty certain that the University will be able to come up with a scholarship package for Brian. I hope he'll give our school serious consideration."

Her mother clutched her throat. The squeal Brian released could be heard all over the field, and just in case it couldn't, then the way he leaped up with his fist in the air sure would.

"I think we should go out tonight to celebrate. I happen to know you like Olive Garden. My treat," Avery said.

"I wish I could, Avery, but I need to get back to College Park." Calvin stuck out his hand to Brian. "You'll be hearing from me real soon, Brian. Stay healthy."

"You bet I will, coach." Brian gushed.

From the corner of her eye, Macy noticed an older gentleman within hearing distance. With the salt and pepper hair and the deep lines etched in his face, he looked older than his years, but she'd recognize her father anywhere.

No matter what happened, Avery wasn't going to let Macy get away without at least talking to him. She was doing a commendable job of standing as far from him as she could and avoiding his gaze. Nor had she spoken one word to him. But that wasn't enough to dissuade him.

What he hadn't expected was her outward anger at the sight of her father. She stormed to the edge of the field while Brian and her mother talked to him.

Avery made his way toward her. "Aren't you going to say anything to him?"

"I don't think that's any of your business." She folded her arms across her chest.

"You're right, it's not."

"I'm sorry. That was rude." She held out her hand. "Thank you so much for helping my brother. From the bottom of my heart, I appreciate all you've done. I was hardly prepared to see you today. Now seeing my father has thrown me." She pushed her hair behind her delicate ear.

"I'm glad I could help," he said.

They stood in silence for a moment, each with their hands in their pockets. Her focus was across the field on her family.

"I've missed you, Macy."

She didn't respond.

"Did you hear me?"

She nodded.

"I've been trying to figure out why we can't continue to see each other. That's the big mystery in my life."

"Better the mystery happened now, rather than a year down the road when we've both invested so much that we ended up hating each other, like those two." She used her chin to point to her parents.

"I don't know. Neither of them has pulled out a gun. Besides, they have two amazing kids that they must feel pretty happy about."

"In spite of everything."

"What if they hadn't taken a chance? If they were afraid?"

"I'm not afraid." She spun on him.

He didn't turn to her. He kept his eyes on her parents and brother. Her mother said something to make them all laugh. "I thought you were tough. Willing to go up against anyone, over anything if you thought the cause was right. But now I see you're only willing to do that as long as you don't have to make an emotional investment."

"You don't know anything about me."

"I know your favorite color is yellow, that you don't wear perfume because you've run out and can't afford the brand you like. I know you wear knockoff dresses better than any woman I've ever seen. I know you push your hair behind your ear when you're not sure what you want to say. I know you snore a little bit when you're exhausted. I know more about you than I thought was possible. My head is so full of stuff about you I can't get it out of the way to think about anything else. Did you get out of your own head long enough to get to know anything about me?"

"Sure, I have. I know you can't get moving without your morning coffee. I know you have to sleep on the right side of the bed, all the time. I know you don't like your shirts starched. I know you think Cabernet Sauvignon is better than Riesling, that you like to fall asleep with the television on. I know you love your mother's meatloaf and will endure evenings with your father just to taste it. I know that and a whole lot more. I…"

"Then you must know how I feel about you. That I love you." He forced his hands to stay in his pocket and his gaze to stay on the field. "How can you know everything, but not that?"

Three Months Later

Avery stretched out on the full-size bed. He could have used more space, but Macy's bedroom couldn't accommodate a bigger bed. Sleeping in the confined space was better than not sleeping with her at all. If he never experienced being without her again, he'd be the happiest man that ever let his feet hang off a mattress.

He stared at Macy while she slept. Today Gayle was returning from Italy, which meant their private love nest was going to get too crowded. Macy had insisted he move into her place, but now he was going to urge her to move into his condo.

He kissed her mouth, which was the habit he'd adopted their first night back together, then climbed out of bed. After showering and dressing, he made coffee.

He carried a cup of coffee to the bedroom. "Today is the big day," he said to Macy before sitting on the edge of the bed next to her. No matter when he looked at her, his heart always reacted the same way. He'd gotten lucky.

"I know we need to make some decisions before Gayle gets here. I've loved living here in our little cocoon." She snuggled close to him, placing her head on his chest.

"You'll move into my place now, right? That's the agreement we made."

She was quiet for a moment. "Yes. But it was easy to agree when it seemed so far off. I know I'm being silly. You've been super-understanding. I'll pack up some clothes today. We can get the rest of my stuff later."

He removed her cup from her hand and placed it on the floor. With her hands in his, he gazed into her eyes. "I love you, Macy.

She sucked in a quick breath. "I never get tired of hearing you say that."

"I figured I needed to tell you just in case you weren't picking up on all the other ways I was trying to tell you."

"I love you, too. I have for months. I thought you'd think I was moving too fast."

"Actually, I think you're moving way too slow. I knew I wanted you in my life after that first night in my club. I'm glad you finally caught up."

She placed a palm on each side of his face. "If you hadn't been persistent, I don't want to think about how things would have turned out." She kissed him. Her passion matched his.

Her phone rang. She left one hand in place and reached for it. She stared at the screen without accepting the call. Her face darkened, and she withdrew her other hand.

"Your father?"

She nodded. Her teeth dug into her bottom lip.

"Do you ever plan to talk to him?"

"I don't know. I want to but…"

"Every time he calls you stare at the phone as if something is going to happen without you initating it. It doesn't work that way."

The shrill ring continued. She moved her index finger over the phone.

"I going to do it," her voice cracked. "I'm going to talk to him.

"I'll give you privacy." He stood and headed toward the door. He heard her say Dad. Sounding like a small child.

In the living room he packed his briefcase. Until Macy resolved the relationship with her father, a part of her would always be stuck carrying extra baggage. After several minutes, she called his name.

He placed his briefcase by the door and hurried back to her. Her eyes were filled with tears, but she looked serene. More content than she had since meeting him. "What happened?" He sat beside her and draped an arm around her.

"We're going to meet for lunch, next week."

"Because you want to, right?"

"Yes. I think I'm ready. I know we won't erase all those years with one meal." She wrung her hands. "But I might get some answers to the questions I've always had."

"Who knows, you might even invite his to the wedding," he said.

"What wedding?"

He lifted her chin. "Ours."

She studied his face. Her lips turned up. "Are you asking me to marry you?"

"Unofficially, yes. But I don't have the ring yet."

"Then I'm withholding my answer until it's official." She rested her head on his shoulder. "You know today has turned out ten times better than I could have guessed when I woke up. I wonder what my horoscope is for today."

"Later." He ran his fingers through her hair. "Gayle's not back until later today, so we got some time." He pushed her down on the bed, covered her small frame with his body. The warmth of her skin was enough to turn his blood hot. He cupped both of her breasts in the palms of his hands. With his tongue, he circled each nipple until she moaned the familiar sound he'd come to cherish. She captured his mouth. Together their tongues danced a waltz of their own making. Every minute with her mouth locked on him was like a moment in heaven. He released her breast. "I am the luckiest man in the world."

"Then that must make me the luckiest woman. I'll never understand why you put up with me. I have so much baggage, I feel hopeless at times."

"I'm here to help you carry it."

She drew back. "Are you serious?"

"Yes. I want to spend the rest of my life with you. When I get down on one knee and ask you to marry me, you will say yes, won't you?"

"Yes. Of course." She threw her arms around his neck. Her tongue plowed into his mouth with a force that matched her words.

Author Bio

Jacki Kelly has been writing since her fourth-grade teacher made her keep a journal for a grade. Now she does it to keep track of all the fascinating and heartbreaking moments that life throws our way. Poetry, personal essays, short stories and novels have all occupied space in her heart and her hard drive.

Jacki loves to read almost as much as she likes to write. When she's not reading or writing, she's walking her adorable cocker spaniel or on the golf course. Her idea of bliss is squeezing all this stuff into one day. Happy Reading!